# WHEDONISTAS!

WHEDON, J.
48 - 152342

A CELEBRATION OF THE WORLDS OF
JOSS WHEDON BY THE
WOMEN WHO LOVE THEM

EDITED BY
LYNNE M THOMAS
DEBORAH STANISH

mad
norwegian
press

Published by Mad Norwegian Press (www.madnorwegian.com).
Edited by Lynne M. Thomas and Deborah Stanish.
Editor-In-Chief: Lars Pearson.
Cover art by Katy Shuttleworth. Jacket & interior design by Christa Dickson.

ISBN: 978-193523410-4
Printed in Illinois. First Edition: March 2011.

Also available from Mad Norwegian Press...

*Chicks Dig Time Lords:*
*A Celebration of Doctor Who by the Women Who Love It*
edited by Lynne M. Thomas and Tara O'Shea

*Resurrection Code*
All-new prequel to the AngeLINK novel series
(1. *Archangel Protocol,* 2. *Fallen Host,*
3. *Messiah Node,* 4. *Apocalypse Array*)
by Lyda Morehouse

*Redeemed: The Unauthorized Guide to Angel* (ebook forthcoming)
by Lars Pearson and Christa Dickson

*Dusted: The Unauthorized Guide to Buffy the Vampire Slayer*
by Lawrence Miles, Lars Pearson and Christa Dickson

*Wanting to Believe: A Critical Guide to The X-Files, Millennium*
*and The Lone Gunmen* by Robert Shearman

*Running Through Corridors: Rob and Toby's Marathon Watch*
*of Doctor Who* (Volume 1: The 60s)
by Robert Shearman and Toby Hadoke

*AHistory: An Unauthorized History of the Doctor Who Universe*
[2nd Edition now available]
by Lance Parkin

*More Digressions: A New Collection of "But I Digress" Columns*
by Peter David

The About Time Series
by Tat Wood and Lawrence Miles

*About Time 1: The Unauthorized Guide to Doctor Who* (Seasons 1 to 3)
*About Time 2: The Unauthorized Guide to Doctor Who* (Seasons 4 to 6)
*About Time 3: The Unauthorized Guide to Doctor Who*
(Seasons 7 to 11) [2nd Edition now available]
*About Time 4: The Unauthorized Guide to Doctor Who* (Seasons 12 to 17)
*About Time 5: The Unauthorized Guide to Doctor Who* (Seasons 18 to 21)
*About Time 6: The Unauthorized Guide to Doctor Who*
(Seasons 22 to 26, the TV Movie)
*About Time 7* (forthcoming)

*This book is dedicated to Joss Whedon,*
*who created worlds that touched us all.*

# Table of Contents

# Table of Contents

# Introduction

### Lynne's Story:

You may know me as a Chick Who Digs Time Lords, but I'm also an avowed Whedonista. Although Whedon fandom is not my primary active fandom (that belongs to the Doctor), the Whedonverse has been a part of my life for just about as long.

I mentioned in *Chicks Dig Time Lords* that watching *Doctor Who* got me through much of my pregnancy; *Buffy the Vampire Slayer* got me through oh, I dunno, my whole adult *life*. As an ex-cheerleader who grew up to be a rare books librarian (no, really), it seemed, well, *appropriate*, even if the collections I'm responsible for aren't located on a Hellmouth, and I don't rock tweed quite as well as Giles. I landed my current job as a pop culture librarian/archivist through my knowledge of librarianship and *Buffy* in equal measure. Now if I can just get our subscription to the "Demons, Demons, Demons" database up and running...

For me it's less about the Big Bad, and more about the heart. As I struggled with my life's challenges, like my mother's death, and the hospitalizations of my daughter with special needs, I could hold on to Big Damn Heroes, folks who took on Alliances or demon armies with quips, determination, and a posse of their friends. And looked good doing it. There are worse role models. Joss, we love your work so much that we made you this book. I hope you like it.

### Deb's Story:

On a September morning in 2003 I nervously checked my hair in the rearview mirror, smoothed down my Gap sleeveless turtleneck, locked my car and walked into a hotel in downtown Philadelphia. Meeting an illicit lover would have made me less nervous but the truth is I was a suburban mom in my mid-30's meeting "Internet people" for the very first time.

I was going to my first fan convention.

While working on this book I discovered two things: Everyone has a story to tell on how they found "their" Whedon show and, once discovered, that show helped them form a community, provided inspiration or tossed them a lifeline when they needed it most.

Much like women who feel compelled to share their birth stories, Whedonistas feel compelled to share this wonderful and powerful thing that changed their lives.

I know it changed mine.

Through *Angel* and *Buffy the Vampire Slayer* I discovered online fandom. I learned Internet etiquette, found a community of smart, fierce women who argued with abandon, and created with joy.

The thing with the Whedonverse, it's about connections. Both on the screen and off. I'd made my online connection, and when I walked into that hotel in 2003 I made a real life connection. On the surface we had little in common, but a shared passion united us.

I became a more knowledgeable and compassionate person. Issues of tolerance, racism and homophobia weren't just concepts, they were real and affecting my friends. My complacent, soccer-mom life was shaken and I learned to question, to accept, and to embrace.

In return for flipping my life upside down, the Whedonverse has been very generous. I traveled, met more fantastic "Internet people" and learned that while actors are nifty, writers are my heroes. I volunteered at cons, co-chaired a con and learned that sitting at a dais and talking to a roomful of people about the thing you love is the most terrifying, exhilarating experience in the world. (Other than sitting next to Catherynne M. Valente in a New York radio station at 5 a.m. and attempting to be witty and insightful about fandom.)

The great thing about connections is that, with a little nurturing, they continue to grow. Whedonverse fans led me, kicking and screaming, to *Doctor Who*, which led to publishing opportunities, meeting yet *more* amazing "Internet people," and drinking mojitos on New York's Lower East Side after my first book-signing experience.

So thank you, Joss Whedon, for creating the universe, to our contributors who shared their stories and to everyone who dared to make a connection to this wonderful and powerful thing called the Whedonverse.

### The "Whedonistas" Story:

So what is a "Whedonista", anyway?

Beats us. We burned through a lot of titles when struggling to find one that accurately described this unique collection of essays by women writers, artists and fans, but nothing seemed quite right. Just like the worlds of Joss Whedon, this volume contains multitudes. Much like Joss Whedon the man, it's nearly impossible to put in a neat box. Finally, Lynne came up with the word in the shower one day, and we knew we had a perfect fit.

We're not the first people to use the term, but we liked that the word has a distinctly feminine feel, perfect since this book turns the female gaze on Whedon's work. He built a career on creating strong female characters and now we're flipping the table and looking at the creator's works through our own lenses.

It's not only strong female characters that have built Whedon's reputation, it's also his delight in turning tropes on their head. Within the first two minutes of his breakout show *Buffy the Vampire Slayer*, he made us re-examine our perceptions of what goes bump in the night. In *Buffy*, the innocent school girl was the monster we fear, the flighty cheerleader was the savior of the world, and a delicious bad boy hid just below the surface of the prim and proper *male* librarian. The trend followed in Whedon's later offerings. From Kaylee to Zoe, Cordelia to Echo, Willow to Fred, we have strong women making their way through extraordinary circumstances with style, wit, and heart. They didn't wait around for rescue. They strapped on a stake or sword; used a magic spell, science lab or database; and *kicked some evil ass*.

We're all for heroines who kick ass and take names. We're also pretty fond of female engineers who can appreciate beauty in all its forms, deadly assassin teens, lady vampires who are off their rocker and computer nerds turned witches. And let's not forget the menfolk – broody vampires with souls and badass vampires without them, The Evil League of Evil (helloo, application form!), space captains with tight pants and large... hearts, and so many other examples of characters that we would never see anywhere *other* than in the Whedonverse's... tight embrace.

Is it any wonder that female viewers fell in love with these worlds?

We embraced the characters, the shows and their creator. More than simply thinking this was cool television, we wanted to talk about it. Online forums, fansites, conventions and academic conferences proliferated. These shows were important to us, and we wanted to turn them around and around, to examine their details and nuances, to analyze and revel in words and works that have affected us in ways that we're still discovering. What makes this volume special is that it brings us back to the proverbial water cooler.

That's partly what *Whedonistas* is all about.

Quite simply, it's personal. Each of us has had our lives personally affected by our enthusiasm for these shows. And we aren't alone. That deep personal connection with the shows, their fandoms and each other is what makes us Whedonistas.

The essayists in this book – a unique combination of professional and amateur writers – have come together to talk about how Whedon's shows, as well as the fandoms that they inspired, have changed lives for the better. We bring you stories that will break your heart, lift your spirits and make you think about how "just a television show" (or five) can have a huge impact on generations of viewers, merely by making "strong female characters" the default rather than the exception.

To sum it up, *Whedonistas* is an eclectic and exciting collection of essays that touch on nearly all aspects of the shows, the fandoms and the people to whom they made a difference.

Industry insiders have kindly given us insight into the production of the

Whedonverse. SF/F authors take on some of their favorite tropes, series, stories and characters, and tie them to their lives and their work. (Hint: Spike is rather popular.)

Other essayists outline the process and impact of shifting the Whedonverse from television to comics, the transition from fanfiction to professional publication, and what happens when you cheat on your muse with Spike (did we mention *popular?*). Our writers take on feminism in the Whedonverse, show us how Whedonista families and communities are made, discuss fandom across the pond in the UK and help us to understand Buffy's calling. They also look at coming to a fandom late, and how they brought new fans into the fold.

See? Multitudes.

So join us. No matter how you choose to define "Whedonistas," you're on our crew.

# The Girls Next Door: Learning to Live with the Living Dead and Never Even Break a Nail

In addition to being a rabid media consumer, **Seanan McGuire** is a distressingly prolific novelist, with three books out in 2010 (one under the name "Mira Grant," to make it look like she sometimes sleeps) and three more coming in 2011. She won the 2010 John W. Campbell Award for Best New Author. It came with a tiara. When not writing or watching television, Seanan releases albums of original music, draws an autobiographical comic strip and goes to way too many conventions. Her cats disapprove of all these things – except for maybe the television, since at least then, she sits still.

I have a confession to make. Unlike what seems like the majority of *Buffy* fandom, I didn't start with the television show – I almost didn't even *watch* the television show (although we'll get back to that in a moment).

I started with the movie.

Like all children, I spent a lot of time looking for idols. I grew up in the 80s, during one of the periods where media representations of blondes fell into two categories: the bimbo and the bitch. Being a deeply weird little girl, neither of these particularly appealed to me. I eventually grew into a pre-teen Marilyn Munster, that being the only option I could find that allowed for a) blonde hair, b) a fondness for frilly pink things and wearing ribbons in your hair, and c) hanging out with monsters. Like I said, I was a deeply weird little girl. At least answering "Who do you want to be when you grow up?" with "Marilyn Munster" didn't get me sent to the principal's office... unlike my previous answer to the same question, which was "Vincent Price."

My quest for idols carried me into my early teens, and it didn't get any easier. I *enjoyed* being a blonde and I *enjoyed* my monsters, but I didn't want to be a victim, and I didn't want to be rescued. I wanted a more modern idol who could combine the two. My quest seemed hopeless...

And then came 1992, and a little movie called *Buffy the Vampire Slayer* opened at the dome theater down the street from my friend Tiffany's house. It looked... promising. Weird, but promising. I liked the poster a lot, which showed a clearly badass blonde girl providing a human shield for that guy from *90210*. I liked what I could glean of the concept from the commercials. Eventually, I begged for movie money and decamped myself to a matinee – figuring that at worst, I was out five bucks, and at best, I'd have a little fun.

I snuck back in for the next showing (the statute of limitations on movie-hopping in the 1990s has long since expired, right?). I went back the next day. I rapidly reached the point of being able to recite large stretches of the script, complete with hand gestures and vocal inflections. Mysteriously, this did not make me more popular at school, although it probably didn't make the other kids consider me any weirder than I was before all that happened. By the time *Buffy* finished its Bay Area theatrical run – including a two-month stint at the dollar theater – I had seen the movie well over three dozen times. I was in love. I was in love with Buffy's world, with the concept, and most of all, with a bubbly California blonde girl who knew how to punch out the forces of darkness and never even break a nail.

Now let's skip forward a few years, shall we? When asked to list my favorite movies, I reliably identified *Buffy the Vampire Slayer* as one of the top three (the others being *Little Shop of Horrors* and *Beetlejuice*). I quoted the film the way other people in my social circle quoted *Monty Python*. And no one had a clue what the hell I was talking about... until The WB started running ads for a brand-new TV show with a very familiar title.

(It also had a very familiar lead actress. I was a huge fan of *Swans Crossing*, the pre-teen soap opera on which Sarah Michelle Gellar played Sydney, the primary antagonist. Amusingly enough, it was on the air in 1992 – the year that I was meeting Buffy Summers for the very first time.)

A lot of my friends immediately started getting excited about *Buffy*, since it looked, well, kinda cool. A roughly equal number of my friends dismissed it out of hand, since they remembered the movie as being, well, kinda lame. I staked out a weird sort of neutral territory between the two camps, since I remembered the movie as being totally awesome, and had absolutely no interest in watching the show. It had a lead actress I adored. It was based on one of my favorite movies ever. The man who wrote the original movie – some guy named Joss Whedon – was in charge. The bits of dialogue in the commercials were witty and well written. And there was absolutely, positively, no way it couldn't be terrible. It had too much going for it. It was designed by the universe to *crush my dreams*.

I was living with my best friend and her family when the show premiered, and her mother – one of Nature's natural-born geniuses if there ever was one – realized that sometimes, when I make decisions about things like whether I should watch a television show, I can be, well, wrong. She set the VCR to record the show's premiere. That Friday, as she was heading out of the house, she casually said "By the way, I taped that new *Buffy* show for you. The tape is on the bookshelf. Let me know if you want me to record next week's episode."

I didn't want to watch the show. I didn't think it was going to be any good. I didn't want it to hurt my memories of the movie. But if she'd gone to the trouble of taping it for me, I might as well give it a shot, right? I mean, I could always turn it off if it was as bad as I thought it was going to be, and everyone was sure it was going to be cancelled anyway. I had nothing to lose. I got myself a soda and some chips, went into the family room, and started the VCR.

Hello, Destiny. How've you been?

If the movie was a beautiful dream, the show was a beautiful reality. Serious – sometimes deadly serious – and well-written, with a unified cosmology and a canvas big enough to encompass just about any story the writers might want to tell. If *Buffy* the movie was the true love of my childhood, *Buffy* the series quickly became the true love of my teenage years. It was everything I'd ever wanted in a show and more.

*Buffy* quickly became an obsession, and, shortly thereafter, became my gateway into an incredible, insane, indescribably wonderful new world: shared media fandom. See, prior to *Buffy*, all my obsessions had been either outdated (like my passion for *The Munsters*, a show that, quite frankly, wasn't inspiring all that much fannish activity by the late 1990s) or totally obscure (like my undying love for *Night of the Comet*, a movie that, for years, no one I knew had even heard of, much less seen). But *Buffy* was everywhere. *Buffy* had people talking! And sure, most of them were talking about how much fun it would be to boink one or another of the main cast, but that didn't matter. I had finally, after years adrift in a sea of solitude, found my tribe. And my tribe really, really cared about whether or not Angel was a vampire.

The early days of *Buffy* were a heady merry-go-round of possibility. I remember spending literally an entire day arguing with my friend Kevin over whether or not Oz was going to turn out to be some sort of a demon. Why did we care? Because we could. Because we had something rich enough, and detailed enough, for us to really sink our teeth into it. It was an incredible feeling, and we all wandered around pretty well drunk on it. I joined mailing lists. I debated (endlessly) whether the selection of a *red* fuzzy sweater, vs. a *yellow* fuzzy sweater, meant that Willow was going to play a larger role in upcoming episodes. (Hint: it actually meant that the costume department had a red fuzzy sweater in the appropriate size.)

Since a lot of us were new to organized media fandom, we were free to create our own rules, etiquette and traditions. I'm sure we seemed like crazy interlopers on the well-manicured lawns of older, more established fandoms, but we didn't care. We were having way too much fun to even really notice. I learned about spoilers, after accidentally blowing the fact that Angel was a vampire; I learned about taking umbrage with canon, after they killed off Jenny Calendar. (It wasn't the fact that they killed her. It was that they didn't follow that by having her family come to town to bury her properly, lest her unquiet ghost rise up and torment Sunnydale for the rest of time. I am occasionally deeply literal.)

These were our passwords into a whole new universe:

"I may be dead, but I'm still pretty, and that's more than I can say for you."

"Books should be smelly."

"Tact is just not saying true stuff. I'll pass."

Seriously – we didn't say "the crow flies at midnight," or "remember the curse of the vampire pumpkin patch." We said "if the Apocalypse comes, beep me" and "oh, hey, juice." Later fans of Joss's work would know each other by the colors of their coats, but in those early days, we knew each other by the caliber of our dialogue. And that dialogue was *awesome*.

After years of looking for a blonde role model on television, I finally had one... even if she did spend the first season or so more on the brunette side of the Force. What was interesting was that after I finally got my iconic blonde girl, I was able to be a little less shallow about my preferences; my characters quickly became Faith, second Chosen but never second best, Anya, who, well... *Anya*, and Giles, because who wouldn't love a sexy British librarian who knew about the monsters lurking in the shadows? My high school librarian was cool, but she wasn't *that* cool. For one thing, she didn't keep weapons in the library.

I learned about fannish panic. When the second season of *Buffy* started, people crawled out of the woodwork to cry that the show's best days were over, and that it would never be that good again. Never mind that the second season was better in so many ways, with the character and plot foundations already securely in place and allowing for bigger, more ambitious storytelling; it wasn't the new kid on the block any more, and that meant it was no longer shiny enough to be utterly perfect. And I learned about fannish obsession, that strange power that convinces each and every one of us that the shows we love would be absolutely perfect if only the creators focused solely on our favorite things, and let everybody else's favorite things fall by the wayside.

As the show matured, so did its fandom. We splintered, going from a single coherent group to dozens of sub-groups – for all I know, the final count may well have been in the hundreds. I lost track after a while, and just keeping track of the groups I belonged to or that my groups were affiliated with was exhausting enough. Half the groups had fannish blood feuds going with each other at any given time, making the fandom an increasingly difficult-to-navigate minefield of conflicting interests, preferences and ideas. It was a little scary.

(This diversification of the fandom is why I have been known to express the somewhat non-standard belief that the cancellation of *Firefly*, tragic as it was, was actually very good for the Browncoats as an organized group. Because their show didn't have time to develop factions, they were able to hang together in a united fashion... and the splintering of a fandom is usually the first sign that people will, eventually, lose interest and let the fandom die. The Browncoats are more likely to endure than the various branches of *Buffy* fandom were. Not only did they develop around a relatively small quantity of established canon, they were promptly given reason to rally together, what with the loss of their show. Fox Network provided the Browncoats with their very own Serenity Valley... and just like the show's Serenity, it can never be anything but a bitter unification.)

I made friends – close, lifelong friends – through my love of *Buffy*. I co-wrote a chain sonnet – a form of structured poetry obsessively detailed enough to border on being a form of insanity – with a fan from New York, spending hours and hours debating symbolism, character, and how many times it was acceptable to rhyme "lives" with "knives." (In the context of *Buffy*, you can do it as many times as you want. So there.) I eventually wound up flying across the country to be a guest at the first BuffyCon, and played Buffy Summers in their cabaret sing-along of "Once More, With Feeling." Let me tell you, you know you love a fandom when you're willing to fly a couple of thousand miles to stand in front of a room full of strangers and sing about how you're just going through the motions. That takes dedication. Or, y'know, some sort of a head injury.

Sadly, all good things must come to an end, and *Buffy the Vampire Slayer* wound up teaching me another, accidental lesson: that sometimes you're so excited to keep going down the road you're on, you drive right past your destination. The show lost focus over its last two seasons, and while all the hardcore fans I'd come to know and love kept watching, the spark was gone, and the fire was in the process of going out. The mythology warped and twisted back along itself until Buffy Summers, the girl who once railed against the unfairness of being Chosen, looked at a squadron of girls who were just like she'd been and took away their right to Choose. It was an interesting statement about becoming the evil we fight against, and it hurt to see it made.

For seven years, I spent one night a week with Buffy and the Scoobies, and I never regretted a minute of it. For six years, I hosted season-premiere parties, watching the new status quo unfold with a roomful of people who cared just as much as I did. Like so many others, I watched the finale alone, and I cried like the world was ending.

Buffy Summers taught me that you can be a bouncy, buoyant blonde in cheer pants and impractical shoes, but still kick ass, chew bubblegum and take names. She taught me that if you do it right, you can punch somebody in the face without ever even breaking a nail. She taught me a lot of things ... but in the end, it was Giles, Xander and Anya who taught me the things I really needed to know, because they taught me that you don't need superpowers, or cool weapons, or a Calling to stand up against the forces of darkness. You don't need to be the Chosen One. Buffy's life was about being Chosen. For the people around her, and for the fans who chose to watch and love her adventures, it was about having the right to Choose.

Over the course of seven years, Joss Whedon gave us a stable, loving lesbian relationship; more redemptions than I really care to think about; fantastic villains; enthralling heroes; and, yes, a few big musical numbers. He created something that was unlike anything else that had come before, and now we look at genre shows the way we once looked at the second season of his first show – having seen perfection, we argue, how can anything be as good, ever again? He gave us monsters, and he made them human, and in the middle of it all was his modern Marilyn Munster in miniskirt and thigh holster, kicking ass without ever ruining her manicure. I am forever grateful to him for that, if nothing else. He changed the landscape. He's pretty good at that.

Still, do I think it was perfect? No, at least in part because Buffy herself wasn't perfect. Maybe it's not fair to ask perfection of our heroines. Still, we grew apart, she and I, as the seasons went by … and when she came back from the dead at the start of Season Six, I was almost sorry. Part of me had really been looking forward to the transition into *Faith the Vampire Slayer* – I mean, you have to admit, that would have been one hell of a ride.

Not that what we got wasn't one hell of a ride all by itself.

In the long run, I think I like *Buffy the Vampire Slayer* better as a television series, because it had so much more time and room and space to grow … but I like Buffy Summers better as a California Valley Girl who got on the back of a motorcycle with her boyfriend, and got the hell out of dodge before someone could ask her to fight some shiny new variety of evil. I like the girl who, upon being told that she was Chosen, decided she still had the right to make a Choice. I'll still take Pike over Riley and, yes, even over Angel; he was a guy who'd let his girl do what she needed to do, and would never judge her for being a little unladylike about the way she went about it. I just wish the movie Buffy had been given the opportunity to meet Willow, Xander and Giles. I think she would have liked them as much as I did. But I guess the TV Buffy needed them more, because she had more to prove.

I'm still a Marilyn Munster girl; I'm still out there looking for monsters. Still, I owe Joss Whedon my eternal gratitude, because by giving me what I'd been asking for all along – a blonde girl allowed to be where the monsters were – he showed me that sometimes, you have to look a little more than skin deep for your ideals. Joss Whedon taught me not to be that shallow. Buffy learned the same lesson, in the end. She just had to die a few more times than I did to get there.

So thanks, Joss, for the hall pass to Sunnydale High.

It was definitely an education.

# Ramping Up for a Decade with Joss Whedon

Before becoming a writer, **Nancy Holder** grew up in California and Japan, and spent time as a professional ballet dancer in Germany. Nancy's work has appeared on bestseller lists such as *The New York Times*, *USA Today*, *LA Times*, Amazon.com, *Locus* and more. A four-time winner of the Bram Stoker Award from the Horror Writers Association, she has also received accolades from the American Library Association, the American Reading Association, the New York Public Library and *Romantic Times*. She lives in San Diego, California, with her daughter Belle; their two Corgis, Panda and Tater; and their cats, David and Kittnen Snow.

Chris Golden and I wrote the first original *Buffy* tie-in novel, titled *Halloween Rain*, in the same month that *Buffy the Vampire Slayer* was going to debut on TV. When we accepted the job, *Buffy* had not yet aired. We were sent about half a dozen scripts, from which we compiled a "Buffy-ese" dictionary of sayings, primarily from the scripts written by Joss. Despite the fact that we had had three and a half weeks to write the novel, we kept calling each other and chortling over the scripts to what we fervently hoped would be a smart, clever show. The scripts were awesome, but a lot can happen between the written and spoken word.

*Halloween Rain* featured all hell breaking loose on Halloween night. Yes, we know. Correction: we know *now*. But the canon that *nothing* is supposed to happen on Halloween in Sunnydale hadn't been established (and besides, Halloween that second season *was* the Slayer's Super Bowl of the Bad).

When I had read that early clutch of scripts, I often stopped to laugh out loud. But as I watched the first episode, I started to cry. I felt as if I "got" it. I experienced a visceral connection to the show that I still have trouble articulating. I can easily understand fans who think of *Buffy* as *their* show. It was my show, too.

Then we were offered *The Watcher's Guide* – the first in a series of official guide books on *Buffy*, offering a comprehensive look at the show.

I'd never actually gotten used to the reality that I was/ we were writing about Buffy Summers and her world. It was always a thrill to find a new script on my porch, beyond exciting to receive author's copies of the finished books, and the best of the best was doing signings accompanied by an actor or two. I was signing *Halloween Rain* when Todd McIntosh, head of makeup on the show, made up James Marsters and Alyson Hannigan as vampires – Alyson for the first time ever. Todd created some other vampires, too, and I have pictures of Spike and crew menacing my giggling, chubby baby daughter. Then they went off to a Halloween party.

Heady times, those. But being handed the job of creating *The Watcher's Guide* was a new level of wonderful. Chris and I would go on set, something we had not yet done, with the aim of interviewing nearly every member of the cast, staff, and crew.

And now, we were on our way to Oz.

I probably spent about a month in total watching production of *Buffy* and *Angel*, and I never got tired of it. That was due in large part to the generosity of nearly everyone involved – affable, friendly, available – and my degree in communications, which served me well as I discussed the minutiae of aspect ratios and overcranking. But let's be real: the real coup was that I got to meet Joss and watch him work.

I felt very shy when he walked toward Chris and me as we were scoping out the high school set. I knew it would be inappropriate to gush, and it would waste time. So I kept all my fangirl behavior firmly under control. And if I had been a proto-Whedonista before, I definitely became one then.

First of all, he worked so hard.

We matched his hours, but we were only going to be there for a short time, and we needed to get as much done: conduct interviews, collect photos and blueprints, and make room for serendipity. But this was the pace he kept for months at a time (and that was back when he only had one show).

The soundstages for *Buffy* were located in Santa Monica, in the Bergamot Station complex. I was given the code for the security gate. Driving onto the property, I would see an art gallery, a deli, lots of parking spaces, and the soundstages, with "Mutant Enemy" painted on the front office. There was a security guard at the door; he would call upstairs to the production offices for clearance.

When we first went onto the lot, we were assigned a liaison named Caroline Kallis, who would facilitate each meeting we had with anyone connected to the production. We'd go upstairs to check in with Caroline – or, if she hadn't yet arrived, with the production coordinator.

One of the first things we'd see was a large square of tables lined up for pre-production meetings, and hallways along which the writers, producers, department heads, and many assistants of department heads had their offices. For on-set and actor interviews, sometimes Caroline would call ahead to arrange interviews; other times, she would escort me from the production offices downstairs to the set. I would stand to one side while she would approach the person I hoped to speak with, and ask if it was all right. No one she approached ever turned me down.

Chris had to leave to fly back to Boston, and I stayed on. After a couple of days, I was given the go-ahead to approach the actors, staff and crew on my own. I went to all the sets on all the sound stages, and someone would always make room for me to watch. In the offices, I'd duck my head in and get a wave, and an invitation to "see something cool." Some of my best interviews were conducted this way.

This "just go ask" policy included Joss. He was directing, and he was incredibly busy. Although I had watched film and TV production before, I had never been so focused on the director, and hadn't fully appreciated what an all-consuming job it was. Everyone needed a decision from him: props showed him several blankets and asked which one he wanted. An actor didn't like his costume, and wanted an alternative. A dangerous stunt was underway and Joss had to be consulted each step of the way – they wanted one take; they had to make it work. I hovered, needing an interview from him, nervous (still!) about being intrusive. Even though I was working on a book about *his show*, it was a *book*, and I wasn't part of the actual show. But he'd see me and take a moment to chat with me. He'd give me head-nod, or a smile.

He knew I needed some time with him, and he'd trot over when there appeared to be a lull. But each time we'd start the interview, he would be interrupted. He'd turn to me with an apologetic smile and I would say calmly, "My time is your time," although I was aware that at some point, I was going to run out of time.

But when he had a moment, he'd seek me out, give me a slightly more hopeful smile, and I'd start my tape recorder and get out my notepad. We sat together on a set in the dark, and he was as smart and funny as his show. I sat amazed, but pressed on with my questions, trying to stay quiet about my own opinions, trying not to connect to him, but to listen to him connecting to his work. I wanted to tell him that I admired and respected him, and I loved *Buffy*, but I needed to do my job.

Too soon, he was called to solve a problem – one of dozens he was confronted with – and when we went outside, I discovered that something had happened to my tape recorder. I swore. He grinned, took my tape recorder from me, fixed it, and did his best to recreate the conversation as we strolled through the graveyard in the brilliant sunshine. He promised to get back to me later, and he did.

I knew the *Buffy* company was putting their best foot forward while I was there, but there really was a sense of excitement about what they were doing, and an awareness that this might be the most magical time of their careers. I appreciated their level of professionalism. Everyone who was there had survived a winnowing process (one that continued from Volume 1 of *The Watcher's Guide* to Volume 2) and they had really wanted to be there – so much so that several key members of the company had gone against their agents' or managers' advice, turning down more stable, lucrative jobs in favor of *Buffy*. Like me, they couldn't explain exactly what it was about *Buffy* that captivated them, but they were under the spell, and happily so. More than one person I interviewed was moved to tears, as I had been, when they talked about what *Buffy* meant to them.

After I got home, I ferried batches of tapes to one of the three local transcriptionists I hired. Chris was doing the same back in Massachusetts. Some of our tapes were garbled. I had to relocate twice while recording my interview with David Boreanaz, first when the crew began breaking down a set; the second time, when someone else began vacuuming. David carried my equipment for me to the second interview location. When the vacuum started up, he offered to move all my stuff again, but I was worried that he would be called back to work, so I made sure I took copious notes. Good thing, too.

The actors became people: Juliet Landau's shoes hurt her feet. James Marsters was very glad for the gig. Alyson Hannigan walked her dog and left happy faces on sticky notes for people. Costume designer Cynthia Bergstrom burned candles in her serene office. Todd McIntosh gave us pictures of Seth Green in his werewolf makeup; without Todd, there would have been no werewolf shots of Seth in the book. Gareth Davies, the producer, gave me a *BtVS* producer's bag filled with goodies and reminisced about Adrian Paul, whom he would see in the hotel bar when they were both shooting in Canada. (Adrian Paul played the Highlander in *Highlander: The Series* – my only tie-in credit before *Buffy* – which, when combined with my horror work and young adult novels, was enough to help me land my *Buffy* job.)

Ironically, by the time I began work on the second volume of *The Watcher's Guide*, this time with Jeff Mariotte and Maryelizabeth Hart, the show had become so popular that many of the actors had employed new protective barriers of managers and publicists. As a result, the casual atmosphere I'd enjoyed during the first *The Watcher's Guide* had faded a little, and I had to go through channels to secure interviews with some (but not all) of the key players. Still, they were people: I was charmed when Alexis Denisof's father came to visit, and Alexis fussed over him. I'd seen Alexis on *Highlander*, of course. But I was charmed most when Marc Blucas brewed me some hot chocolate, and made a point of spending time with me while I drank it, just sitting companionably.

On the other hand, the staff and crew remembered me from the first *The Watcher's Guide*, and it was a pleasure to catch up with them. Our plan for the second *The Watcher's Guide* was to follow an episode from pre- to post-production, and the *Buffy* scheduling allowed for us to observe "The I in Team." There was a lot of chatter about "Hush," which had concluded filming just before our arrival. I finally got to sit at the large square of tables as each department head went through the script, discussing sets, costume changes, locations and the like before filming got under way. We concluded our survey with a visit to Todd AO, a post-production company in Santa Monica, to watch post-production maven David Solomon lay in the soundtracks and talk to the ADR experts – the people who made all the "efforts," such as grunts and moans (Sarah Michelle Gellar usually did her own). *The Sopranos* was working in the next suite over, and a few *Buffy* crew members tried to get spoilers out of them – to no avail.

*Angel* was located at the Paramount lot, except for the writers and post-production, which were back on the *Buffy* lot. Before they were sound-stages, *Buffy's* headquarters had been a complex of dilapidated warehouses, which were cleaned and repaired before being put into service. Paramount – an old and venerable film lot – was more Hollywood, less clubby, complete with tour guides, golf carts and a long history.

While there were some old faces among the *Angel* cast, crew and staff (particularly the staff), most of the principals were new to me. I didn't see Joss at work – not even at the *Buffy* offices – while I was compiling *Angel: The Casefiles* (the *Angel* counterpart to *The Watcher's Guide*) and I missed him. With three of us working, and a more streamlined approach to getting material (faxing and phoning, for example), our *Angel* set visit was shorter.

These were the years of the very active fansites such as the Bronze and CityofAngel.com and the Posting Board parties. I occasionally saw Joss at these functions and I would always re-introduce myself. He would smile and say, "I know who you are." He smiled at everyone. He'd joke and make them feel special.

A pop culture journalist I know had interviewed Joss many times, but a new publicity regime came into play during a press junket, and she'd been relegated to a cattle call-style mass interview rather than a private slot with Joss. When he spotted her in the crowd, he walked up to her, greeted her by name, and told her he would be happy to give her an exclusive interview if she wanted one. She took him up on it, and he did it.

As the series wound down, there were other events – *Buffy* academic conferences and *Buffy* festivals – where I would occasionally run into an actor, a director, or someone else in the company. *Buffy* went off the air, and I grieved. By the time the Wolfram and Hart Annual Review (an *Angel*-themed party attended by some of the cast) was held in Los Angeles, *Angel* had been canceled. *Firefly* was harder to catch than a real firefly.

I began to really mourn the heady days of driving up to L.A. to work on the Matter of Whedon, but then I remembered how I had felt when I read that first pile of *Buffy* scripts. I thought of how it felt to work on my first *Buffy* novel with Chris. Excited, elated. Script to novel, word to word. I had come to these experiences as a writer. And I was still writing in the Whedonverse – essays, short fiction and even a game/novel hybrid. I had sat with my laptop in the foyer of a restaurant in Maui where I was having dinner with a Pulitzer Prize-winning playwright, and she waited for me at the table while I finished and emailed my *Buffy* novel to my editor.

When I was doing *The Watcher's Guides* and *Angel: The Casefiles*, I thought that my life as a writer would never get any better than that. That was probably the most intense part of my life to date as a Whedonista. I hardly slept while we were working on them, first because I wanted to observe and interview as much as I possibly could, and then because the sheer amount of data we had collected had to be transcribed, edited, and arranged on deadline. It was intense in a way that writing a novel was not – and it got me out of my writing room and my head and into the day-to-day world of Joss's work as a director and producer.

When those books were finished, I felt a void for a long while. I missed the interaction and the sense of excitement. I felt a little drifty, as if I'd headed for the black and I was getting transmissions of the action from somewhere far away. But the life of a writer is a life of the mind, and that was where I first connected with Joss Whedon – on the written page. I read his work before I saw his work. And that's how I became a Whedonista – through the medium not of TV, but of words.

I keep track of Whedon alumni as if they were distant relatives. When I see Nathan Fillion on *Castle*, I smile. When I see Marc Blucas in *Night and Day*, I cheer. David Fury contributed books to my book drive after the first big fire here in San Diego, as well as *Lost* and *24* swag to a student of mine when she lost her house in the second big fire.

As I write this, another Comic-Con has just concluded. My daughter and I signed books featuring our collaborative short stories in the Browncoats booth for Joss's charity of choice, Equality Now. I also gave away *Buffy* and *Angel* books that are currently out of print. Felicia Day stopped by the booth while we were there. The Browncoats and I had a chuckle because I was signing while one of Joss's panels was in progress. No wonder our crowds were thin. They had another author scheduled during the "Once More With Feeling" sing along.

Caroline Kallis and I have caught back up with each other, and we're making plans to meet up in Los Angeles. And ten days after I turn in this essay, the second *Buffy* omnibus of three previously published novels – with a new look (and font!) – will be published. It contains two of my *Buffy* novels, including that first, *Halloween Rain*. New fans are discovering the Whedonverse on DVD, and emailing me to talk about my work.

My written work has been my attempt to serve the vision of Joss's shows. Writing is my connecting place, and *The Watcher's Guides* and *Angel: The Casefiles* were a kind of intersection between writing and visual production – and so was the *Sunnydale High Yearbook*, which was an ersatz yearbook Chris and I helped to create.

I loved watching the broadcast episodes of *Buffy*, *Angel* and *Firefly*. And I relished being in that other world while we worked on the *Guides* and the *Casefiles*. But at the end of the day, it's what Joss has written that affects me the most deeply. I admire his ability to produce and direct, but I love the way he writes. And that is what has made me the Whedonista I am today.

# Outlaws & Desperados

**Sharon Shinn** has published 21 novels, one short story collection, and assorted pieces of short fiction since her first book came out in 1995. She has won the William C. Crawford Award for Outstanding New Fantasy Writer as well as a Reviewer's Choice Award from the *Romantic Times,* and two of her novels have been named to the ALA's lists of Best Books for Young Adults. You can find more information about her on her website, sharonshinn.net.

The year is 1971. I am in junior high school, and my favorite TV show is *Alias Smith and Jones.* My school notebook has a three-month calendar on the inside front cover, and I carefully print "ASAJ" on the square for every Thursday. Every night that I can't sleep, I lie awake and imagine adventures that I would go on in the Old West, accompanied by Hannibal Heyes and Kid Curry. Both of them are in love with me, but I haven't yet decided which one I love in return. (The truth is, I can't choose; I want them both.)

When Pete Duel (aka Hannibal Heyes) kills himself in December of that year, I am more devastated by a stranger's death than I will ever be again until I learn of Princess Diana's car crash 26 years later.

The year is 1987, or perhaps 1988, and I am an adult holding down a professional editing job. My local PBS station has started to air the entire run of *Blake's 7* later at night than I can stay up. Fortunately, I own a VCR, and I record all the episodes. And I watch and re-watch them half a dozen times. I make tapes for a friend who lives in some podunk town where they either have bad reception or no PBS station (I forget which), and mail them to her every week.

I am in love with Avon, the show's main anti-hero. These nights, when I can't sleep, I concoct story lines in which this unemotional sociopath is forced to confront the fact that he has feelings for me. I have found a comic book store on the other side of the city – foreign territory for so many reasons – and picked up some back issues of *Starlog* and a bumper sticker proclaiming "I've escaped with Blake's 7." I've also purchased a color 8"x10" print of Avon in a silver-studded black leather costume, aiming a preposterous weapon at someone out of sight. I frame this and put this on my desk at work. A maintenance guy, in to fix a buzzing fluorescent light, asks me if that's my boyfriend. I still retain enough sanity to think that anyone who dressed that way would make a pretty scary boyfriend, and I say no. But I don't put the picture away.

That fall, a friend of mine attends a *B7* convention in Chicago and returns with a full report. More than anything, I wish I'd been there to view a montage video of Avon set to the Eagles' "Desperado." (To this day, missing that video is one of the great regrets of my life.)

The year is 1995. My first novel has just come out, and my editor asks if she'll get a chance to meet me at World Fantasy Convention. "What's that?" I reply.

Because I didn't *know*. I had never been to a convention of any kind. I was vaguely aware that such things as *Star Trek* (and *B7*) conventions happened on a regular basis, but I had no idea what kinds of people attended them. I didn't know what you could buy, who you could meet, what you would talk about. I certainly didn't know about fanfic, or I undoubtedly would have been writing down and mailing off accounts of some of my adventures with Blake and his crew. I was completely cut off from fandom and all its attendant joys.

That changed pretty rapidly once I became a published author. Nervous and disinclined to speak in public, I attended my first World Fantasy Convention, my first WorldCon. I met local authors and joined a writers group – and discovered Joss Whedon. Well, in my writers group, you had to be watching *Buffy* or you pretty much couldn't participate in the conversation. No matter how serious the current debate, no matter how closely we were focused on dissecting the story under review, inevitably at some point in every discussion the topic turned to everybody's favorite vampire Slayer. *Hey, did you see the episode where...* We repeated lines, we analyzed relationships, we argued about endings. We marveled at how very good it was.

But much as I enjoyed *Buffy* and *Angel*, I didn't entirely lose my heart until *Firefly* came along. Obviously, I love both Westerns and space opera; what could be more perfect than a show that married the two? Bonus points because it's so freakin' awesome, featuring fabulously drawn and wonderfully acted characters, a setting both exotic and expansive, and that trademark idiosyncratic dialogue. I regularly change my mind about which episode is my favorite – "Shindig," "Our Mrs. Reynolds," "Trash," "War Stories" – but I think "Objects in Space" is a damn near perfect hour of television.

While I adore each perfectly realized character on the show, it's Malcolm Reynolds – the space-age desperado – who makes me swoon. I can't resist his scruffy charm, his boyish humor, his heartfelt conviction that he's a pretty cool guy and everybody, even Patience, will forgive him his mistakes and indiscretions. I laugh every time I watch the closing scenes of "Shindig," where he grandly claims that not killing Atherton is what makes him a great man. Then he pokes Atherton with his sword. "Guess I'm just a good man."

Pokes him again. "Well, I'm all right." I'm impressed by the way he handles Jayne in "Ariel," trapping him in the airlock, willing to kill him for his betrayal – and relenting when Jayne shows a glimmer of remorse.

I love his varied relationships with the women on the ship. Zoe is the one person he trusts absolutely; he never mocks or doubts her. Kaylee he treats as a younger sister, calling her "mei-mei," kissing the top of her head. Inara fascinates and infuriates him, making him petty, making him kind, making him jealous and proud and thoughtful and edgy by turns. Even so, he's an action hero, a man's man, willing to shoot a bad guy in the head or endure horrific torture or send the rest of his crew to safety while he goes down with his boat. He's loyal, he's audacious, he's determined, he's funny and he's really, really cute. As a friend of mine says: "Best. Captain. Ever."

I'm not quite the dreamy-eyed fangirl I was in my teens. I haven't actually pictured myself joining up with the crew aboard *Serenity*, and God knows I don't have the nerve to attempt fanfic in the Whedonverse. My adult-oriented fandom has been more purposeful and more in the nature of proselytizing; I've poured all my energy outward. *Have you seen this show? It's fabulous. Want to borrow my DVDs?* I've lost count of the number of boxed sets I've given as gifts, the number of people I personally have turned into devotees of the show. *Firefly* went off the air nine years ago, but I'm still recruiting converts.

And I'm still delighted when – in venues both obvious and unexpected – I come across fans who are just as likely as I am to own knitted Jayne hats and Blue Sun T-shirts. For instance, I met a handful of Browncoats in 2004 when I was Guest of Honor at ArmadilloCon in Austin. One of my favorite memories is crowding into a hotel room with ten or 15 others to watch the two-hour pilot episode, played through someone's laptop and projected on the wall. Whoever owned the computer had forgotten his speakers, so we ended up activating the subtitle feature so we could follow the dialogue as Mal and his friends set out on their very first adventure.

About a year later, I was a guest speaker at a "genre fiction class" offered by Washington University's Summer Writer's Institute. A couple of other authors discussed writing romances and historicals; I talked about writing SF/F. Afterward, a young woman in the class approached me to ask if I was a *Firefly* fan. "Of course," I replied.

She had two tickets to the *Serenity* sneak preview that was being shown at a local theater the next day. Problem was, she was from Dallas, didn't know a soul in St. Louis, and none of her classmates were interested in going with her. I had some other commitment that night, but I knew one of the women in my writers group was dying to see the movie. I asked the girl if she was willing to share the ticket with a complete stranger *and* trust me with her phone number so I could arrange for them to meet. She was. The next day my friend Debbie joined the writing student – and hundreds of other fans – to see the movie. It was Joss Whedon's birthday. It was Debbie's birthday too. Best. Present. Ever.

Even so, I think the world would be a better place if that movie had never been made – had never *needed* to be made – because *Firefly* would still be on the air. At times I can convince myself that Fox actually did us a favor by canceling the program so early in its run. There was no time for the show to get sloppy or bloated, to waste hours on subpar stories; every scene in every episode is necessary to tell the tale at hand or hint of a past that will someday haunt the present. But while that's all true, most of the time I'm (still!) really angry that we never got to learn those backstories, never got to find out what lurked in the past for Inara and Shepherd Book, what lay in the future for River and Simon and Mal.

The wild Internet success of *Dr. Horrible's Singalong Blog* gave me renewed hope that Joss Whedon might find another live-action medium for finishing up the series. Yes, Nathan Fillion and Adam Baldwin and Christina Hendricks have new high-profile gigs now, but surely they'd all make time for something as important as the second, third and fourth seasons of *Firefly*, whether they're broadcast on network TV or over the interwebs. I own the comics, I saw the movie, but I want more.

I know what you're thinking. "But Wash and Book are dead." Sure, but how many times has Joss Whedon killed off key characters, loving that sucker punch to the gut, and then relented, rescuing them from parallel universes, from graveyards, from *ashes*? My friends and I have spent countless hours coming up with theories about how Wash can be brought back to the show. (He's been cloned! He's got a twin brother, who dresses in Hawaiian shirts and plays with toy dinosaurs! He was in the presence of a fantastically powerful psychic when he died, and all his memories were downloaded into River's brain...) Book – well – maybe he left behind digitally recorded or holographic diaries. Maybe his spirit was captured in some form back at the monastery. All I can say is, Whedon swore that all nine characters had signed on for a movie trilogy. That tells me that he expected them to show up – in one form or another – in the sequels that never were.

I'm a writer; it's my primary goal to create characters so compelling that readers wish they were (and sometimes believe they are) real. Despite that, I am constantly amazed at how deeply my emotions can be engaged by wholly imaginary people. I don't understand the synergistic magic that allows an actor, a writer and a few technicians to create living, breathing human beings whose lives sometimes matter to me as much as my own.

If *Firefly* is never brought back to the screen, if we never hear the rest of the stories, I have to believe they are happening anyway. Inara and Mal are still flirting and bickering, sidling closer and closer to consummation. Kaylee and Simon are still doing their dance of attraction and misunderstanding; Zoe is suspicious of a man who looks *just like Wash* but has to be some kind of imposter. Shepherd Book is offering advice from some otherworldly plane, and maybe even spilling a few of his secrets along the way. Jayne, God love him, hasn't changed at all. And River – well – as always, even when we didn't realize it, River is propelling the whole storyline. Wherever she goes, people are bound to misbehave.

They're still alive somewhere in the 'verse, arguing, running, tangling with Reavers, outsmarting the Alliance. Even though I can't follow them anymore, they still exist. For people who make up stories for a living, that is the ultimate success: knowing that, when the book closes, when the series ends, the adventure is not over. It goes on without the creator, in the minds of the people who love it. *You can't stop the signal.* Once it's broadcast, it continues on forever, pulsing past star clusters, lighting up new worlds, collecting new fans, till the end of time itself.

# An Interview with Jane Espenson

**Jane Espenson** has written for a number of TV series, including *Buffy the Vampire Slayer, Angel, Firefly, The O.C., Gilmore Girls, Dollhouse, Battlestar Galactica, Caprica* and *A Game of Thrones.* She also co-wrote and executive-produced the Emmy-nominated *Battlestar* webisodes, and co-created Syfy's *Warehouse 13.* She is currently proud to be on the writing staff for *Torchwood: The New World.*

**Q. How did you get into television writing, and how did it lead to you working on *Buffy*?**

A. Those questions are separated by about five years. I got into TV writing because it was always my dream, and then I found out you could submit scripts to *Star Trek: The Next Generation* without an agent. Later, I got into the ABC/ Disney Writing Fellowship, which allowed me to move to L.A. I spent a number of seasons writing for sitcoms such as *Dinosaurs, Monty, Me and The Boys* and *Ellen* before I decided to make the transition to drama. I was already a *Buffy* fan, and focused on getting that job. I wrote an *NYPD Blue* spec script – it seemed logical at the time – and used that to get a meeting with people who worked for Joss, and then with him personally. Getting hired there was lucky, dizzying, exciting and terrifying.

**Q. You've written for many non-SF comedies and dramas, but your resume is also heavy with credits in the science fiction/fantasy genre. (Congratulations, by the way, on the announcement that you'll be working on *Torchwood*.) Does SF/F writing come naturally to you?**

A. I always loved *Star Trek,* and I grew up reading a lot of Ray Bradbury and a fair number of *Wonder Woman* comic books – it was always something that appealed to me, this idea of creating a different world into which to put characters. I loved comedies just as much, though – when I was a kid, it was *M\*A\*S\*H,* not *Trek,* that first had me trying my hand at writing scenes. Of course, you can make the case that for a teenager growing up in Iowa, war-era Korea was every bit as alien as outer space. This isn't a digression, it's sort of the point of the thing – I like writing stories that aren't set in an ordinary world. I like a different setting: a period piece or SF or just the heightened world of an unusual job. It makes the universality of human behavior stand out, I guess. So I started my career with equal parts SF and sitcom. SF won, but I'm glad that my career has included lots of non-SF things too: *The O.C.*, *Gilmore Girls, Jake in Progress, Andy Barker PI, The Inside*, etc.

And yes – I'm so excited about working on *Torchwood*! It has strong amazing characters (I love Jack and Gwen and Rhys), and it's not your standard US science fiction show; the Welsh origins of the series are so unique and interesting to me. I want to write all the Welsh-US culture clashes, and all the humor that comes out of *that* kind of alienness! And I adore the way that *Torchwood: Children of Earth* took on this incredibly real tone – most shows shy away from scenes involving the corridors of power, because it's so hard to do it well and make it interesting, but those scenes in *Children of Earth* were riveting. You were watching huge horrible decisions being made, and you just *believed* that was how these things really would happen. We're going for that same brand of realism in *Torchwood: The New World*, and we're all going to be writing our hearts out to make you believe every word of it.

### Q. Is there a special skill set needed to succeed in science fiction/fantasy television, or is it the same as more mainstream writing, but with different window dressings?

A. If you can write character-driven episodes, it doesn't matter if it's an episode of *Friday Night Lights* or *Mad Men* or *Battlestar Galactica* or *Torchwood*.

### Q. Switching gears to *Buffy* for a bit... is there an episode of which you're particularly proud?

A. I was always very fond of "Band Candy," but I do see all the mistakes in it now – I wrote the principal's lines with pop culture references from the 70s, when I probably should have gone a little earlier. And I'm not happy with the old lady teacher's stoned rambling – I have never been able to write stoned rambling, and I've decided since then to just declare that as something I cannot do. So, with all of that in mind, I think I'm more proud of "Harsh Light of Day," "Superstar" and "Storyteller."

### Q. Are there any episodes that make you cackle with fannish glee when you see them?

Hmm... maybe "Pangs"? I love that it almost feels like it's become a holiday tradition for some people. That gladdens my fangirl heart.

### Q. Were there any *Buffy* episodes that proved exceptionally difficult to write?

"Doublemeat Palace" was hard from beginning to end. Joss wanted a very specific tone, different from that of a normal episode. I wrote a first draft that missed the mark tonally, and I had to do a complete rewrite in something like 24 hours. It's very hard to write that much that fast, and it's even harder when you're feeling bad about the first version. But Joss liked the rewrite, so that was good. The episode was not beloved at the time, but it's starting to shine a bit with age. I think the original intention of the strange languorous tone is clearer now that you can see the episode in the context of the whole series, rather than it was at the time.

"Earshot" was more fun to do than "Doublemeat Palace," but it was also pretty hard to write...

**Q. How so?**

A. For one thing, we had to make decisions about the rules of Buffy's new mind-reading ability – would we the audience hear what she heard? Always or just sometimes? Would we hear the voice of the person whose thought it was, or would we hear it in Buffy's voice? It seems obvious now, but it didn't seem that way at the time. There was also the challenge of the delicate writing of the Jonathan-with-a-gun scene. What you see in the finished version of that scene is largely Joss's writing, and I love it.

**Q. What is it about Joss's work that you think resonates so strongly, particularly with female fans?**

A. Innovation, fearlessness, humor. And female characters who are written as real people. It's surprising how rarely that is done, even now. You hear the idea a lot – often from stand-up comics – that women are "better" or "smarter," by which the comics mean "responsible," "sober" and "clean." In other words: uptight, unfunny and unreal. Joss – and also Tina Fey – have done a lot to counteract that by making women just as endearingly foolhardy, brave, flawed and hilarious as men.

It's just my theory, but I think Joss makes women heroes by making them vulnerable first, like all humans, and then giving them strong hearts that allow them to be brave despite that.

**Q. In some of the commentaries and interviews on the *Buffy* and *Angel* DVDs, you joked that whenever someone came up to you and mentioned a favorite line in one of your episodes, it was usually Joss' work. Did it take you a while to accept the value of your own work because of experiences like that? Or to put it another way, have you ever experienced "imposter syndrome"?**

A. The experience you've described about someone singling out a line that Joss wrote wasn't unique to me, actually – at the time, all the *Buffy* writers talked about it. It's just simply the case that the most memorable lines in any script came from Joss, usually during the process of plotting out the episode. But any discussion we had about those experiences was always more a source of comedic angst, exaggerated for effect, than of any real stress. Writers are used to being given credit and blame for things that aren't strictly our contribution. In fact, sitcom shooting scripts often contain not a single line of the original writer's draft, and you're taught early on to simply thank people for any compliments without getting into the details of who did what. So it's not a big deal. If anything, I sometimes feel that I'm given undue credit for having come up with the *idea behind* an episode, which can be a bit lowering. But even that's all right. My career is long enough now, and my bosses have been happy enough, that I figure I'm bringing something valuable to the table.

### Q. Did working for Joss change your writing "voice" at all?

A. That's an interesting question. It certainly does when I'm writing for him, because I use his voice on those occasions. I think I've maintained my own distinct voice, but it has always had some natural overlap with Joss's style.

### Q. In an interview on IO9.com about writers' rooms[1], you mentioned that working with Joss had taught you a lot about writing for television, but it was interesting that you tended to break down your answers by genre – i.e. comedy vs. drama. Is the writers' room on a "mixed" show like *Buffy* different from that of a single-genre series like *Battlestar Galactica* or *Warehouse 13*?

A. Actually, I think *Warehouse 13* is a very mixed genre show... it's run by the great Jack Kenny, a comedy veteran, with a lot of comedy writers in the room. It's run more like a comedy than *Buffy* was. I understand that *Desperate Housewives* has a room with a lot of comedy elements in it – I think the writers there might even do group rewrites. But there is still a huge gulf between the way a multicam sitcom (like *Two and Half Men*) works and any other kind of show.

Sorry, is any of this answering your question? I've never really thought of shows as being "mixed" or "single genre," so I'm trying to work this out as I go. Comedic elements can mean that a one-hour show will develop a more collaborative room, but they don't require it. *The X-Files* had very funny episodes, and it didn't even have a room. Instead, the writers worked one-on-one with the showrunner. So I think the character of the room has more to do with the preferences of the showrunner than the nature of the show.

---

1. http://io9.com/5555114/inside-the-tv-writers-room-a-place-of-magic-and-mystery-and-making-shit-up-for-money

**Q. What was the most important lesson you learned while working on *Buffy* and *Angel* that carried over into your later work?**

A. The main lesson I learned was about needing a reason to tell a particular story. A ripping yarn is not an excuse to take an hour of someone's time. You have to make a point. And your main character should ideally be right at the middle of it, undergoing a change.

**Q. In addition to the *Buffy* TV show, you've also written for the *Buffy* comics. Given that your TV scripts have been acclaimed for their verbal dexterity, and comics are such a visual medium by comparison, how do you manage the disconnect between the two media?**

A. Comic writing in general is hard for exactly the reason you state – it's more visual than verbal. It's really frustrating when you want to settle the characters in for a funny and emotional conversation, and then realize you've just condemned the artist to drawing two people on a bench for a couple pages. I think I'm only just now getting the hang of it. The trick, I think, is to actually tell a different kind of story, one that unspools naturally through images. Then you can add back in little portions of the funny and emotional conversation.

**Q. Do you work in close collaboration with the comic-book artists you're paired with? Or is it more a matter of handing over the script and seeing what happens?**

A. It depends on the script and the artist, but mostly it's the latter. I turn it over, then I might have a call or email exchange with the artist to clarify certain points, or I might not. Then I get to look at the art as the pages are completed, so I can ask for changes at that point. I haven't had many occasions where there was an interpretation I didn't like. Usually, what I see far surpasses what I was picturing.

**Q. In fandom, writers as well as actors have their own followings. What is it like to be treated like a rock star? How do you feel about the "cult of the writer," and does this have any real-world implications in terms of cachet and bankability?**

A. This question made me laugh... I wouldn't say that I'm treated like a rock star! Where are my hookers and blow? (Don't send me any, please.) But, yeah, I get what you mean. Genre writers – and *Buffy* writers in particular – get a lot of fan love. I certainly find it hard to complain. I think writers are often overlooked, and it's great to see fans being curious about all the behind-the-camera stuff. And yeah, it's had a lot of real-world implications for my career – it's fun to walk into a meeting with a young exec who grew up as a *Buffy* fan. I think my job prospects are all the better for it.

**Q. Writers today have more accessibility to fans – and vice versa – via social networking sites such as Twitter, Facebook and blogs. What do you consider to be the pros and cons of this, and has it changed the creative process at all?**

A. It hasn't changed the creative process as much as you might expect. The secret to writing things that the audience likes is to write things that you yourself would like to see, not to try to aim at some target inside someone else's head. I see my blog as a way to just have fun exploring small aspects of the writing craft. And I see my Twitter account, usually, as a way to amuse myself and others with things that make me laugh or ponder.

All in all, I love contact with fans – especially aspiring writers – because I am a fan myself of other people's work. It's simply fun to cycle the love the around. The downside of interacting with fans? You have to be a little guarded, of course. And you can easily stumble on vicious criticism or personal attacks. If anything about Internet contact with fans affected my writing it would probably be that – I could see a writer starting to write defensively, shying away from topics or plot turns that might bring on that sort of reaction. That would be a shame. I haven't caught myself doing that yet, thank goodness!

**Q. What is it about "dead" shows such as *Firefly*, *Buffy* and *Angel* that, even long after they have left the airwaves, still attract new fans? Is it frustrating that some finished shows you've worked on continue to have a life of their own, while others – such as *Jake in Progress* – have disappeared so quickly from the public consciousness?**

A. I think the difference has to do with the cluster of properties that define "cult" television. The more a show fits the cult show category, the longer it lingers. Genre shows, shows about ideas, complex and challenging shows... they stay.

**Q. What are you personally "fannish" about? What currently tickles your fancy?**

A. I dearly love *Project Runway* and a few other competition-type reality shows, such as *Work of Art*, *The Amazing Race*, *Top Chef*. I like thinking of challenges they should do – [*Battlestar Galactica* producer] Ron Moore and I had an idea that the *Project Runway* contestants should be challenged to design the native clothing of one of the 12 *Battlestar* colonies. Another *BSG* producer dearly wanted the *Top Chef* people to come cook for our crew. And I'm totally lobbying for the *Work of Art* contestants to be required to design art that passionately expresses an opinion they disagree with. Wouldn't that be interesting?

**Q. As you're such a fan of reality shows, is there a part of you that worries about their prevalence diminishing scripted television writing jobs?**

A. It did for a while, when the reality shows seemed to be squeezing scripted stuff off the air, but now I feel like a balance has been reached – the pendulum even seems to be swinging back the other way again. But even when it seemed like they were taking over, I still enjoyed the best of these shows. *Project Runway* just makes me happy.

**Q. We're dying to know: who is cuter? John Stamos or David Boreanaz? Discuss.**

A. They are equally adorable.

# My (Fantasy) Encounter with Joss Whedon (and What I've Learned from the Master)

**Jeanne C Stein** is the author of six (soon to be seven) *Anna Strong Vampire Chronicles* and numerous short stories. She is an ardent Whedonista, prefers Spike over Angel and believes in every young girl beats the heart of a Slayer.

I'm writing this right after returning from Comic-Con 2010, still basking in the glow of all things Whedon. There's no doubt that Comic-Con is a Joss love-fest. Although I didn't get to connect with him personally this time (I was lucky enough to win a place in his signing line two years ago), there's nothing wrong with a little hero worship (even if it is from afar). I've given a lot of thought to what I'd say if I met Joss again face to face – say in an elevator, or on the convention floor. In reality, I'd probably be too tongue-tied to make anything but incoherent animal sounds. Since this is a *fantasy*, though, I'd like to think it might go something like this:

> **Me:** Hello, Mr. Whedon, I'm sure you don't remember me, but I'm the person who gave you an advance copy of *Many Bloody Returns* two years ago. It was an anthology dedicated to you.
> **Joss:** Of course, I remember. You're Jeanne Stein. You write a vampire series called the *Anna Strong Chronicles*. I love Anna. She reminds me a lot of Buffy. Except for the part of Anna being a vampire and not a Slayer.
> **Me:** You have a phenomenal memory. I'm flattered.
> **Joss:** Well, you impressed me.
> **Me:** I did?
> **Joss:** Not too many people try to jump over the counter during a signing.
> **Me (blushing):** Sorry, about that. I got a little excited.
> **Joss:** Think nothing of it. Two weeks in traction and I was good as new. Gave me time to read your books.
> *Awkward pause during which we are surrounded by other fans who spy Joss and hurry over to offer tribute. It gives me time to slink away. Still, he did say he read my books. And he loves Anna. Perhaps if he's*

*looking around for a new series to... I float away on a cloud of dream-
like optimism.*

Well, that's *my* Joss Whedon fantasy. Why? He's the writer I'd most like
to emulate, both in story and character development. Because of that, I
thought about all the things I knew about him and realized there's a heck
of a lot more about him and his process that I didn't. So in search of answers,
I did some homework.

### The Write Environment

I don't know how many of you have had the chance to watch the interview Jeffrey Berman did with Joss for a series called *The Write Environment*
(it's available on DVD). It gives great insight into Joss's writing process as
well as a peek into his writing space. I thought I'd share some of the high-
lights of that interview and see how I could apply some of Joss's genius to
my own writing.

Some logistics first. Joss doesn't work in an "office." He works in a house.
"A tiny house," as he puts it. "But a house nonetheless." He likes it because
it offers him space and he likes to pace while he writes. From a counter to
the living room and back again where he can just perch and write. The need
to move is an important ingredient in his creative process.

For me, a desk, computer and no distractions work best. I have a very
short attention span. Joss has a Starbucks he frequents to write, as well.
When I go to Starbucks, it's to *look* like I'm writing. See the note about distractions above.

The walls of Joss's writing space are hung with comic book art. The only
award he displays is his Nebula – which he dreamed about winning since he
was a boy. The other awards he stashes "in drawers." He has stacks of comics
around, too. And lots of books.

I like to keep "things" around me, too. No Nebula, unfortunately, but I
do have a plaque naming me Rocky Mountain Fiction Writers' Writer of the
Year for 2008. That counts as an award, doesn't it? And I have my signed
copy of the *Buffy* Season Eight, Volume 1 graphic novel. Always right there
in sight as I work. It's inspiration.

Joss's philosophy on writing is simple. In his own words, "You should
need to write. You should *have* to write. Or you shouldn't be writing."

Don't know a writer out there who would disagree with that statement.
Most of us write because we have a vision we want to share. The few who
also find fame and fortune are the exception. But don't all writers approach
their work much the same way? We bring life experience, dreams, fantasies,
and the assimilated knowledge of years of education into play when we plot
a book.

We all understand that writing books is very different from writing scripts for television. But the basics are certainly the same. All the ingredients – plot, characterization, setting – need to work together for a story to click. From studying Joss's work, I've come to a greater appreciation of what it takes to bring fantasy down to earth. It's not enough to *tell* a story. You have to immerse the reader in the dynamics of your world.

## Transforming Vision into Reality

Now armed with the facts I learned in the interview, I started rewatching the *Buffy/ Angel* series on DVD, trying to understand how Joss transforms his visions into reality. Joss's visions are uniquely his own. They come from mixing genres – of realizing the funniest things often happen at the worst of times. They come from his love of horror movies, his job in a video store (the title *Buffy the Vampire Slayer* was designed to catch the eye of video seekers looking for movies like *The Attack of the Bimbos*) and a feminist bent that wanted to show a strong woman who *survives*. Buffy was the ultimate secret superhero. Who hasn't shared the fantasy of "I'm awesome but no one can know"? It got many of us through high school, including Joss, who says in the interview that he was a geek before it was cool. My heroine, Anna Strong, like Buffy, is a prototype for all women – strong, loyal, protective of those she loves. She would make a good friend.

Joss views television and film as distinctly different: TV shows offer questions – movies offer answers. I agree. A series, whether on the screen or the written page, is always in pursuit of the next question. Joss plots his series out carefully, developing a two year, four year and six year arc. The farther out, the more nebulous the details in the beginning, but he has a clear vision of where the story will go. (That and the ability to drop a line in Season One, episode two that we recognize in Season Four to have been prophetic!! Genius!!) He develops a goal for each season, then lets his writers take over. He describes it as letting them "paint" instead of merely coloring in the lines.

It's different in novel writing, of course. Which brings me to something I wish I'd learned earlier – to develop a story arc covering the first two or four or six novels. I had no idea when I started the series that books one to six would end up covering one year of Anna's life – her first as a vampire. Since I was new to the publishing business, I looked only from one contract to the next. Now that I'm about to embark on the second round, I plan to have a definite game plan. Thank you, Joss.

## With a Little Help From My Friends (and Enemies)

*Buffy* and *Angel* were Urban Fantasies in the finest sense. They were set in a world we recognize with the added elements of the bizarre. Vampires, demons, werewolves, big bads of all sorts haunted high school and college campuses. Buffy's Slayer duties were often overshadowed by mundane things like homework and family responsibilities and she didn't have the luxury of monitoring evil from a computer center. She was out in the middle of it every hour of every day.

And yet, she had a *life*.

She had the Scooby gang – Willow and Xander were the heart; Giles, the guardian; and later Oz, Cordelia, Anya, Dawn and Tara all played supporting roles. They sustained Buffy when she needed to keep going even when things were the darkest.

We see Buffy's strongest attributes when we examine the character of her friends. Which is the role of secondary characters. They are a mirror in which we see our protagonists more clearly. They are the way our protagonist sees herself. The most important (and painful) truths often come to light through disagreements with those we hold most dear. Joss used the technique often.

They were reflections of Buffy – her nature and her strength. Only someone special could inspire the kind of loyalty that would make her friends willing to risk their lives to fight alongside her. Joss might have called it a moral compass – drawing to Buffy others who shared her belief in good and the importance of fighting evil.

In my own writing, there have been several instances where characters who were supposed to be throw-aways take the reins and run away with the story. Just like finding the perfect actor to fill a part (James Marsters, for instance), finding the right ensemble to complement your protagonist is just as important.

For example, most of the secondary characters in Anna Strong's world started out with bit parts and like Spike, soon commanded a bigger role. And, again like Spike, became mirrors through which we saw Anna. Culebra, Max, and David reflect Anna's true character in a way that's unique. It's truly "showing" and not "telling."

It's what we need to give our protagonists to make them come alive. Our characters have to have a life as well as a mission. Joss does that so well. He mixes all the elements of everyday life: humor, pathos, stress, fear, hate, love and makes them appropriate to the action.

Joss identifies with all of his characters – even the villains whom he gives a perspective all their own. Most good writers understand the difference between a cartoon villain who is evil for evil's sake and a three-dimensional antagonist who has a reason for what he is doing. Spike is the perfect example. He is the hero of his own story. Spike, in the beginning, was the ultimate bad boy. But we soon learn he had a reason for his actions – his love for the damaged Dru and his plan to make her well again. He might have been just as magnetic had he remained purely evil. But I doubt it. For one thing, he never would have had a relationship with Buffy. He would never have made the choice to seek out the return of his soul. Spike evolved, even more than Angel, who had his soul forced on him, and we loved him for it. He became a hero. He did it for Buffy. He did it for himself. He became a part of the whole.

No piece of writing about the *Buffy* saga would be complete without a mention of Angel. Now I know there are two camps. The Angel vs. Spike debate rages still. I am a Spike fan. I guess the thing about chicks liking the bad boy applies to me, too. But Angel actually had more influence on my own writing than Spike. When I decided to make my protagonist a vampire, the vampire with a soul was a theme I embraced. I see Anna as the "good" vampire who has to fight her true nature in order to retain her humanity. It's a recurring theme in all my books. Sometimes she wins, sometimes she loses. But that moral compass thing is part of her. And, like Angel, she fights monsters – both human and not.

The concept of evolving villains is something I still struggle with. So far most of the antagonists in Anna's world, while not two dimensional, are certainly evil. And that applies to both mortal and otherworldly foes. I've yet to find a character I can turn from antagonist to friend through actions of his or her own. It's a challenge for every new book.

### Writing without Boundaries

If I had to pick one thing from studying Joss Whedon that most influences my writing, I'd have to say it's the way he mixes genres. In some circles, being called a genre writer is looked down upon (look at sales figures for genre versus "literary fiction" though and just *why* that is is a mystery to me). In any case, it is no longer unacceptable or unmarketable to write something that combines horror, humor, fantasy, romance, and mystery in one book. In fact, it's the defining characteristic of most Urban Fantasies, one of the reasons I love writing it. There are no formulas, no boundaries. Joss shows us how it's done in every episode of *Buffy* and *Angel*. It's what makes his stuff so good.

The last thing Joss says in his interview is perhaps the most important to new writers: "Be the geek you are. Not the geek someone else wants you to be."

My translation: write the book you love, not the book you think you should be writing for the market. Be the geek you are. When I turned from writing straight mysteries to developing a series around a protagonist I could look on as a friend, it made all the difference. And most importantly, it was fun.

Again, thank you, Joss Whedon.

# The Ages of *Dollhouse*: Autobiography through Whedon

**Sigrid Ellis** earns her living as an air traffic controller. She writes about comics at Fantastic Fangirls (*http://fantasticfangirls.org/*) and about everything else at her blog, Thinking Too Much (*http://sigridellis.wordpress.com/*). Her short story, "No Return Address," was published in *Strange Horizons* in 2010. She and her partner raise and homeschool their two children in Saint Paul, MN.

At different points in my life I have wanted to be, or wanted to date, most of the characters of *Dollhouse*. They embody the fantasies of power I have held throughout my life.

When I was nine years old I wanted to be Victor. *Dollhouse* wasn't on the air but had I known of him at the time, Victor is who I would have wanted to be. My fantasies were of a direct and physical competence. My best friend and I made elaborate plans to live our adult lives on a ranch in Montana, where we would raise horses and dogs and be entirely self-sufficient. We would train all our own animals, raise most of our own food. We would survive nuclear war there, and nuclear winter. Or, if the Soviets invaded instead of nuking us, we would defend our ranch with profligate use of firepower. We would shoot well, make our own ammunition, and be unafraid to bury the enemy dead.

Victor captures my nine-year-old goals and fantasies. He is an expert at weapons and a natural leader (at least, his imprints are). In the paradigm of the Dollhouse, he can be good at anything chosen for him. Victor's skills and talents are, in the first season, largely a lie. But it's not his skill set that I wanted to be, to have, at age nine. It's his nature. Victor is stalwart, Victor is loyal. Victor embodies romantic and selfless love.

Victor is more romantic than sexual or sexualized, which appealed to my childhood self. Even in Season One's "A Spy in the House of Love," Victor's sexual engagement is extremely romantic, full of long talks, playful banter, fencing – *fencing*, for goodness' sake! – and British accents. (British accents being exotic, sophisticated, and immeasurably adult to Sigrid, age nine.) Victor's love for his fellow doll Sierra is nearly chaste, clean and pure. His feelings for her are largely structured in an enabling manner. Victor wants to see Sierra get what she wants more than he desires anything for his own needs or goals. When I was nine, I thought this was the pinnacle of human emotion. To want nothing for one's self, but to merely strive to make others happy. I also wanted to be Galahad when I grew up. The best knight in the world, the one whose purity makes him holy. Not the leader, not the best at straight-up combat, but the one whose will cannot be shaken by doubt or fear.

When I was 13, I wanted to be Topher Brink. I still wanted power and control; that hadn't changed since age nine. But by 13, it wasn't good enough to have power and autonomy, out on my isolated ranch with my dogs.

I wanted other people to know just how good, how powerful, I was. I wanted to grind the faces of the kids who teased me in junior high into the dirt. I wanted to see their pain, wanted them to cower. I wanted the people of the world, and especially my junior high school classmates, to know how thoroughly I had bested them through science, intellect and wit. Lacking physical and social skills, I wanted my brilliance to win. To win everything.

If I had been able to control the kids around me as Topher does the Dolls, I would have. I would have blasted new personalities into the heads of people I feared and hated. New, weak personalities. Like Topher, and unlike the clients of the Dollhouse, at age 13 I would not have gone in for sexual degradation. I would have done something far more insidious. I would have made everyone like the things I liked: *Max Headroom*, *Star Wars*, Stephen King and *Uncanny X-Men*. They would not have known as much as I did about those topics, of course, but enough to appreciate how much I knew. In eighth grade my English class was required to write a radio play. I wrote about four runaway teenage kids with elemental-based superpowers who were captured by an evil school-slash-government-agency, from which they then escaped. If I could have given my classmates new personalities, they all would have liked my radio play and performed it in front of the class with enthusiasm. Like Topher in Season One's "Haunted," I would have used my genius and power to make people into my friends.

I don't think Topher is a sociopath. I think Topher is an incredibly selfish being. He is someone for whom the playing field is so uneven, so not-level, that he tries to make every interaction a contest he can win. For Topher, everything is about how smart he can be. When confronted with physical threats and violence, Topher is still plotting how he can be smarter than the person attacking him. When his genius can't save him, Topher's got no other course of action.

Topher wants the world to be right for *him*. He wants what *he* wants. Yet, when that expands to include the happiness of other people, Topher participates in plots that do not meet his short-term goals of safety, acclaim and comfort. They meet his longer-term goals of safety for himself and others and comfort for everyone he reluctantly cares about. When I was 13, I thought the whole world could go hang – except for the people I loved.

I was Paul Ballard when I was 15. More of Victor's white-knight tendencies had stuck with me through junior high school's Topher years than I'd thought. I loved my friends in high school, and desperately wanted to save them. Save them from pain, from stress, from their parents, from the cruelties of high school romance, from their internally generated standards of failure. From the system, from the school. From themselves. I was utterly certain that I knew what was best for them. I knew how to save them all, if only they would let me.

As with Paul Ballard, my rescue fantasies were all about myself and had oh-so-very-little to do with the objects of said fantasy. Yes, it would have been nice if my friends stopped expressing their stress in complex and counter-productive ways. But my attempts at mothering and caring for my friends were always about my own feelings of powerlessness. I was overwhelmed and stressed, finding my own way through webs of relationships and expectation. How much easier for me, for Paul, to simply pick a goal and work towards it. Whether the object of the attention wanted it or not.

Paul Ballard is presented in the early episodes of Season One as heroic. Sort of. He's the hero red-herring. He does and says all the typically heroic things. That it's not right to enslave people. That a person should not have their body used without their permission. That stealing someone's life is wrong. But Ballard acts as though the Dollhouse story is about *him*, not the Dolls.

His stated goal is to "bring down the Dollhouse," to defeat a worthy villain and thus make himself great. He takes the machinations of the Dollhouse personally, welcomes the attacks. The resistance of the Dollhouse to Ballard's probing validates him. It means he's on the right track, it means he is powerful, that his actions have weight and authority. Ballard needs to be a threat to someone – *anyone* – in order to not feel like a victim himself. This is clear to the other characters on the show. From Ballard's FBI peers, to Adele DeWitt, to Echo herself – everyone can tell that Ballard's quest to destroy the Dollhouse is about Ballard.

In college I wanted to be Echo, sort of. Or maybe date her. Or, perhaps, be her friend? Rescue her? During college I wanted such contradictory things.

I wanted to be completely autonomous, without needing anyone. Some days I went through my life callously careless of the people with whom I had connections – much like Echo's original personality, Caroline. She's not a very nice person. When I watched the show, I was pleased to see that. I like Echo – I like her stubborn insistence on remaining who she is, regardless of how she came to be that person. I didn't want to see Echo vanish, lost to Caroline's prior claims. Caroline will cast aside people who don't serve her goals, even if she likes or loves them. Caroline uses people in the service of that which she deems most important. Caroline is a lot like Paul Ballard that way; I expect they wouldn't have gotten along at all.

But I also wanted to make connections with people. In spite of who I was, who they were, and the fact that all of us used each other to greater or lesser degrees. Used each other to experiment on, to find out how this whole "being an adult and having relationships" thing worked. I often didn't know who I'd be talking to, the next time I saw my friends. Would they be kind? Ingratiating? Dismissive? Would I be on the inside of the group conversation or the outside? It wasn't that my friends were particularly rotten people. We were all kind or cruel to each other in the same ways, to the same degree as most everyone is in college. I spent too much time and energy pretending I knew who I was to notice that everyone else was wearing masks. Yet, like Echo and Victor and Sierra, some things would hold through. I still have friendships from that time in my life. The three Dolls learned to like and trust each other despite all their masks and false personalities. True identity glimmered through the erasures and imprints.

When I was in college, I craved to be special. (Who am I kidding? I wanted to be special most of my life. Now I have kids, though, and the world no longer revolves around me.) But when I was in college I no longer wanted to be Topher, with his arrogance and demand for recognition. Nor did I want to be Paul, precisely. I still wanted to rescue people, but not for the power it granted me. Like Echo, I wanted to rescue people because I wanted to remake the world. From a geeky kid who wanted to run away from the world, to a young adolescent wanting to force the world to acknowledge me, to a high school kid wanting to be the center of my friends' lives, I had managed to progress to some sort of sense of universal justice. I wanted the world to conform to the principles I thought best. Personal freedom, freedom from coercion, ownership of one's body and sexuality. A very American, middle class, privileged view of social justice – but still, social justice. In college I signed petitions, I attended a few rallies. I spent a lot of time talking to my friends about how we obviously knew the answers to the world's ills. I was never quite an activist. I admired the people who were. Particularly the women I had crushes on, with their passion and energy. But I never managed to commit to anything.

These days, I identify with Adele DeWitt. Of all the characters on *Dollhouse*, she seems the most adult. Adele accepts her actions and their consequences. She apologizes when she is wrong. She stands her ground when she is right. She changes her mind and her plans when a convincing argument is made that she should do so. Adele can be wrong, and she does harm in the world. But she also has a code of ethics that leads her to use her power in the Rossum Corporation for the greater good.

None of which is why I respect her the most. I respect Adele DeWitt because she lies to herself least of all the characters on the show. Adele knows why she participates in the Dollhouse. And as those original and compelling reasons are eroded away, Adele changes her position to remain in congruence with her internally generated sense of right and wrong action. She remains true to herself in a world and on a show dedicated to the idea that everyone and everything is false. That character is for sale, that anyone and anything can be bought. Adele doesn't pretend, like Ballard, that she can't be bought. He knows she can be; knows she has been. But she also has the strength to walk away when the cost is too dear. This ability to navigate a complex and ambiguous world while remaining true to one's self is what I most admire. I hope that I have some of it. I also hope to never be in a position like Adele's in which I have to find out.

I still find Victor and Sierra's relationship sweet. (This is made easy by incredibly good acting on the part of Enver Gjokaj and Dichen Lachman.) But I can see the problems with it. When Victor and Sierra leave the Dollhouse and return to their identities as Tony and Priya, they don't know each other. Not really. I've dated enough, had enough relationships, to understand that falling in love isn't love. That love is hard work, and that as much as you like and respect someone, you may not be the right person to date them. I was pleased beyond measure to see that Priya and Tony had broken up in the future of "Epitaph Two: Return." And I was more pleased to see that they still obviously cared for each other. Respected each other. Loved each other. They just hadn't been able to move through the world as partners – though perhaps, after the world-wipe, they might be able to. People grow and change. It's a truth that the Dollhouse's imprint process attempted to deny. The imprint kept the Dolls unchanged, unable to learn. But Priya and Tony had a chance to live in the world. I hoped, at the end of the last episode, that they had grown enough to be good for each other. To see each other as the people they really are.

I love watching Topher on the screen. He's the frenetic, arrogant sort of geek around whom I still spend a lot of my social time. The one who professes not to care about having been picked on in third grade, but who manages to make every possible interaction a contest. Who is smarter? Who is more right? Who wins a fight held 25 years ago in a playground far, far away? I no longer share those views, but I understand them. A great part of the glee I have in watching Topher is seeing those playground fantasies of power and prestige come true. But I no longer believe that my self-worth comes from the accolades awarded by others. My power and autonomy are not prizes handed out by an admiring crowd. They are built by my own actions, whether those actions are public or private.

Watching Paul Ballard these days makes me wince as I remember my own past actions. I find him so creepy, so manipulative, so *blind* to anyone else. Watching him try to rescue Caroline makes me want to call up all my high school friends and apologize for not truly seeing them. There are many levels of evil in *Dollhouse*. There's Topher's power-mad evil, using people as components in his power fantasy, but Topher never believes he's doing it for the Dolls' own good. There's Adele's evil, as pimp and madam and broker in human beings, but she also doesn't think the whole thing is in the Dolls' best interest. She thinks it probably doesn't hurt them too much, but Adele points out that the Dolls are paid for their loss. Paid for the loss of their time and autonomy. It's a deal in which everyone gets something, but it's not altruism.

Ballard thinks he's an altruist. He thinks everyone should be pleased at the way he's putting himself on the line, risking it all for people he doesn't know. He thinks if he rescues Caroline, his life will be worth something. It's a pervasive and almost-impossible-to-root-out form of insecurity, the feeling that one isn't worthwhile unless and until someone else owes one something. But Ballard doesn't realize that making people indebted to you is not the same as having their respect, in much the same way that Topher doesn't understand that humiliating people with your skills doesn't make them respect you. Rescuing someone, the way Ballard intends to, doesn't make the object of the rescue any stronger. It doesn't make them autonomous. It merely trades one form of dependence for another. If Ballard had actually broken Caroline free of the Dollhouse, how could she have ever balanced the debt between her and Ballard? Would she have thanked him at all? From what we know of Caroline, I rather suspect she wouldn't.

Watching *Dollhouse*, Echo was my least favorite part of the show. As much as I disliked Ballard, I still found his character engaging and interesting. Echo was... neither of those things, to me. Part of that disinterest on my part was due to the nature of the show's premise – it's hard to like a character whose principle trait is that she has no personality. But part of my lack of caring was due to my own experience of the world. I'm 37 years old as I write this. I have a better, though still imperfect, understanding of personal relationships than I did when I was younger. I no longer think I'm the center of the universe, nor do I want to be. And I know, now, that I can't rescue anyone.

I rooted for Echo to get all the Dolls out of the Dollhouse. I loved the Season One episode, "Needs," in which Echo gets to succeed at this goal and save everyone. Yet I applauded the fact that the whole thing was a huge trick. *Yes*, I thought. *It's not that easy. You never actually get to save anyone.*

In everyday life, the lives lived by the majority of people who watched *Dollhouse*, most people are not enslaved. We're not being trafficked to rapists. We're not coerced into selling our bodies to avoid a prison sentence. For *most* of us, most of our problems are both solvable (with effort and sacrifice) and of our own making. Our problems are real, they are difficult and painful. But they are not problems from which we can be *rescued*. We can be helped, certainly. But no one can swoop in and make everything better for us. To do so trades our autonomy and power for the temporary and illusory relief of not thinking about the problem. Our lives get better when we take steps. When we leave the emotionally abusive partner, even though we're scared of what happens next. When we get a second job to cover the tuition, and stop smoking so much pot. When we ask a coworker for help and get rides to and from work for a few weeks. When our power is taken away from us, *we* have to take it back. Autonomy is not a gift. It *cannot* be a gift.

Rescue is a gift one can only give to one's self.

I love this fact about *Dollhouse*. I love that the attempts to rescue people fail so miserably. Ballard's multiple attempts to rescue Mellie fail. She remains part of the Rossum web. Echo's effort to free the Dolls in "Needs"? A huge trick, and a failure. Alpha's attempts to free Whiskey, and Echo? Failures. As for the attempts by the characters to improve their lives or save themselves? Just like in real life, the results are mixed. Whiskey's fate was a shock to me. I had been so pleased when she walked away from the Dollhouse. I was happy when she was living with Boyd in an apparently consensual relationship between free adults. And there she is in Season Two's "Getting Closer," a puppet and tool and slave all along. And Topher finds madness and death. But Priya and Tony make lives – not the lives they would have chosen had the world remained sane, but lives built of their will and their hands.

I have always loved and identified with fantasies of power, in different ways at different times in my life, as my needs, fears, and desires have changed. *Dollhouse*, with its story of overt slavery, coded and overt rape, economic coercion and devaluation of human life, is a platform designed specifically to discuss the human craving for control of self. The show presents us with an absolute imbalance of power. The Dolls are people so powerless they no longer have their own names. And their abusers are a secret society of the world's most powerful elite, untouchable by any means. Yet the story told in this setting is one of reclamation of identity, a story of people regaining their autonomy and finding their responsibility to humanity. Our gang of Dolls and Dollmakers, slaves and owners, pimps and whores, the cast-aside and forgotten, the broken and abused – and the bought collaborators who abused them – these people conspire to make their own freedom. They drag themselves into autonomy and power. They save themselves, and in doing so save the world.

# A Couch Potato's Guide to Demon Slaying: Turning Strangers into Family, *Buffy*-Style

**Heather Shaw** is a writer, editor, gardener, aikidoka and Joss Whedon fan living in Berkeley, California, with her husband and son. She's had fiction in *Strange Horizons, Polyphony, The Year's Best Fantasy, Escape Pod* and other nice places. She just finished her first middle-grade novel, *Keaton T., Junior Gene Hacker*, and is looking for representation. She considers *Buffy* to have been her gateway drug to the world of Joss Whedon. She loved *Angel* almost as much, adored *Firefly*, loyally watched every episode of *Dollhouse* and wishes they'd make *Dr. Horrible's Sing-Along Blog* into a series, already.

I came to *Buffy the Vampire Slayer* after the second season, drawn in by my post-collegiate roommates who made it a weekly ritual to gather and watch each new episode as it aired. I had been turned off by the name "Buffy," I think – it conjured up images of perky girls in Izod shirts with sweaters tied around their necks who spoke as if they had lockjaw. I thought it had to be stupid fluff at best, and more likely insulting dreck.

How very wrong I was.

I was desperately lonely in those days – I'd moved over 2000 miles from Indiana to live in Oakland, CA, with only one of my own college friends around to ease my transition. I'd made some new friends, but they were still "weekend friends" mostly because they lived in a part of Oakland that you needed a car to get to, and I didn't have one. My roommates were strangers to me when I moved in. I'd answered an ad on Craigslist for a room in an already-occupied house – a pretty standard living situation in your mid-20s, but still a daunting prospect. I'm not terrible in social situations, but I'm also sometimes very shy, and I spent a lot of my after-work time locked in my room, trying to write, or read, or just stay out of everyone's way.

I think, being so far away from my own family, watching the camaraderie of the group of friends on the screen – how they formed their own, created family – made me feel a little less lonely.

My roommates and I crammed on a tiny, hard futon – one of those that didn't have arms on the sides – to watch. Two of us balanced on the futon, while the other would sit on a big floor pillow on our scratchy plastic carpet. Our landlord had apparently never heard of carpet padding, and had installed the cheap carpet over concrete, so we quickly started up a rotation so no one was stuck on the floor pillow every week.

We actually still didn't have that much in common, but every Tuesday night, we gathered together and spent a happy hour watching the created family of Buffy, Xander, Willow, Cordelia and Giles solve much more difficult problems than a housemate forgetting to buy toilet paper this time, or how Luis took more time in the bathroom than Diana and I combined. (He did have great hair tips, though.)

When Luis[1] moved out and Diana invited Julie to move in before asking me (or even introducing us), our small created family took a big hit. It's hard to get off on the right foot when you only find out you're losing your old roommate when a stranger starts moving her furniture in right in front of you. But I was raised in the Midwest, so I was polite even though I was furious. It wasn't until a few minutes later when Julie brought in a new, overstuffed, full-sized couch big enough for three or four people to sit on that I began to see the upside of our new arrangement.

Still, it was awkward the next Tuesday when the three of us sat down for our first episode of *Buffy* together. The episode was "Faith, Hope and Trick," where we meet Faith, the new Slayer and Buffy's rival.

Diana squirmed as we watched the Scooby gang try to deal with this new arrival, but Julie, who was watching her first-ever *Buffy* episode, seemed oblivious to her counterpart on the screen. When we finished the episode, we didn't celebrate the fact that someone got through it without their butt being numb from having to sit on the floor, because Julie announced that *Buffy* was stupid. Diana stared at her, aghast. I shot Diana a triumphant look. Clearly, if she had let me vet our new roommate, this would never have happened.

Thankfully, though she never became a part of our *Buffy* family, Julie didn't mind if we used her couch to watch *Buffy* every week. And when she finally moved out, it was her couch that we were the saddest to see go.

Diana and I picked our next roommate, Michael, together, and he was a great choice. Diana insisted we get a guy this time ("a *straight* guy"), because she was sick of how long Luis and then Julie took in the bathroom in the mornings. Even though we were back to the old, now rickety (from being in storage) futon, our new roommate came preinstalled with *Buffy* fandom. We started Season Four together, and when we watched the second episode, "Living Conditions" – about Buffy's horrible new roommate who turns out to be an actual demon – we bonded over past bad roommates, telling Michael all about Julie's spontaneous parties and how she planted an ornamental plum tree in the front yard, shading the sunny garden spot, without asking us. "Living Conditions" became part of our canon – if one of us was annoying, we would label the eggs with their name as a funny way to let them know they were "becoming a Kathy."

---

1. Some names have been changed, to save us all from embarrassment.

Even though we watched every week and were enthusiastic about preaching our love of *Buffy* to everyone who would listen, it wasn't until "Hush" that it really hit us how amazing the show was. In "Hush," a group of demons called the Gentlemen come to Sunnyvale and steal everyone's voices, and most of the episode is performed in perfect silence. That episode made us aware of the genius behind the show – that Joss could build a group of characters and give them complicated relationships and funny interactions and painful growth experiences was one thing, but his being able to maintain and even improve on the intricate interactions while taking away everyone's voices drove home how intensely connected the little family on the screen had become. That sort of unspoken communication takes years to develop in real life, and he'd made it seem not only possible, but utterly believable, on the screen. Our reaction, after the final moments of the show, when Buffy and Riley try to talk but sit together in their own, non-demon-created silence, was to jump up on the poor futon and shout at one another about how freaking *amazing* the show was that we'd just watched, ending in a group hug.

Another thing we bonded over was our dislike – okay, outright hatred – of Riley. What was fascinating about our shared resentment was that we each hated him for very different reasons. Diana didn't like him because he was too goody-goody. Michael agreed with that, but also resented his patriarchal representations of manhood – how he was always trying to protect Buffy when she was clearly more than capable of not only protecting herself, but of also saving his own sorry ass at the same time. I definitely agreed with that – though I thought Joss was playing around with this notion of traditional gender roles to make his outstanding use of strong women elsewhere in the show stand out; Riley provided contrast. But what I really resented about Riley was that I thought the actor playing him just wasn't all that good. (At least in that role; I've seen him in other stuff and didn't hate him in it, so maybe he just didn't click with the character? Who knows.) Also? I am from Indiana, and even though Riley was from Iowa, it was near enough for me to feel he was giving my own background a bad name. Why couldn't someone *cool* come from the Midwest, dammit?

Looking back, I think we were missing what really caused our extreme discontent with Riley as a character. One of the best things about Joss Whedon's work is that he not only assembles a brilliant ensemble cast of unique and fascinating characters, but that he *uses* each and every one of them. No character is used as window dressing in a group scene in *Buffy* – everyone is active and fully participating in the scenes. But even though Joss included Riley in this, he never felt fully a part of the team. Now, you could argue that Joss understood this, and even played with the idea (in "The I in Team," Buffy's involvement with Riley and the Initiative makes Willow worried that she won't have enough time for her friends), but even if it was deliberate, it felt perilously close to a false step with the series. It made us uneasy; we were invested in the little family of characters on the screen, to the point where our own invented family relied on it not only as a family ritual, but as a common language and source of metaphors (a broken glass might elicit the quip, "This is the crack team that foils my every plan? I am deeply shamed," and a request for privacy for a date would always get the reply, "Oh, you mean an orgasm friend?") used to lighten the mood as we navigated the trick of living together without killing one another.

I'm not saying it was a deal-breaker. I can't imagine Joss Whedon creating a deal-breaker. But one of the things I've always loved about *Buffy* was this sense of unity, of creating a family from your friends, and while he added other family members to the original Scooby gang with success, we never felt Riley was among his more successful attempts.

Summer is a drought of reruns, of course, but as autumn (and Season Five) rolled around, Diana moved out and Michael's girlfriend, Kim, moved in. I was a little nervous about this, as before the three roommates had always initially been strangers, but now two of them not only knew one another (they'd gone to school on the East Coast together), but they were *romantically involved* (and thus, the potential for Real Drama was much bigger). Not only were they college friends and dating, but the force of the two of them living in one space (and the fact that we had a house and not a tiny apartment) meant that all of their local college friends (a surprising number, considering the college in question was over 2,000 miles away) would often descend on our house, turning *Buffy* night from an intimate, created-family bonding experience into... well, a party.

But before the party atmosphere took over, there were a few episodes of *Buffy* with just the three of us. Diana had taken the rickety old futon with her when she moved out, and Kim didn't come with living room furniture, so I got a... well, to call it a "couch" would be giving it too much credit (I hesitate to even call it furniture). It was a cushiony thing that would inexorably lower you slowly onto the floor when you sat on it. It didn't take long before we were fighting over who got the floor space and who was forced to sit on that melty slanty cushiony thing.

In retrospect, adding Kim to our little created family sort of reflected what was happening on *Buffy*. The second episode of Season Five introduced Dawn as Buffy's sister, an "actual" family member addition and not just a friend that became like family. There was a *lot* of speculation over this in our house – what was she really was, could Joss really mess with canon like that and make us buy it (answer: yes, of course), and so forth. We did grow to love Dawn (though Michael always reacted to her as you would an annoying little sister – pretending to hate on her, but affectionately) and I grew to love Kim as one of the very best roommates I've ever had. She was funny, sweet and not at all annoying. Okay, the analogy is breaking down here – I never liked Dawn as much as, say, Willow or Xander – but it was sort of neat how our own household family sorted itself out with a "real" family member (in the form of a girlfriend) at the same time our Scooby gang was accepting theirs.

But, as I said, with Kim came, eventually, a whole gaggle of people – and once that started happening, my shyness kicked in. My roommate's friends already *knew* each other, and college in-jokes from years back trumped *Buffy* quotes. They were loud, raucous and fun-loving, and – most damning of all – they took up all available seating and most of the floor space.

I hate to admit it, but for a few weeks it drove me back into my room, even during *Buffy*.

But there's something compelling about a group of people who travel from all around the San Francisco Bay Area on a "school night" (which we called them even though it was work instead of school we had to get up early for the next morning) to gather for a TV show. Shy as I was, there was some serious shit going down that season, and it was all wrapped up in a mystery, too. Soon, I was standing off to the side, watching. That episode was "Family" – the one where Tara, a relatively new character (as far as Scooby gang members go), is convinced she has a demon inside her and is almost persuaded to go with her (rather restrictive) "real" family back home where she can be locked away to keep others safe. Maybe it was the way the created family on the screen was more willing to accept Tara for who she was than her "real" family did, or maybe it was the glorious way the entire Scooby gang stands between Tara and her father when he tries to force her to leave with him at the end, but that episode helped shoo away most of my shyness. Sure, my roommates had bonds with their friends, but that didn't mean I couldn't make my own.

The next week, I was claiming my right to sit on the floor with my housemates. Sure, some of their friends had to watch from the side, but I paid 1/3 of the rent, dammit. And, soon, our shared *Buffy* experiences made it even easier to get to know this extended family that came with my roommates. In Season Five, my social circle blossomed.

This seems as good a place as any to mention that at some point around then I interviewed for a job where, when interviewing with my potential coworkers, I was asked by more than one person, "And do you watch *Buffy*?" When I answered "yes" the first person interviewing me said, "Oh good! We talk about the last night's episode every Wednesday; it'll be great to have new perspectives on it in the office!" Is it any coincidence that I still work at that company now, over eight years later? I think not!

Meanwhile, in my own personal life, I was dating. I'd been in relationships and dated in the past, of course, but romantically, I was really lonely around this time. While I'd had some fun, lighthearted flings, they weren't relationships that were going to last and I was determined to find myself one... maybe even *the* one.

But dating isn't fun. The number of guys that you go out with who end up being complete duds skyrockets when you're looking for someone to really click with. I quickly learned things such as "if he's a bad kisser, just cut it off after that first date; it's a good indication of bad chemistry in other areas, too" and "facial hair goes right up your nose, ew!!!" (This was later amended to "hippie facial hair goes right up your nose, ew!!!" as well-trimmed facial hair is actually kind of nice. But I digress...)

*Any*way, as I was in my own whirlwind of looking for chemistry, I had a lot of interest in Spike's ongoing infatuation with *Buffy* during Season Five. Not that I was pining after any one in particular, but those two had great chemistry on screen, and even though she wasn't giving in (that season, at least), it was a glorious thing to see. And, I might add, much easier on me than watching my disgustingly-happy roommates smooch all the damn time (that's from the perspective of a single girl, mind you; I'm very happy for them now). I could project myself onto Buffy, and boy, was I ever... appreciative of Spike's, um, gifts to womankind.

So I had a lot of sympathy when, in a misguided attempt to create love for himself, Warren makes a robot woman to be his girlfriend (and, of course, I was furious and devastated at how he treated her). And Spike's commission of the BuffyBot, while also misguided, was a brilliant stroke of storytelling. I mean, if your "real" family doesn't work, Joss has shown us that it's possible to create your own, yes? So, in a way, Spike was just taking that idea to the next, very wrong, level.

Alas, in my own life, I knew no mad scientists (well, no crazy scientists, or evil engineers), and wasn't really that interested in forcing anyone to love me. I wanted to be loved for who I was by someone I could love for who he was.

And then, on St. Patrick's Day, 2001, I met Tim Pratt on my doorstep at a *Strange Horizons* tea party for author Nalo Hopkinson.

Now, I must confess, I didn't see him wholly for the wonderful man he was at the time, but that's not entirely my fault. For one thing, *OMG Nalo Hopkinson was in my house!!!!!!!* I get flustered when I'm hero-worshipping, and I was helping Mary Anne Mohanraj (the original editor-in-chief of *Strange Horizons*) host a party full of editors, writers and *Nalo Hopkinson*!!! What I'm saying here is, I was distracted.

But he noticed me, and it wasn't long until he was sending me nice long emails, and driving up for our first date in the Oakland Rose Garden.

No, this part doesn't have anything to do with *Buffy*, except that sometimes when you're creating your own, eventually "real" family, you don't have time for your created ones, not even the ones you can set the VCR for. It didn't help that Tim was not preinstalled with the Buffy-love. And I was too busy falling head-over-heels with him to worry about it. The fact that he lived an hour-and-a-half drive away in Santa Cruz didn't help me make time for other leisure.

But then he moved in with me the summer of 2001. (And, for those keeping track of couches, he brought a couch with him! A real couch! With springs in it and everything! Sure, it was from the Salvation Army, but it was the best couch since Julie.) Michael *and* Kim moved out – I think someone got into Columbia for grad school – at exactly the same time Tim's job in Santa Cruz ended. One of Kim and Michael's friends "moved" in at the same time, but she ended up staying with her boyfriend for most of the month (seriously, she only came by to drop off the rent check; Best. Roommate. Ever.), so Tim and I had the place more or less to ourselves. And because he was living with me, we had more time, and we got one thing out of the way right away.

I turned him on to *Buffy*.

It didn't hurt that Season Six was my favorite season. (I know, lots don't like it for various reasons, but shh!) Spike and Buffy finally get together! And at the end of a *musical episode*!! I have always loved musical theatre (I did some in high school and college), so I was thrilled by "Once More with Feeling"; it's definitely the episode of *Buffy* that I've watched the most times. I got a pirated version of the soundtrack from a friend, but don't worry – I bought a copy of the official version as soon as it came out.

The Spike/Buffy romance was seriously hot, hot, *hot*. And, since we were in the middle of new relationship energy, it was a *nice* counterpoint to our relationship. Sure, it was rocky, but then we were both learning to live with a romantic partner for the first time in our lives (hoo boy, was that not easy), so we grokked the rocky. And when they were sexy while we were rocky, it helped remind us (in part) of what we were in it for.

How much did Tim get into *Buffy* with me? We scoured eBay for pirated VHS versions of the seasons he missed. We learned both parts to "I'll Never Tell" (the song Anya and Xander sing in "Once More with Feeling") and sang it together – me doing Anya's part, and Tim doing Xander's. When the DVDs started coming out, we bought up each season as soon as it was available.

Now, it's hard not to focus almost entirely on Tim, but I should note that around the end of Season Five, I started to become close friends with Susan Marie Groppi, who lived around the corner. She was at that brunch where I met Tim, and she was an editor at *Strange Horizons*. And, she too, loved *Buffy*. It wasn't long after Tim moved in that she was making a regular night of coming over to watch *Buffy* and drink wine with us. This not only kept us from missing too much *Buffy* by turning it into a make-out fest (easy to do, but it would have been tragic, especially considering how much we loved that season), but it started our own, new, little family.

We watched Seasons Six and Seven together, but we were a little bummed about the latter. Maybe it was because the series was obviously ending, and that was such a downer. Maybe it was because we were getting really into *Angel* instead. But, no matter what, when *Buffy* aired its last new episode, at least we had one another to help us through that dark time.

A few years later, Tim and I got married, and Susan was one of my brides-maids. A few years after that, Tim and I had a son, River; we're debating how old he should be before he's old enough to sit down and watch all seven seasons of *Buffy* (and *Angel*) with us. Not yet, alas. But our little created family has become one of those "real" ones we disparaged years before. Funny how that works.

Now, over nine years since I met both of them, Susan is still a close friend of ours – in fact, I wrote part of this essay this while flying home from being the maid of honor at her wedding. We certainly would have met, and would probably have found other ways to bond even without *Buffy*, but those regular nights, sitting together in front of the screen, brought us together and taught us a bit about how families – really good, interesting and witty ones – work together, treat one another and create a lifelong family where before there were just friends.

# Smart Is Sexy: An Appreciation of *Firefly*'s Kaylee

**Laurel Brown** is a senior engineer who works at a major aerospace defense firm in the Midwestern United States. She has been a science fiction fan for almost all of her life and has participated in conventions, writing fan fiction, and general squee for just as long.

Close your eyes and picture your ideal mechanic. Who are they? What do they look like? Are they male or female? Clean or dirty? Who would you rather work on, your car? When I imagine a mechanic, I tend to see a man, covered in grease, buried underneath my car. It's a stereotype, but that's my fallback image, and – as much as I love it – I'm still startled whenever I see a female mechanic.

*Firefly* is one of the few television series that defies this stereotype, and while all of its lead women are mould-breakers, there's something unique – and something deeply personal for me – about Kaylee, the mechanic on *Serenity*. As much as I love all the *Firefly* characters, it was the instant that we were introduced to Kaylee that made me stop and say, "Oh, yes..." So, this essay is written in celebration of her.

Science fiction television, films, and books tend to cast engineers and mechanics as men, whether you're dealing with a planet-based science fiction series (e.g., *Eureka*) or a starship-driven universe such as *Star Trek*. Want your warp drive to go faster? Here's Scotty or Geordi LaForge. Is there a strange, improbable invention that needs to be created or fixed? Again, it's generally a man such the Doctor on *Doctor Who* or James Bond's Q who will solve the problem for you. This is even true for shows outside the science fiction genre (e.g., *Gilligan's Island*'s Professor). You'll rarely – if ever – find that the person who makes your ship travel through the black is a woman.

There's a reason for this. The public's preconceptions regarding engineers and mechanics for a long time got fed into Hollywood (or elsewhere, as the case might be), and influenced any number of television shows, whether they were outside the science fiction genre and firmly rooted in it (such *Star Trek: The Next Generation*, *The X-Files*, *SeaQuest DSV* and their ilk). It's only relatively recently that we've seen shows where women – specifically intelligent women – were playing any role other than the nurturer. But thanks to *Firefly*, I can finally watch television and see women who are a lot more like me, and it's brilliant.

What do I do for a living? Well, I'm a female engineer. I could go a step further and say why, yes, I *am* a rocket scientist. I don't work for NASA or on any actual rockets, but my degree is in aerospace engineering. I do work on aircraft and spend most of my time trying to make them work better. I just don't work on anything as amazing as *Serenity*. (Yet.)

Kaylee is clever, beautiful, witty, and works in a technical position on this amazing ship. This is probably the point where I should make some bad joke about how engineers don't really have the best people skills, but I'll abstain. We've seen clever women shown on television before – Dana Scully on *The X-Files* and Samantha Carter on *Stargate SG-1* come to mind – but they weren't same sort of character as Kaylee. Her technical skills rather than her educational background are what's important. Generally, before you can get some sort of technical position, you have to have an education to get your foot in the door. Without that piece of paper, you don't have much chance of becoming the equivalent of a chief engineer. The most you could ever hope for would be some sort of fabrication job.

The *Firefly* universe changes that; to get a berth as an engineer, you have to prove yourself. Kaylee doesn't flash a degree; she first earns her place on *Serenity* (as shown in *Out of Gas*) by pointing out where another mechanic went wrong.

> **Kaylee:** Grav boot ain't your trouble. I seen the trouble plain as day when I was down there on my back before. Your reg couple's bad.
> **Mal:** You got much experience with a vessel like this?
> **Kaylee:** I never even been up in one before.
> **Mal:** Wanna?

One thing that I've learned in my years as a practicing engineer is that an education is just a threshold you have to cross to get to where you want to be. To be truthful, I have used what I learned at university maybe a grand total of three times in the past ten years. Education isn't what counts in engineering. What counts is having good instincts, the will to use them, and the knowledge that can only be earned either by being a savant or through years of on-the-job training.

The knowledge that I'm speaking about – the knowledge that's gained through experience rather than education – is the sort of gut feeling that strikes you when you look at something and think, "Something's wrong with that." It can be as complex as picturing whatever you're working on in your head – seeing all the gears and gizmos at work and realizing how they interconnect – and knowing what might be wrong. It can also be as simple as following a gut feeling that something is wrong and going about proving it.

I can close my eyes and imagine how I might react in any given situation Kaylee is thrown into. I'm invested in this character because I can identify with her. We have some things in common.

Kaylee is a savant who learned at her father's knee and through on-the-job training. In "Out of Gas," she says that she doesn't know how she does what she does. Machines just seem to talk to her. She can make just about anything work when she's got the parts and the time. Education isn't what counts in the *Firefly*verse. It's being able to do something with yourself. Being able to take something that's broken and fix it, even if it means getting down and dirty to do it.

Kaylee is an engineering savant, but she's also a woman and refuses to let us forget it. Women like Kaylee tend to get assessed by what they wear, what they do and how they talk. Kaylee likes her frippery – pink lace and frills – and she likes men, but she also happens to be a mechanic. She's inclined to walk around in coveralls and loves to tinker about with machines, but she also can appreciate and – yes, covet – beautiful things. That doesn't make her any less a woman.

*Firefly's* characters are apt to judge Kaylee by what they see. Even Mal, who normally is an understanding type, can only see the technician in Kaylee and not the woman. And so in "Shindig," Kaylee – who is all dressed up – is obviously hurt by an unthinking comment on Mal's part:

> **Kaylee:** I like the ruffles. Inara gets to wear whatever she wants.
> **Mal:** What are you going to do in that rig? Flounce around the engine room? Be like a sheep walking on its hind legs.

Here is a man who works with her, day in and day out, and cannot see who she is beyond what she does in the engine room. Mal *does* apologize later by bringing her with him to the shindig, but the damage is done.

At the party, in one of my favorite scenes of the entire series, Kaylee wears that dress she so fancies, truly showing who and what she is. She's not afraid to be herself. She doesn't try to fit herself into other's preconceptions and, instead, makes her own way rather than the one expected of her. She might be wearing clothing that was bought at a store, but she knows her worth – and so do the infatuated men surrounding her for the sake of hearing her opinions on machinery. The women who scorned her at the party do not get even half the attention she earns simply by being brilliant. It doesn't matter how fancy her dress is – or how many slaves dressed her – what matters is what she knows and how she conveys it and that's what those men respond to.

I also love that Kaylee doesn't get drowned in technobabble. She tells it like it is in simple terms that anyone can understand. She's not hampered by her cleverness. In "Out of Gas," she tells Mal:

**Kaylee:** Catalyzer on the port compression coil blew. It's where the trouble started.
**Mal:** 'Kay, I need that in captain dummy-talk, Kaylee.
**Kaylee:** We're dead in the water.

This is what makes me want to jump up and say, "Yes, this!" Kaylee flies into the face of convention, which makes her one of the best role models I've seen on television. She's a woman in an alternative role and doesn't mind that fact. She's not a nurturer like *Star Trek*'s Doctor Crusher or Counselor Troi. Nor is she a leadership type, who tend to be portrayed as more unattainable and, in some cases, less than a woman. For example, on *Star Trek: Voyager*, Captain Janeway was a woman, but she was asexual and abrasive. She didn't tend to wear "frippery" or get into romantic entanglements, nor did she tend to pamper herself. But Kaylee's life both before and during *Firefly* is something we can all relate to – she's someone we could meet on the street every day and not give her a second glance because, truly, she's extraordinary in her ordinariness.

Kaylee isn't only defined by her mechanical skills. She's defined by her relationships with others, both friendships and romantic entanglements. It's not possible to discuss Kaylee without talking about her relationship with Simon Tam. From the instant Simon ended up on *Serenity*, Kaylee had him firmly in her sights. She wasn't afraid to let him know she was interested, and not above needling him into giving her some sort of reaction. Simon was, after all, remarkably innocent of the way things go in the black.

There is a distinct class difference between Kaylee and Simon and a lot of their interactions reflect that. Simon has a tendency to talk down to Kaylee and dismiss the way she lives her life and sees the world as somehow being beneath him. Does she just sit down and take those insults? Does she storm off, insulted? No, she gives him what-for. She tells him that he has no right to insult her and hers. I love that she's gutsy enough to stand up for herself, even against someone who sees himself as superior simply because of his background.

Their relationship starts slowly and builds throughout the series. We know that Simon cares deeply for Kaylee, despite his insulting her with his "proper" attitudes. We never did get to see their relationship consummated on the small screen, though I know I was rooting for them – even when Simon was being a prat. Thankfully, we got to see their relationship reach its natural conclusion in the motion picture.

**Simon:** My one regret in all of this is never being with you.
**Kaylee:** With me? You mean to say, as in... sex?
**Simon:** I mean to say—

*Kaylee cocks her gun, with determination.*
**Kaylee:** Hell with this. I'm gonna live!

Even though this is a relationship only seen on television (and the silver screen), it seems so very real. The pitfalls of romance are portrayed well – she fancies him, he fancies her, there are arguments, teasing and insults. There are times where they aren't speaking to one another. The writing of this relationship – and of the characters involved – was so incredibly rich, and I do wish we'd gotten more of it before the show was cancelled.

I've spoken about how three-dimensional Kaylee is – her background and her abilities are clearly conveyed on screen, along with her chipper personality. She's always got a smile on her face and a strongly positive attitude. She might live with a group of criminals, but she doesn't let that sort of thing get her down. Instead, she's always a "ray of sunshine" amongst the rest of the crew. It would have been easy to make a character like Kaylee bitter. She's clever with machines, yes, but that doesn't necessarily mean she's as clever around other people. She could've been the rogue genius, unable to communicate with "normal" people. She could've been a morose woman, saddened by her treatment by the rest of the universe, and thus separating herself from it through aloofness and bitterness. She would've been a completely different character had they gone that route, and I'm so very glad they didn't.

She can always see the bright side of life. That is inspiring, especially to someone like me. I've seen how tough things can get. It'd be easy to let myself grow jaded, smile a little less, and cry a little more. Not Kaylee, though. As Mal remarks in the *Firefly* pilot: "I don't believe there is a power in the 'verse that can stop Kaylee from being cheerful."

The universe shown in *Firefly* isn't an easy place to live. There's an authoritarian Alliance in power, a failed rebellion, and struggles to make ends meet day to day. Smuggling is a way of life simply because prices are either too high or goods are not available out in the Rim territories where Serenity tends to travel. Bad things happen to good people and that's hard to deal with. Somehow, though, Kaylee can still see that silver lining despite this difficult world. There are instances where she's discouraged, or can't fix something ("Out of Gas"), but for the most part, she just remains cheerful. It always makes me smile when Kaylee chases River through the ship, all to get back an apple. Little moments like that make things seem a little better, even in a harsh universe. If only more of us could be like her – at least in that outlook – I suspect we'd have a lot less wars and a lot more laughter.

Now, we return full circle to the beginning. I want you to close your eyes again. Don't picture a simple mechanic. Picture someone who you'd like to have at your side, fixing your ship, in a world like *Firefly*'s. Who do you see? I see Kaylee.

# Teething Troubles and Growing Up

**Caroline Symcox** is currently in her final year of training for ordination in the Church of England at Ripon College Cuddesdon, and all being well will be ordained deacon in July 2011. When she's not studying theology and ministry, she enjoys writing fiction: her previous efforts being in the realm of *Doctor Who*. Her published work includes the audio dramas *Doctor Who: The Council of Nicaea* and *Doctor Who: Seasons of Fear* (with Paul Cornell) for Big Finish Productions, and the short story *A Question of Identity* in the first Bernice Summerfield short story anthology *The Dead Men Diaries*.

One of the things about being married to a TV writer is you realise how few people know who the writers of their favourite TV shows are. Or what they do. You have to be a pretty major fan of a show to know the names of the writers, despite the fact they're the ones who start the magic.

Joss Whedon is the exception to this rule.

Even my non-SF friends recognise the name Joss Whedon, and yes, plenty of my friends not of the genre faith were watching *Buffy*, *Angel*, and to some extent *Firefly*. What is it about Mr. Whedon and his work that means in his shows it's the writer who defines the product, rather than the actors?

My first introduction to Joss Whedon's shows was reading an issue of *SFX Magazine* I had picked up because I recognised the *Doctor Who* episode they were doing a retrospective of that issue. On the cover was a picture of Buffy in all her Season One glory. The show hadn't even been picked up in the UK at that point, but the *SFX* crew knew a good thing when they saw it. I read through the article and immediately knew I was going to be watching this show.

I was excited. I don't think I have, before or since, ever been excited by a show I hadn't even watched before.

And then *Buffy the Vampire Slayer* arrived in the UK. Sky One showed it. More importantly for me at the time, the terrestrial BBC 2 showed it, and my love for the work of Joss Whedon was born.

For those not from the UK, let me take a moment to explain what I'm talking about. At this point, if you bought a TV you would immediately have access to four, and later five, free channels. The first two were BBC1 and BBC2 – paid entirely through the License Fee, which is essentially a UK tax on television that goes towards running the BBC. So, no advertising breaks, but often a certain by-the-book reluctance to try new things. The final two channels were ITV and Channel 4 – both independent stations financed through advertising revenue. Later came Channel 5, running on the same lines. These are referred to as the UK's "terrestrial" channels.

However, if you had the free cash, and your town council didn't object to you sticking a satellite dish on the side of your house, you could get satellite TV, which usually (though not always) meant you got Sky One, among other channels. Sky, of course, got subscription fees as well as advertising revenue, and gained a reputation for buying up new American shows and showing them well ahead of their terrestrial competitors. *Buffy* included.

### *Angel* in the UK – When TV Executives Attack

By the time *Angel* arrived at the end of *Buffy* season three I knew I was ready to see more from Mr. Whedon. I had access to satellite television now, and could finally watch episodes as soon as they were shown in the UK. It was good to finally be at the cutting edge, and the prospect of a new, darker show definitely appealed. I was on the edge of my sofa as *Angel* prepared to hit our screens.

Unfortunately, that's more than I can say for the TV executives over here in the UK, which made for a frustrating time for British fans. This was during the period when the morally dubious phenomenon of Bittorrent hadn't yet appeared, and the internet, although a good place for discussing US shows, didn't actually make it possible to procure them. Audiences in the UK were entirely dependent on TV channels to see the latest episodes of *Buffy* and *Angel*.

And the UK channels didn't seem to know what they had.

*Buffy* hadn't done too badly in terms of programming slots. Sky One showed uncut episodes at 9pm, and made everyone happy. The BBC, on the other hand, stuck this new US import in the same place it stuck all its other US genre imports – at 6pm on BBC2. Problematic, given that the UK "watershed", the time before which no "adult" content (think of an American PG-13 level of violence, sexual content, swearing and so on) is to be shown, falls at 9pm. Unsurprisingly, this meant a large proportion of material had to be cut from the show to allow episodes to be shown so early. But still, things could be worse, because the BBC had enough sense to show repeats of uncut episodes a day or so after the original broadcast, and much later in the evening. Sure, there was a delay to see the real goods, but this was *Buffy* we were talking about, and it was worth the wait.

Unfortunately, yes indeed things could be worse. We discovered how much worse when *Angel* appeared on the UK scene.

If you were one of the lucky ones (like me, thanks to an advantageous marriage to a man with a satellite subscription), you had Sky One, and got to see new episodes of *Angel* immediately after *Buffy* on a Friday night. All well and good, especially for those key Season One crossover episodes. Less good later on when the shows had more or less firmly diverged, and suddenly you had two hours' worth of TV to watch at a sitting. Oh yes, no TiVo back then. No Sky + hard drive. You watched episodes when they were shown, unless you were organised enough to set the video recorder on the off chance you wouldn't have the mental energy to watch two episodes back to back. Because let's face it, watching TV for a couple of hours at a time erodes the concentration somewhat, even when those two hours are made up of *Buffy* and *Angel*.

But if you didn't have a Sky subscription, you were in trouble. In a surprise development, the BBC had been outbid for *Angel*'s terrestrial rights. Rather than episodes being shown alongside *Buffy* on BBC 2, new episodes of *Angel* were shown for the first time on Channel 4. Why the sudden competition? Who knows, because sadly, it was only when the deal was done and Channel 4 executives had *Angel* in their hands that they realised what they had actually bought. And they had no idea how to handle it.

*Angel* was not *Buffy the Vampire Slayer*. Producers and writers on the show, notably David Greenwalt and Joss himself, had been saying since the new show was announced that it was going to be a different beast from its parent programme. It was going to be darker. Grittier. More violent. And they weren't kidding. Adult themes and material appeared from the word go. Family viewing this was not.

So when Channel 4 chose to air episodes at 6pm, worried UK fans knew something had to give. There were cuts. And not just little surface cuts – a particular moment of violence here, an incidence of offensive language there – but deep, unsustainable cuts of material vital to plotlines. Episodes saw 10 to 15 minutes being cut from their duration. Plots actually became difficult to follow. In one epic case, the necessary cuts to show the episodes at the prescribed timeslot were so extensive that the episode wasn't shown at all. *Somnambulist* was never seen by Channel 4 viewers in the advertised slot for the first showing of episodes. A couple of weeks later a complaint was received by Broadcasting Standards, and before we knew what was happening, *Angel* was buried in an irregular post-midnight slot.

Predictably enough, UK fans exploded.

I was pretty new at the whole fandom game. All through my school years I'd been a thoroughly closeted fan of all things SF, on the understanding that science fiction in particular (and genre in general) weren't things that nice girls watched or read. Going to University brought a whole new lease of life, as I realised what I could enjoy with other people without needing to be embarrassed that I was enjoying it. And though I had gotten into *Doctor Who* fandom, it never felt as if I had any level of ownership, on a fan level. The new show had yet to come along, and most of the old series had been shown before I'd been born. *Buffy* and *Angel* were here and now, being shown for the first time, and I was a fan of them right from the beginning.

So it was a shock to the system to find that these wonderful new shows weren't quite as much mine as I had imagined. Rather than receiving and viewing the episodes in a wonderful direct line from production company to network, as with *Doctor Who*, suddenly there was this distance between production and audience. Sadly, a distance that was entirely open to unthinking abuse by the folk in the middle, in the form of UK channels. For the first time, I was seeing fans having to work to gain the full experience of a show that they loved.

Perhaps these initial teething troubles with *Angel* on UK television were what meant the show didn't seem to take off as much as *Buffy* had done over here. The mass appeal that had happened with *Buffy* simply didn't happen. Your average man in the street, or student at university, would happily recognise the name *Buffy* and sit down to watch an episode. Not so with *Angel*. But again, perhaps because of these initial difficulties, the folk who did become enamoured of the new show became a rock solid core of fans. There's nothing like weathering trouble together, and actually working for a show to give you a stake in it, if you'll forgive the pun. It was entirely possible to be a fair weather fan of *Buffy*, but when it came to *Angel*, there was no middle ground. Either you were a fan or you weren't.

### Different show, different fandom: *Angel* versus *Doctor Who*

All of this felt a long way away from my experience of being a *Doctor Who* fan in the early days of watching the show, and not just because I was an adult fan this time, and not one of the legions of small children watching the good Doctor on the BBC. For a start, it felt like it was harder to get to grips with *Angel* simply because I wasn't surrounded by people who knew what I was talking about. In the UK, *everybody* watched *Doctor Who*. If I wanted to talk through an episode, all I needed to do was show up to school and get chatting with the girl at the next desk. With *Angel* though, the audience was small enough that you had to go out of your way to hunt down other viewers.

Just as the difficulties managing to even *watch* a more or less intact episode cemented those who weathered the troubles into a solid core of fans, so did the sense of being an isolated audience. There's a tremendous sense of ownership that comes with the awareness you're part of a select band of people tuning in to watch on a Friday evening. Nothing forges a fandom like adversity, and watching *Angel* had adversity in spades.

This was compounded by two factors. Obviously, I was in the UK, which made the source of the show distant both in terms of the time it took for episodes to reach me, and in terms of the bulk of the fandom. I was internet savvy enough to check for online news, and to follow some of the discussions, but I was never much into posting on community sites, so the conversation was all one way. When it came to actually interact with someone, I wanted to do it face to face – a hard thing to realise when most of the fans of the show were on the other side of the Atlantic. *Doctor Who* fans I could find to speak to in person. *Angel* fans, not so much. But on those rare occasions that I managed to meet someone who was as into the show as I was – there was an instant bond.

That said, I experienced seeing a fandom shaped by adversity and isolation later in my *Doctor Who* fandom days, when the show was taken off the air, waiting for Russell T. Davies and his fellow writers to re-introduce the Doctor to the television-viewing public over a decade later. The numbers of people counting themselves fans seemed to drop in this time, but the level of commitment to fandom rose exponentially. Books were published; audio plays were written, produced and acted; fanzines were produced in ever-increasing numbers. Because now it was *our* show – not a television show for the masses. It was our secret.

The difference with *Angel* fandom was that our show was still being shown on the TV. *DoctorWho* needed to be off the air for several years before its fandom was hammered into shape – not so with *Angel*. It felt like it was a cult production even while it was still being made and shown.

## Cultural Clash?

The distance between the show's source and its UK viewers wasn't purely geographical, either. *Angel*, like *Buffy*, was set in southern California, which is worlds away from day to day life in the UK, or even the rest of the USA, come to that. But whereas *Buffy* was a school-based show, which ensured the majority of its themes and motifs were familiar to those who had experienced life as a teenager at school, *Angel*'s setting was the dark side of Los Angeles. For the majority of *Angel*'s UK viewers, this was a step into an alien world.

In interviews, David Greenwalt has spoken about an early desire on the part of the show's creators to consciously echo noir themes. Raymond Chandler's 'mean streets' found a new home in *Angel*'s Los Angeles setting. In a city made wealthy by its fascination with showbusiness, the notion of superficial impressions hiding danger and darkness underneath must be a continual fear.

Of course, as *Buffy* made use of school-age fears, so *Angel*'s screenwriters and creative staff used the same technique to address adult fears – to good effect. After all, who isn't afraid of betrayal, of manipulation, of being used for someone else's ends? This is a setup that speaks across cultures, and across oceans. California may be worlds away from Oxfordshire, but betrayal is the same no matter which side of the Atlantic you're on. Everyone is equally ill-at-ease, with no idea who or what to trust.

The noir atmosphere was one of *calculated* alienation, where nothing and nobody could be trusted, and any value system you came with goes out of the window. This isn't something directed at or for a particular culture, but rather aims to shock and alienate all viewers. Universal alienation, if you like.

Is being ill-at-ease, being alienated, a bad thing? It could be. Why watch something that's going to make you feel uncomfortable? Something that makes you unwilling to root for a character on the off-chance that they'll suddenly turn out to be evil? Or that they'll be on the receiving end of shockingly sudden death? *Angel* seemed to play with making its audience uncomfortable, and I can imagine there are a fair few genre fans out there who tuned out on that basis.

Perhaps the most obvious example of this use of alienation was the appearance and disappearance of one of the key members of the ensemble – Doyle. In hindsight, it seems thoroughly in character for Joss and his team to lull the audience into a false sense of security and then undercut their expectations by killing a title sequence character in only the ninth episode of a new show. But at the time it was profoundly shocking. After the episode had been shown I headed to the internet to check the online community's response. There was one question on everyone's lips. "Is it for real?"

## A Risky Investment

Good drama demands that its audience feel something as a result of their experience. *Angel* makes demands on its audience, and one of those demands is that the audience become emotionally invested. This can be risky; the feeling of being pushed to some emotional state that hasn't been earned by the material is deeply annoying. When a show uses emotion with skill and care, it can make the resulting payoff one of the most memorable moments in a show. *Angel*'s use of emotion was what cemented my love for the series. By its fourth and fifth seasons, *Angel* had got this down to a fine art.

Adult themes can be divisive; as what may appear to one person as a mature presentation of a difficult topic such as violence against women, may seem to another to be glorifying the thing it seeks to explore. For me, *Angel* sailed close to the wind on this issue in particular, especially in the first season in its handling of Cordelia, but on average managed to stay on the right side of the line.

Three moments in *Angel* stick out for me – they're what I automatically think of if you name the show to me. They are all character deaths, and they are all vastly emotional. Lilah Morgan. Cordelia. Fred. Even at some of *Buffy*'s real low points I never found myself tearing up, but three times I was bawling at *Angel*. I have vivid memories of sitting through the final montage of the episode "A Hole in the World" set to Kim Richey's *A Place Called*

*Home*, staring at the screen in floods of tears. I bought the track. It still gives me a lump in my throat every time I listen to it. How many shows can you say have done that to you?

It can be tough, watching a show that wields the emotional power to make you break down. A show that makes you ask hard questions, to which there may be no answers, and even if there are, you might not like them very much. A show that never makes it easy for you as a viewer, but asks you to both care for the characters and be ready for anything – because you never know when the worst is going to happen. But it's worth it. It's so worth it.

And if the show itself needed to grow into its potential to be an adult show, to cement its audience and earn its place in our hearts, so we needed to take the plunge and take the risks to watch it as part of an adult audience. Growing up never felt so good.

# Transgressing with Spike and Buffy

**NancyKay Shapiro** is a writer who lives in New York City. Her novel, *What Love Means To You People*, was published in 2004 with Saint Martin's Press and can be purchased as an ebook for the Kindle and Kindle iPhone app through Amazon.com.

Before I ever watched *Buffy the Vampire Slayer*, I had a history with fandom and fanfic via classic *Star Trek*, and was certain I'd never return to it again. Not because I'd had a bad experience, but because it felt like a kind of enthusiasm that went with being in my early twenties, never to return.

In the long-ago-and-far-away time before the Internet, before DVDs – before, even, you could buy *Star Trek* episodes on VHS tape – I watched the show in its 6:00 daily reruns, on a black and white TV. This was against the will of my mother, who wanted to serve dinner sans Spock, and with that of my father, who would stand behind me imitating the *whoosh* noise the Enterprise's sliding doors made every time they opened, until I'd turn around and shout at him to Leave Me Alone!

A few years into that, I attended a science fiction convention in Manhattan one summer weekend, and someone who should've known better put a fanzine into my 15-year-old hands, and let me buy it. (*Ob'zine* #1 and 2, my first zines, contained sexually explicit stories and art, most of it slashing Kirk and Spock.) Before my years of obsession with *Star Trek* were done, I'd written reams of fic that never made it into any zine, and then drifted back to writing novels. "Serious," "literary" novels.

I missed the *Buffy* bandwagon by a good few years, only deigning to give the show a try when it first went into syndication in 2001. Even though various friends had recommended it to during the first few years of its run, I thought I wasn't interested because I perceived it to be campy, or teeny-ish, or sitcom dumb; a perception based on no input beyond seeing a few still photos of Sarah Michelle Gellar and deciding she looked too much like a cousin of mine whose company had annoyed me when I was 14.

The beginning of the show's syndicated run in New York City occurred at the same time as the destruction of the Twin Towers in lower Manhattan, an event that left me and everyone else in the city reeling, disrupting all sorts of routines and changing the whole tempo and tenor of daily life for months afterwards. I found myself in a befuddled emotional state – one where, even though I wasn't personally involved with the violence and destruction and grief, I couldn't listen to music, had trouble focusing on my usual refuge in books and, other than working, didn't quite know what to do with my feelings or myself. The early evening showing of *Buffy* quickly became the event my day hinged on. As if answering some psychic request for More Escapism Please from its New York Metropolitan-area viewers, WPIX soon began running two *Buffy* eps each weeknight, and I sank into that daily saga with total absorption and rapture. I watched both Season One (in reruns) and Season Six (airing for the first time), even though a number of people suggested I TiVo the new eps and wait until I'd caught up to watch them. I couldn't wait, and so my introduction to the character of Spike, who was to go on to obsess me for some years, was a little unusual – I saw him first in his gentle guise as Dawn-protector and Welcomer-of-Buffy-Back-from-the-Grave before I ever saw him in his initial Big Bad persona from Season Two.

He at once become my woobie[1]. Spike's beauty, his grace, his tragic-comic actions and, most of all, his role as a desolate, hopeless and yet unswervingly resolute lover hit my kinks – as we say in fandom – hard.

As his fucked-up anti-romance with Buffy developed on screen in those early episodes of Season Six, my imagination raced ahead, looking for ways to make it functional, to make it all right. Something in my psyche, always attracted to "transgressive" relationships, became intent on inventing a Big Misguided Doomed Romance That Succeeds Against All Odds. That the show's writers clearly had different ideas imposed an exquisite frustration on me and plenty of other fans who were eager to 'ship the slayer with Spike – as well as those who were disgusted by the whole subplot.

By the time of the first hiatus of the season, I'd found my way to online fandom (the Buffistas), and, with a freelance gig that left me with a lot of time on my hands at the office and no one looking over my shoulder, I took the plunge into fan fiction. I wanted attention and approbation from the fan community – I wasn't getting it from that "serious," "literary" fiction I was struggling with. At the time I was stalled out on my novel-in-progress, so when this inner prompting to write about Spike took hold, I didn't fight it.

My first foray into *Buffy* fic was about Spike only, and not Buffy. My job at the time was near Grand Central Station, one of Manhattan's classic public spaces. I've always treasured Grand Central for its stylishness and beaux-arts beauty, and as a sort of portal into New York's past – suggestive of the work of writers such as John Cheever and John O'Hara, whom I adore. In those raw post 9-11 weeks, I was especially in love with New York City, busted up but unbowed – New York was my woobie too. That love, born out of

---

1. Per tvtropes.org, a woobie, named for a child's security blanket, is that character you want to give a big hug, wrap in a blanket and feed soup to when he or she suffers so very beautifully. Woobification of a character is a curious, audience-driven phenomenon, divorced almost entirely from the character's canonical morality.

a sense of how precarious everything was, was at least 50% of the impetus that went into that first Spike story. Starting with an arrival by train at Grand Central Station, I took Spike on a whirlwind tour of Manhattan one cold winter night in 1928, bringing him to some of the spots from that enticing jazz-age time that are most vivid in my imagination – the bohemian streets of Greenwich Village, the public baths that even then were a major cruising spot for gay men, and the segregated nightclubs of Harlem, with lots of slashy, porny, blood-soaked and sentimental Spike-ish doings along the way. "Manhattan Nocturne" was my paean to a precious endangered place, with all its layers of atmosphere and history – as much as to Spike, who, unlike the characters in my stalled novel, was free to do every single appalling thing I could think up for him. I won't say that writing that fic was cathartic so much as that it filled me with a naughty thrill, not merely that I could put such things down on paper but that I could then post them on the Internet, to be seen by... well, *anyone* and their grandma. The story *was* seen, and I was welcomed to the fandom by some active fans who probably thought they were present at the advent of an exciting new dark slash ficcer. Sadly for them, I veered off from that opening gambit straight into the heart of Spike/Buffy, never quite to return so full-throatedly to Spike-as-bad-ass-vampire.

Writing is a lonely business – often I wish I'd chosen a more collaborative art form, though in truth I think the art form chooses the artist – but in the case of fanfic, my readers were wonderfully interactive. On a few occasions we did collaborate, as when I'd revise long fics-in-progress in response to thoughtful feedback received along the way. But mostly I published my fan-fic stories in a way that contemporary writers no longer do, but nineteenth century writers did – on the fly, in parts, composing along the way and trust-ing to the white-hot energy of it to keep the momentum going. Working this way, I was thrilled to find readers who, like those who met the new install-ments of *The Old Curiosity Shop* as they came off the boat from England, were eager for each new part. (After the first few stories, I found my way to LiveJournal and began to post my fics in chapters, as I wrote them.) This making-it-up-as-I-went felt like a daring act to me. A big part of the exhila-ration of putting out these stories was the showmanship, trusting in my cre-ative subconscious to make the whole thing come together in some unfore-seen way at the end. I wrote without a plan or an outline; each tale began from a premise, or a situation, either stemming from the one before it, or in response to some fanfic trope that was going around – such as amnesia, or time travel – but in every case I had to trust to my imagination to give me what I needed when I needed it.

Along with being in dialogue with my readers, I was in dialogue, also, albeit in a one-way fashion, with the writers of *Buffy*. My long saga about Spike and Buffy, *The Bittersweets* series, arose from my dissatisfaction with the anti-romance between the two presented on the screen. What if, instead of being a disaster, a shameful secret for Buffy and a big mistake, the relationship between Slayer and vampire could somehow be incorporated into their lives, be out in the open, be challenged continually and coped with? Wouldn't that be *more* interesting? I produced a story cycle a couple of novel lengths long out of that idea, because it continually stimulated my narrative kinks. It was no coincidence that my novel was also about a "transgressive" relationship that ultimately succeeds.

While it was Spike who first started "talking" to me in a way that made me want to write, it was that Spike/Buffy romance that fueled most of the subsequent work. I don't know that I'd have written fanfic about *Buffy* without that particular spur. It seems unlikely that, had I started watching the show when it first aired, I'd have been moved to write about Buffy/Angel either (though when I did see those episodes, I was 100% bought into the storyline as it unfolded). While I loved watching and thinking about other Joss shows – *Angel, Dollhouse*, and especially *Firefly*, which seemed to me to be nearly perfect in many ways – they lacked that unique combination of compelling character and incendiary relationship that made me want to take hold of the characters and move them around myself. I was content to be an observer. Spike functioned for me as a sort of perfect storm of a character, intriguing on multiple levels, irresistible. He came alive in my imagination just as fully as any I'd ever invented for myself. Some of it had to do with his antecedents – he was English (I'm an Anglophile) and a Victorian gentleman (I'm also a nut about Victorian novels). Spike brought me to find a way to write fiction set in the nineteenth century, which was something I'd always wanted to do and couldn't quite find an impetus for. (The classic Victorian novels are a constant inspiration and re-reading pleasure to me, and I loved a chance to create that atmosphere and play with that sort of language myself). Spike as a character was both extremely strong and extremely malleable – it was possible to make him do all kinds of unlikely things while retaining the essence of his personality, his voice and his manner. I wrote a Spike who was often good, and a human William who definitely wasn't.

In Buffy, I had a heroine who was so invulnerable and sturdy that I could use her to explore the messiest and most outré emotions. I could make her play out those romantic fantasies that were maybe all the more alluring to me because they came up to the edge of being "Feministically Incorrect" – or occasionally plunged right over.

My stories about Spike, Spike/Buffy, and (in a few cases) Spike/Xander are still available online for all to read[2], so I won't outline them here. What began as an impulse, spurred by the events unfolding week by week in

2. www.echonyc.com/%7Estax/Buffy/herself/index.htm

Season Six, kept burgeoning with each round of attention and encouragement my writings received. The first Spike/Buffy story was a quickie, a sort of inter-episode filler. I thought, having dashed it off, that I was done, but almost immediately I began another that branched off from the first. I've been a writer all my life, but I've also struggled with avoidance, with feeling stymied, with a tendency to endlessly rework the same patch before moving forward. All of that difficulty evaporated once I plunged into what turned into my fanfic odyssey, a run of some eight years when the narrative impulse around those characters just flowed through me with an ease that was joyful and wildly exhilarating. What made the difference has always had an element of mystery to it, while also being obvious – for the first time as a writer, I didn't have to importune people to read. My work was in demand. I had an avid audience, and those readers rewarded me with commentaries, responses, recommendations, dialogue, *attention*. Fanfic brought me camaraderie and community, and friendships that have outlasted my engagement with fandom.

Through this entire wonderful creative period, I didn't give up on my original novel. A couple of years after I made my online fanfic debut online, I figured out how it needed to end and finished *What Love Means To You People*, which was published in 2004 with Saint Martin's Press. The novel was years in the writing and revising, and the publication experience could not have been more different than online fandom – the book received no promotion or critical attention, and was lost in the great sea of unheralded publications. To my great disappointment, my publishers didn't even give it a paperback edition. It's no wonder that I continued during this time to put a lot of energy into writing Buffy stories – whenever I finished one, I'd get numerous emails from readers asking me for another. For me as a creative being, there's nothing more stimulating than the presence of a ready-made audience. I kept on writing as long as the characters kept on challenging me. But once that creative thread unraveled, not even importunate messages from readers could get another story going. I did finish up *The Bittersweets Saga* with a satisfying and hopeful ending, and, with a strong sense of nostalgia, laid it to rest.

As I write this essay, it seems to me – as it did in those years before I plunged into *Buffy* – that nothing again could entice me back into writing fan fiction. But among the many self-discoveries I made during my time of Spike-obsession, I've learned to embrace never-say-never. Another character (and fictional world) as compelling as Spike *may* come along, and seize me by the scruff of my imagination. I doubt it. I'm not looking for him. But if such a situation comes along, I won't resist.

# Brand New Day: The Evolution of the *Doctor Horrible* Fandom

**Priscilla Spencer** is a character designer, 3D modeler, and texture artist at Launch, a New York firm that creates animated pre-visualizations for television commercials. She designed and illustrated the map for Jim Butcher's bestselling Codex Alera series, beta reads Butcher's other work and serves as a thematic consultant/continuity monitor for *The Dresden Files'* Hugo-nominated graphic novel series. She is the founder of Books for Boobs, which raises money for the Avon Walk for Breast Cancer while promoting noteworthy authors. She also enjoys photography, costuming and bursting into Broadway show tunes at the slightest provocation.

I came at the Whedonverse backwards.

I discovered *Firefly* in that awkward, torrent-tastic span between cancellation and the release of the DVDs. I watched the episodes in the order in which... in which my good friend who recorded the show as it aired lent me her completely legal tapes, let's say. "Serenity"-the-episode was among the last I received, and "Ariel" was among the first, which put me only slightly higher on the confusion scale as those who experienced it live.

I watched the first episode of *Buffy* the night the last episode of *Angel* aired. Unfortunately, I'd watched the musical episode in my high school's Sci-Fi Club a few years prior, and I had all the lyrics memorized by the time I watched anything else, which gave me frustratingly spoilericious insight into Dawn's existence, Willow's fondness for the ladies, Xander and Anya's approaching nuptials and Buffy's imminent fling with Captain Peroxide, for a start. Not to mention all the spoilers I osmotically absorbed through casual conversation with *Buffy* fans who'd assumed I'd never watch the show. While the majority of the show was fresh and new and wonderful to me, I couldn't help resenting those spoiled moments that should have been surprises.

When *Serenity* came, I had the opposite experience. In the months leading up to the film's release, I approached the movie in an awkward dance, trying to learn everything I could about it without actually spoiling myself. I was lucky enough to score tickets to the advance preview screenings in June and July, months before the film's September release, but when I left the theatre in a state of shock, I had precious few people I could discuss the film with. I felt stifled by my knowledge, and I was afraid to discuss the movie online for fear of inadvertently spoiling someone.

For *Doctor Horrible*, however, I had the opportunity to catch each episode the moment it was online, just as everyone else did. Finally, a Joss production I could both theorize about with my friends and analyze immediately afterward! I wouldn't be scrambling to catch up to everyone else, too late to speculate on where Joss might take us next, and worse, too late to avoid spoilers for which the fandom had long since stopped warning. Nor would I be teetering beneath a burden of knowledge I could only share with a limited subset of the fandom – this chronically un-punctual Whedon fan could finally engage with the fans on equal footing. I would have a nice, normal fandom experience, or whatever passed for normal when fandom is involved.

"Normal." Heh. The gods of fandom love straight lines like that.

Not only were the show and fandom borne of the bizarre circumstances and unyielding solidarity of the Writers Guild strike, but the brothers and fiancée Whedon motivated the fans to take on a role that was anything but conventional. The strike instilled in fans a political fervor to support independent productions, and the absence of studio involvement freed the creators to invite fans to participate in that world.

Let's rewind to the winter of 2007-2008.

When negotiations broke down over the rate of residuals on DVDs and new media, television and film writers united by the Writers Guild of America called a strike against the Alliance of Motion Picture and Television Producers. Production of scripted shows trickled to a halt, finally shutting down entirely as key actors refused to cross picket lines or when shows ran out of scripts. The writers took to the streets, demonstrating outside major studios and media centers, and steeled themselves for a long battle.

Over the duration of the strike, I watched the Whedonesque blog in awe and admiration as fans organized in California to show their support. They fused with literally dozens of other TV fanbases into a great fen Voltron called Fans4Writers, which conspired to channel fans' support of the writers as effectively and visibly as possible. They brought pizza to the picket lines, organized letter-writing campaigns to networks and advertisers, held auctions and raffles to raise money to support non-WGA professionals left unemployed by the strike, and otherwise demonstrated their commitment and gratitude to the writers' sacrifice.

I wasn't aware of any equivalent fan mobilization action on the East Coast, and my 9-7 job rarely gave me permission to leave work during lunch, but twice over the course of the strike, I brought pizza to frozen writers picketing at Columbus Circle and Rockefeller Center. I added my voice to the cheering crowds as Tim Robbins, Danny Glover, Kal Penn, and other Hollywood notables called New Yorkers to arms at a rally in Washington Square Park, organized by then-Presidential-hopeful, now-late-night-punch-line John Edwards.

I felt some ironic amusement as small teams of writers created short films on the web to bring attention to the fact that they weren't being paid for creating short films on the web, but their actions only served to underscore the vital importance of the web short as an advertising and communication tool. As the videos made their rounds on the net, their humor, eloquence, and stark enumeration of the writers' grievances triggered a more forceful, more immediately galvanizing reaction among those they reached than any press release could. However, perhaps the bleakest message came from the studios themselves. Back in 2001, *The Daily Show* ran a segment called "Pitch," which parodied the then-nascent Reality TV phenomenon, proposing shows like "Super Chore Island" and "Sexy Hill Teens Go Up A Hill To Fetch A Pail Of Sexy Adventure! In Space!"[1] As I read a real-life list of game shows that would take the place of scripted shows during the strike, including Fox's *Moment of Truth*, "where contestants are strapped to lie detectors and asked personal questions in a quest for cash,"[2] I couldn't help feeling that every one of *The Daily Show*'s nightmare scenario ideas had more intellectual rigor than what was playing out in reality. Truth was stranger than fiction. And it was fiction I wanted back.

Finally, the strike came to a close, with more whimper than bang. The precious residuals the writers fought for were a mere shade of what they'd hoped to secure. Newspapers cheered the end of the strike and Hollywood ramped up their great studio machines once more, but fans and the dissenting WGAers looked on in blank incredulity – all that sacrifice, for chump change?

Enter *Doctor Horrible*.

Between sessions on the picket lines, the Whedons had begun work on a new project to fill their time, communicating with WGA leadership to make certain that they weren't violating any strike protocols or undermining the WGA's position. A few short weeks after the strike ended, production began, and details began to trickle out to the public: the title, the cast, and oh, the fact that it was about a low-rent super villain with a blog. And it was a musical.

I rejoiced in giddy excitement. Something positive had emerged from the strike after all! In the wake of disappointment, empathizing with the writ-

---

1. Stewart, Jon et al. "October 11, 2001: Pitch." The Daily Show With Jon Stewart. October 11, 2001. Web. Accessed May 30, 2010. www.thedailyshow.com / watch/ thu-october-11-2001 / pitch

2. Kinke, Nikki. "Network Coming Attractions: Game Shows." *Deadline Hollywood.* November 13, 2007. Web. Accessed May 30, 2010. www.dead line.com / 2007 / 11 / network-coming-attractions-game-shows/

ers' losses of funds and morale and dreading the grim prospect of months without new material, we needed something to celebrate, and Joss Whedon had provided it. Joss repeatedly assured interviewers that he wasn't doing this as a flip of the bird to studio execs, but the narrative in my mind was far more satisfying – not to mention somewhat rather more consistent with the scathing tone of Joss's strike blogs.

Now, Team Joss had given us fans the chance to support and celebrate the creative spirit the AMPTP had tried to devalue. The studios had spent months creating game shows and reality TV that didn't require writers[3], so it seemed justified that a group of writers should create a production that circumvented the studios. It wouldn't help downtrodden writers recoup their losses, but distorted through my hopelessly hopeful eyes and tinted with the colorful language of politics, Joss' creation became linked with a hypothetical future avenue for writers in the motion picture industry. I decided that in the wake of the strike's failure, the writers and their supporters needed an independent production like *Doctor Horrible* to succeed on so monumental a level that it could not be ignored, to show there was life outside the corporate machine, and the monopoly was not absolute.

It was, in essence, a high-profile test case: what kind of fiscal success could a man with Joss's résumé, name recognition, industry contacts, and financial resources yield? Not to mention his reputation for creating vivid new worlds and lovable, memorable characters. Would a big-name creator be able to add legitimacy to a medium that hadn't garnered much respect?

Perhaps in a not-so-distant future, this crack in the corporate hegemony might grant writers a little more leverage to bargain. In this way, the *Doctor Horrible* fandom came pre-packaged with a sense of solidarity and belonging.

Of course, as trailers and posters and interviews poured onto the web, the project went from hazy concept to full-blooded reality, and fan enthusiasm for the project soon took on its own momentum, powered by more than nebulous ideals and leftover enthusiasm from the strike. These tantalizing teasers served as compelling reasons for fans to want the project to succeed – reasons completely unrelated to the circumstances of its inception.

I watched the first episode with two of my oldest online friends, one from Alaska and one from Sweden. Through great and fluffy divine intervention, we managed to hit the site before heavy traffic crashed Hulu's server[4], and we scrunched together on my futon so we could all see my laptop.

---

3. HAHAHAHAHAHAHAHAHAHAHAHAHA.

4. Which brought back fond memories of crashing Fandango with my fellow Browncoats as we continuously hit "reload" on the page for an unlabeled sneak preview screening we hoped was *Serenity*, waiting for tickets to go on sale. In Dallas, it sold out in four minutes, and I was among the triumphant. Booyeah.

The *Doctor Horrible* theme pounded through my speakers, Neil Patrick Harris's awkwardly cackling visage filled the screen, and you couldn't wipe away our manic grins with an acetylene torch.

I loved it. Loved it, loved it, loved it. The three of us managed to score student tickets to *Spring Awakening* on Broadway that night, but throughout the next week, it was *Doctor Horrible* whose tunes I incessantly hummed. In the absence of an official CD release, I ripped the audio myself and divided the song tracks so that I could listen at work (And on my way to work. And at home). I sang my own rendition in the shower. I shared the audio tracks with my friends, with the rigid caveat that as soon as an official release was available, they would buy it to support Team Horrible.

Thus bound by a Girl Scout pinky-promise to be un-lame and give back to the creators whenever possible, we rejoiced in the delightfully catchy music. I did the same for part two, whose music I loved even more than the first batch, and finally for part three as it aired. As I connected with other fans eager to discuss the music, we laughed at the variety of folks' invented names for the songs. We looked forward to the Whedons handing down something official.

Between each episode, speculation abounded as to where the Whedon crew would take us next. Parts 1 and 2 had surpassed my wildest hopes, and I couldn't wait to see how it ended. It being a Joss production, many of us anticipated a major game-changer in the third act; I set my sights on Penny and wondered what Joss had in store for her. I had difficulty reconciling the meek-natured love interest with Joss's gallery of powerful women – particularly in a world populated by superheroes – and I wondered if Felicia Day had been cast for her performance as Vi on *Buffy*, transitioning seamlessly between shy, nervous Potential and formidable Slayer. I wrote in my blog, "It's by JOSS WHEDON. The sun rises in the east, fangirls squee at UST-y[5] subtext, and Joss writes kick-ass female characters."

As musical tragedy struck and the Doctor gained and lost "everything he ever," I was livid. While I quickly came to love where the story left Doctor Horrible and Captain Hammer, I remained furious that Penny never got a chance to shine[6]. I hated that her character was exactly as she appeared on the surface – she had no layers of personality to peel away, pie-like or otherwise. And as someone who kept returning to the soundtrack, I resented that she'd been given such short, humorless solo numbers. Moreover, I saw yet another spontaneous character death from Joss's pen as being uninspired – was he capable of writing a single show where he didn't kill off a main character? Some of my LiveJournal friends grimly pointed fingers at the "Women in Refrigerators" trope, in which a woman is brutally killed solely

---

5. Unresolved Sexual Tension
6. Ouch. Sorry about that, folks.

to advance the male protagonist's storyline, and I puzzled over how a writer with such strong feminist credentials and awareness of genre tropes would do such a thing.

I rewatched Act III a fraction of the number of times I rewatched the first two parts. In huffy annoyance, I spun out elaborate zombie revivification schemes with one friend and egged on another as she dabbled in crossover fan fiction with *Pushing Daisies*, shoving the story back into a place where the world could regain the prior acts' dark-tinged whimsy and be fun to play in again. But there was no satisfaction in denial. I began to recognize the arrogance in the idea I knew better than Joss, and that Joss had ended it *wrong*. Not to suggest that Joss is infallible, certainly, but my frustration wasn't leading to anything productive – it was only getting in the way of my enjoyment of the work.

So I shifted my focus from "why didn't Joss do (blank)?" to "why may have Joss decided to do what he did?" Rather than joining in the lambaste for what many perceived to be problematic gender issues, I chose to scrutinize what was effective in Joss's storytelling, so that I might be in a more receptive frame of mind to guess why he made the choices I objected to, or at least make my peace with them. I couldn't read Joss's thoughts, and my conclusions were only as valid as the next fan's, but framing my analysis in more positive terms was far more appealing to me.

My gaze fell upon Penny once more. And during my next watch, I found myself appreciating her much more. She's the only genuinely good character in the series, I realized. She is defined by her selflessness, wanting to change the world not for herself, but for others. Sure, she's meek and soft-spoken, but it's dangerously hypocritical for those of us who identify as feminists to cheer creators for giving us kick-ass women, and then criticize them when they give us women whose value rests elsewhere on the emotional spectrum. Penny has less self-confidence, and her strength isn't as immediately apparent, but shouldn't characters like her be just as valid?

Rather than emphasizing female empowerment as *Buffy* does, or featuring strong-willed women in a future culture where their competence is unquestioned as *Firefly* does, *Doctor Horrible* illuminates the dangers of unchecked masculine ego in a dark inverse to the Hero's Journey, tracing the path from ordinary man to supervillain. Doctor Horrible is motivated by a desire to impress Penny, but he allows himself to be sidetracked by his idea of what is expected of him as a man. In Act I, she approaches him for his signature, and they converse briefly, but he's so wrapped up in his Wonderflonium heist and raging insecurity that he barely notices when she leaves. When he realizes this, he pauses, and his decision dictates his trajectory for the story – rather than take this opportunity to pursue Penny directly, he tells himself "a man's gotta do what a man's gotta do," and he goes forward with the heist. He is so consumed by his notions of masculinity that he discards his most direct route to the attention he craves.

Soon after, Captain Hammer arrives on the scene. He is a charismatic, womanizing bully who makes no secret of the fact that his dalliances with Penny are nothing more than a new means of torturing Doctor Horrible (though he admits the prospect of The Weird Stuff has its appeal). Doctor Horrible drifts further and further from his original goal of winning Penny's admiration, driving himself deeper into his villainous work. The two men reduce Penny to a mere prize to be won, denying her humanity – and, as a result, all three are destroyed. Doctor Horrible claims to love her, but he knows nothing about her other than her laundry schedule. Each time they converse, he can't be honest with her; he pretends to believe in whatever stance he thinks she'll approve of, be it a fondness for laundry or taking inspiration from Gandhi over Bad Horse. Intoxicated by visions of destroying his nemesis, he imagines her horror over his true identity being cured by the gift of "a shiny new Australia." It becomes clear his infatuation has nothing to do with who Penny actually is. Worse, Doctor Horrible blames Penny for breaking his heart when he'd never given her any indication that he was interested in her romantically, muttering that "The dark is everywhere, and Penny doesn't seem to care that soon the dark in me is all that will remain." It's easy to miss or laugh off the darkness in Doctor Horrible's words in "My Eyes," paired as they are with hilarious visuals, but the Doctor is taking himself seriously. The academically brilliant yet socially stunted misfit we readily empathized with in Act I evolves into something frightening before we know it.

In time, I learned to stop worrying and love the bomb Joss dropped on us in the third act. Some of the aspects I'd initially taken for oversights began to feel deliberately planned. Penny and the two competing men become foils for each other – her groundedness makes Captain Hammer and Doctor Horrible's attitudes seem all the more cartoonish and overblown, and their rigidly Manichean definitions of good and evil underscore the uniqueness of Penny's ability to see shades of grey. "Even in the darkness every color can be found, and every day of rain brings water flowing to things growing in the ground," she sings. Our heroine wasn't the girl we were expecting, but Joss is known for gleefully subverting our expectations.

The next phase in my fandom experience came a few months later, when the Whedons engaged the fans yet again. Over the various stages of the product's completion, they'd called upon us to help advertise through word of mouth, and they'd communicated with us directly through Twitter, which was a relatively untapped commercial resource at the time. They'd been able to learn about fans' unexpected needs, like international viewing rights on Hulu (which is traditionally limited to Americans), and fans were put directly in touch with those able to produce the Groupie t-shirts and other swag they coveted. The Whedons were able to deliver, no rights to negotiate, and no pesky studio middlemen involved. This next challenge, however, was beyond swag. At the *Doctor Horrible* panel at San Diego Comic-Con, the creative team announced a contest for the DVD release. Joss and his team invited fans to create their own application video for the Evil League of Evil. The lack of studio control meant that the usual network paranoia about the erosion of intellectual property rights via fan creations – be they fanfic, fan art, fan vids, filk, or more – was tossed out the window, and treatment of derivative works was instead left to the Whedons' discretion.

I'd fooled around amateurishly with musical theatre songwriting in high school, and I couldn't have been more thrilled at the contest's direction. A character began to form in my mind, a young woman who traffics in petty cruelties with the goal of bringing out worst in the personalities of the people whose lives she touches, and whose hunger to prove herself as a credible villain is whipped into a frenzy when her partner in crime ditches her in favor of a second-rate superhero wannabe.

Creating her was an absolute joy. I spent the bus rides to work brainstorming for her song, gleefully fabricating tiny acts of wretchedness, calculated to chip away at someone's faith in humanity[7]. I watched and rewatched *Doctor Horrible*, looking for ways to tie her story to the original source and bring new meaning to throwaway jokes. As I wrote, I kept in mind the show's blend of wordplay, visual gags and slightly sinister camp, in hopes that my project might recapture it. I reveled in the space creators of all fannish works delight in exploring, where imitation and innovation converge.

Unfortunately, despite the early warning, the official announcement of the contest caught me by surprise, and the deadline was far sooner than I expected. The combination of an unfinished script, dire warnings of a preponderance of weekend overtime at work, and a garden-variety fear of asking anyone to collaborate with me conspired to thwart my plans before I even attempted liftoff. But as entries poured in from around the world, I was awestruck at how many people *Doctor Horrible* had inspired to pick up a camera and create something.

Team Whedon's favorites can be seen on the DVD, but that represents only a tiny fraction of participants. Producer Michael Boretz claims that there were over 650 submissions in all[8], which fans happily waded through in search of the best of the bunch. Countless fan blog entries were dedicat-

---

7. A fun discovery: "I'd serve a ham at seder" rhymes with "change your vote to Nader."

8. Doctor Horrible Fan Site. "Exclusive Interview: Producer, Michael Boretz." Dr. Horrible's Sing-Along Blog Official Fan Site. Oct 18, 2008. Web. Accessed August 22, 2010. doctorhorrible.net/exclusive-interview-producer-michael-boretz/438/

ed to Top Ten lists, and their comment fields abounded with exchanges of links and opinions. Fans cheered on these creators, celebrating the spark of inspiration that had passed from one group of minds to another. In the two years since, who knows how many people saw the fans' creativity on parade and the outpouring of support it generated and became inspired to create something of their own? Team Whedon's gambit to raise the public profile of the web short seems to have succeeded.

Looking back, I realize something that should have been obvious to me from day one: fandom experience has little to do with when you join it, early or late. It's about what you bring to the table, what you create, and what you take away from it. There is no "equal footing." So get a pic, do a blog. Find something that inspires you. Heroes are far from over with.

# We're Here to Save You

**Elizabeth Bear** was born on the same day as Frodo and Bilbo Baggins, but in a different year. She lives in Connecticut with a giant, ridiculous dog and a presumptuous cat. Her hobbies include rock climbing, kayaking, and playing incredibly bad guitar. She's the author of more than 20 books and close to a hundred short stories, and is a recipient of the Sturgeon and Hugo awards, among others.

I come not to bury Joss Whedon, but to praise him. No, really – to praise him. And in particular to praise the character of Daniel "Oz" Osbourne, whose full name has enjoyed exposure as limited as that of Angus MacGyver.

Oz is about my favorite thing ever to come out of the consolidated Whedonverse. I'm pretty sure he needs no introduction, but for those of you who somehow missed Seasons Two, Three and Four of *Buffy the Vampire Slayer*, here's a brief one.

A student at Sunnydale High and aspiring musician played by Seth Green, he first appears in the early Season Two episode "Inca Mummy Girl," and Wikipedia tells me he was intended as a throwaway character. However, Green's charisma and his deadpan, laconic approach to the character won him a recurring role that eventually morphed to series regular.

In his next substantive appearance, Oz is discovered to have been bitten by a werewolf, and only the timely intervention of the Scoobies prevents him from being converted into a throw rug by an overzealous werewolf hunter. Eventually, Oz's level-headedness, practicality and laissez-faire approach to life win him an entry to the Scooby Gang, where he rapidly proves a valuable team member.

He eventually becomes Willow's steady boyfriend, a relationship that lasts through to Season Four (though the course of true love through various plot devices never does run smooth), when he leaves the Scooby Gang to seek enlightenment and control over the wolfish aspect of his personality, incidentally clearing the road for Willow's later relationship with Tara (Willow has a track record for awesome in her dating life).

I love Oz. I want to take him home and feed him cookies. I would like one of my very own, and I'd even be willing to work around the werewolf thing.

If we treat *Buffy* as a mythic construct, an allegory – as in some ways it is unabashedly intended ("High school is Hell. Literally.") – then we're left with mythopoetic methods of analysis. One of the most effective of these is to treat all of the characters as aspects of the same personality – elements of the same mind.

Oz emerges from this particular thought experiment as the stabilizing center of the group, the weighty keel that holds them steady against rough seas. (I imagine that it's accidental that Seth Green's departure from the show coincided with what I tend to think of as the *St. Elmo's Fire* plotlines, in which the group becomes more and more fragmented as adult concerns begin to pull apart their high school friendships, but it does support the metaphor nicely.) Oz is calm; Oz is rational; Oz is accepting. He has *sang froid* – literally, cold blood – and he is also nearly egoless. When he finds Willow (who, as much as I love her, does tend to misuse her mates) snogging Xander in the middle of a rescue mission ("Lover's Walk"), his reaction is to set aside his emotional reaction and concentrate instead of getting everyone to safety. When (in "Gingerbread") an attempt by him and Xander to save Buffy, Willow and Amy from being burned alive atop a pile of books ends in a rather spectacular fall through a drop ceiling into the arms of the mob, he deadpans, "We're here to save you."

Part of Oz's charm is this maturity, but another aspect of it is his rich internal life – revealed (as if we hadn't all suspected all along) in the beloved episode "Earshot," in which Buffy develops psychic powers. Among the babbling minds of everyone around Buffy, Oz's inner musings stand out as a paragon of calm, linear, nuanced thought – but which he only expresses to the group aloud as a considering "Huh."

So Oz thinks a great deal, but shares very little of it. This is reflected in his moral certainty. He knows what's right and he generally does it, a trait that sets him apart from the rest of the characters in his corner of the Whedonverse. He is himself, not a performance. He manages to balance emotional honesty with laconic delivery: he doesn't say much, in other words, but what he says he means – and his detachment and self-appraisal is such that what he *does* say cuts right to the heart of the matter. "Why don't I believe him?" Angel asks sarcastically of a hostage-taking demon at one point, to which Oz answers, "Because he lacks credibility." He's not self-destructive or angst-riddled in the least, which allows him to be a refreshing counterpoint to his teammates and allies.

Of course, the extended allegory of the *Buffy*verse provides a counter-point to this: Oz's supreme – even evolved – humanity, his sense of responsibility, his phlegmatic personality, his practicality, his ability to forgive and accept, to consider nuance and pass on assigning blame... all of these are washed away by his wolf persona, which is a raging beast. He's the perfect guy... with a terrible, murderous, uncontrollable temper. He's not just a metaphorical werewolf: he's a real one.

Somehow, that externalization of the problem makes it more forgivable. We can tell ourselves that Oz really can't control that monstrous aspect of his personality. We can externalize it. We can even cheer it, when Oz, being brutally beaten by an implacable, supernatural enemy, sees the rising moon and snarls, "Time's up. Rules change." And in his werewolf form, proceeds to kick the baddie's ass.

But as time goes by, the show takes pains to problematize this separation – to assign human-Oz responsibility for wolf-Oz's actions, to force him to seek ways to integrate his personality and control his monster within. In the arc that leads up to Oz leaving Sunnydale, he gets involved in a relationship with a female werewolf – which Willow responds to rather badly (and rather hypocritically, considering her own trespasses, but that's beside the point). So he leaves, in order to get his wolf side under some kind of control.

By the time he returns, Willow's moved on, however, and that's the end of Oz for viewers of the TV show.

*Buffy* was never the same for me without him. I admit, it's my opinion that various aspects of later seasons of *Buffy* most resemble a controlled flight into terrain, but it was the lack of Oz (and later Giles) that disappointed me most.

So here's to Oz – the best thing ever to walk away from Sunnydale.

# Imperfectly Perfect:
# Why I Really Love Buffy
# for Being a Pill Sometimes

**Mariah Huehner** is an editor at IDW Publishing. She co-wrote and edited the *Angel* run for IDW, and is co-writing the *True Blood* comics. She was born a long, long, long time ago in a very wild and faraway place called Brook-Lyn. She has a passion for well-told stories, muppets and the color blue. She edits, writes, paints and makes a lot of things with tentacles on. Her hair is not very polite and she's given up on teaching it any manners. She loves dark chocolate in a completely cliche sort of way, and is pretty sure that all cupcakes are made with magic. Also, aardvarks.

Over the course of working in comics, I've had to answer a lot of questions about how I reconcile my feminism with the sexism in the industry. To me, you might as well ask how I reconcile it with the sexism ingrained in our culture. My view of feminism is that it's an ongoing conversation: imperfect, but ultimately a worthwhile philosophical and social goal you implement whenever you can. Not as an agenda per se, but as a way to consider things like characters and their stories, and a way to focus what you want to convey in your work. Most of the time the best you can do is try, knowing that you might (and likely will) fail. So you get up and dust yourself off and try again because no one is perfect.

Which gets me to the point: *Buffy* is all about trying, failing, and trying again. It's about doing what you believe is right, even when it's difficult and even when it doesn't come out quite like you planned. It's about striving to be perfect – the perfect hero, the perfect teenager, the perfect girl – and eventually realizing that there's no such thing. You're just you. That's a pretty big thing for women, given the expectations heaped on us practically from the moment of conception.

Buffy is not perfect. The revelation of that while watching the show was a pretty profound moment for me. Because really, how often is that true of any hero, let alone a teenage girl hero? How often are they allowed to be, you know, obnoxious? Wrong? Self-centered? And yet, she's still brave. She's still kind. She's still a hero. All without devolving into stereotypes. Sure, Buffy gets emotional. And then she kicks something through a wall or stabs it in the chest. She is strong and vulnerable. She is powerful and loving and clever. And sometimes she makes epically bad mistakes that have big consequences for herself and those she cares about. You know, like real people who have full lives. Granted, I've never had to save the world from a vampire army and I'm not likely to. But I can recall things feeling that important at different times in my life, and knowing that I was the only person who could do anything about them was often isolating and confusing. But Buffy soldiers on and so do we. The lack of relatable examples of that in pop culture for young girls and women is, I think, why I fell in love with the show almost instantly. It just took me into my twenties to realize it.

For me personally, *Buffy* is a perfect show, mostly because it tackles so many different issues, has a major supernatural element, but still focuses primarily on developing characters and their relationships. Friendships like Buffy, Giles, Willow and Xander are pretty much the ideal. And allowing Buffy to grow up steadily through each season is what long form narrative is all about. Well, that and really cool plotlines and sisters out of nowhere. Do I have issues with some storylines or character choices? Yeah, of course. But it's not my story and they weren't my choices to make. And I'd rather Buffy struggle and try and have me disagree with something she does, than have another female character defined by how closely she matches a tired stereotype.

Mind you, there is no such thing as a perfect feminist character or story. This is a good thing. Without critical analysis, without thoughtful dissent, you don't get interesting and compelling conversations about anything. There's a tendency in certain circles to dismiss the analysis of pop culture as pointless or frivolous. But when you actually consider the level to which pop culture permeates our lives and influences and perpetuates cultural concepts like gender roles, the Whedonverse, which has always been rife with both references to pop culture and a multifaceted critique of it, starts to get a lot more important.

To me, a story can be feminist in a variety of ways. The most important being how it treats its female characters: are they as nuanced, and dynamic as the male characters? Do they get good lines? Are they flawed? Are they, in short, like a real person and not a collection of easy feminine stereotypes? That's a good place to start. It's equally important to me that a feminist story tackle real concerns about gender and equality in a way that legitimately attempts to explore it for the complex issue it is. Which may seem like a tall order for, say, a show about vampires, but the best genre fiction has that element, exploring serious "real" issues through a fantastical lens. It helps us remove ourselves a little and see them in a different context.

One of the most revelatory things about *Buffy*, for me, was watching a show that clearly took feminism and the issue of female characters in genre fiction (most obviously Horror) seriously while still creating a fun, funny and entertaining show. What I loved most was that it tricked people into thinking about these things without ever having to say, "We're a feminist show and we think the way female characters are often treated is pretty terrible." It was rarely, if ever, heavy handed. Organic and relatively seamless, it just did what it needed to do and slipped some incredibly complex issues right on in with the demon fighting and the staking puns.

Of all the things I love about *Buffy* – and there are so many I could write about it until I'm 90 – it's what I call the Female Heroic that really touches on something I hadn't known I was missing until I saw it. While I could cite Ripley, Xena, Sarah Connor and Starbuck as other examples, Buffy hits a chord that few others ever have. Buffy screws up. A lot. She's flawed in a way I have very rarely seen explored. While she's certainly based on the archetype/stereotype of the petite blonde cheerleader, the multi-faceted nature of her character is complex. Even if she does something stereotypical, like comment on shoes, it's playful and never gets in the way of the overall layering.

Buffy gets the best lines most of the time, the quickest comebacks and the ability to be strong and completely kick-ass, while also being conventionally pretty and occasionally concerned with very mundane things like the prom. She isn't weakened by those typical desires. It's not difficult to see why a teenager would crave normalcy when her nights are spent battling the undead. Buffy can enjoy makeup and clothes and shoes and still be a strong fighter and caring friend. Buffy's heroism doesn't rely on needing to be like a male character. Her femininity isn't played down or diminished or ridiculed. It's just another aspect of who she is.

One of the reasons the Female Heroic is so important to me is that it is rather rare. Most stories about heroes are by men for men. That's not a bad thing, but it does mean that if women want to identify with the hero they often have to identify with a male character. While there's a discussion to be had over whether identifying with a character via gender *should* matter, I think it makes sense. Gender is probably the first difference we identify by and with, and I doubt that's going to change anytime soon (not unless our culture really gets away from such rigid ideas as the gender binary, anyway). The male perspective is not only dominant in most mainstream stories of heroism, but also the default neutral. The expectation is that everyone will just be able to identify with it.

Stories either by women or about women as main characters face a challenge their counterparts don't: the perception that there is something so strange, alien and *other* about the female experience that men can't relate to it. So no one expects them to. And there is a negative connotation to the word *girly* that the word *manly* doesn't have. Things that are coded as "for women" are automatically tainted, because it's that much harder to get people (including women) to view it as more than just an estrogen extravaganza (anything with romance in it, or period pieces that either focus mainly on women or are clearly *for* them). Many women want to distance themselves from the stereotype of being girly, and that's fair. I've done that myself. But Buffy takes the idea of being girly, with her individual style and tendency to wear lip-gloss in battle, and makes it just a part of who she is. Not the antithesis of being a hero, nor a requirement for one. This can make it challenging, in the sense that selling the idea of a strong woman that doesn't rely solely on butt kicking is difficult as is.

I think this is particularly true of stories and characters like Buffy where a woman is the chosen one and has more power, especially physically, than almost any other character. We view women as weaker, and for some people it's a stretch to see a woman punching walls and staking vamps. I've seen the criticism that Buffy being special somewhat undermines her ability to be an empowering icon, because without it, she's just a regular girl who could never do these things; she's only a hero because she's special.

While Buffy does require that bump up in powers, it's about context. In a supernatural world, everyone who is not supernatural is at a disadvantage. While some men in *Buffy* may be able to take on a single vampire, no one but Buffy or other supes (supernaturals) can take on armies of them. In a supernatural setting, your hero needs to be special. She's more than just a supe with a great right hook; that tempers the way she needs to be more than ordinary, and allows for a greater exploration of what being heroic really means. It's not just about physical strength.

Getting that from the perspective of a female character is incredibly important because it takes something that is typically identified as male, codes aspects of it female, and makes it more universal. We all feel love and pain and loss. We may have different individual experiences with it, some having to do with our gender, but we're connected by our shared experiences. I don't think there's a single person, male or female, who can't relate to the awkwardness of adolescence. Or grief over the loss of a loved one. Or understanding when you need to take control of your own life and not let it be governed by others. These things are not gendered. They're human.

This is something that's been interesting for me on a personal level since I started working on the *Angel* comic series. It's no secret that comics is, at least in terms of how it's perceived, a male dominated industry, not unlike television or film. And it *is* true, although there's an element of frustration women like me feel because sometimes it's like we're invisible. It's been decided by the mainstream media that comics are by, for, and about men to a degree that's disheartening. Especially when you've been working on them for the better part of ten years alongside many other women, whether we're talking about creators or fellow editors. The invisibility factor of women in this industry is not unlike the invisibility of girl geeks. We know we exist, but everyone else seems to think we're an enigma every time they get the notion to write about us and what we apparently want. What we want isn't any different than what anyone wants. Good stories. With characters we can relate to or identify with or that are interesting to read about.

And we'd like to feel welcome, not the perpetual *other*. We don't want to feel excluded or like props in every narrative. We don't want or need every story to be about a girl character. But we'd like them to be treated with the same care and attention male characters are. And it is possible, even in male dominated narratives.

When I started working in comics, I hadn't actually watched *Buffy* yet. I was fresh out of college and had largely missed any relevant pop-culture phenomenon with it up until that point. I was too busy learning how to paint and draw naked people. But a friend was so enthusiastic about it that I said, okay. I promptly went through all seven seasons in about two weeks, which I followed up directly with *Angel*. I loved it. But I never dreamed I'd get to actually work with the stories. What it did do, however, was open up the possibilities for long-form narratives on TV, something I hadn't really seen handled that way before. I've loved genre fiction since I was little, but you don't often see it used to so effectively capture so many metaphors and themes on mainstream TV. It gave me hope that something can be fun and yet still socially and personally relevant.

Getting to edit *Angel*, and contribute to it as a writer, has been one of the most agonizing, challenging and ultimately rewarding experiences in my career so far. Here's this world I love, with characters I adore, and I have the opportunity to tell more stories within it. Who wouldn't be thrilled with that? However, there's a lot of responsibility that comes with this power. Angel isn't Buffy, and you have to consider that character and who he is. But I think a lot of the same ideas still apply. Female characters are complex and nuanced. What happens to them matters, and they're important not just for Angel's narrative, but for their own. For me, this was especially true of Fred. Of either show, "A Hole in the World" is probably my favorite episode. Which likely makes me a bit of a tragedy junkie, but, it's more than that. Stories should make you feel. They should make you laugh or cry, elevate you, or break your heart.

Fred's death is one of the most excruciating scenes in an excruciating episode. "Please, Wesley, why can't I say?" may be one of the most profoundly existential statements ever uttered in a show that, on the surface, looks like it's about magic and vampires and stuff. That moment stuck with me, that you could move people like that, and I hope to one day do that with a story of my own. I think one of the great things about *Buffy* and *Angel* is how much they inspire the people who watch them to strive for the things they want to accomplish. Because chances are, nothing you want to do is going to be as hard as fighting armies or dragons.

There are other challenges to working on the comics. For one thing, there's the change of medium. And the fact that "Not Fade Away" is probably the most perfect ending for that character. But it's also about the contrasts between the characters while still being beholden to similar rules, and of course, the influence they've had on each other's development. *Angel* isn't quite the same as *Buffy* for a lot of reasons, one of them being that the story's perspective is not only largely male, but also a quest for redemption by a once-evil vampire. Angel, unlike Buffy, is not inherently good, so as a character he comes from a very different place and has a different set of issues he must face. *Angel* plays on many similar themes of heroism as *Buffy*, but the tone is different, and again, some of it has to do with gender. For instance, women are more often in peril in *Angel*, and many of the female characters (Cordelia, Fred) had terrible things happen to them, like being impregnated by demon offspring, or used as incubators for other creatures to use themselves. There's even an entire episode that was dedicated to a young man that brought out the virulent, horrifying misogyny in any male he touched.

To me, bad things happening to female characters is not inherently anti-feminist. If it's done thoughtfully, critically, and not just flippantly so a male character has something to motivate them, it can be incredibly feminist. While *Angel* may be about a male hero, the female characters are hardly second class. Cordelia's evolution from incredibly vain, ex-rich girl, wannabe actress to a hero in her own right was nothing short of spectacular. Fred's lack of power but incredible emotional range and resonance made her death one of the most painful episodes of any show ever. I'll admit it, it still makes me cry. As does the comparably heartbreaking episode of Buffy's mother dying. Both shows were not afraid to deal with real grief, with unbelievable loss, and even the most fundamental, existential question: where *do* we go when die?

I see feminism as being, at least in the context of pop culture, a lens for exploration and criticism. If nothing bad ever happens to women in a story, you end up with something that plays it too carefully and never realizes its potential. Which, to me, is far worse than trying something and not getting it quite right. Most shows steer clear of anything controversial, and it's only when you risk something that you transcend being just another show about vampires.

Taking the old horror trope of the victimized little blonde girl and turning it around into something clever, funny, tragic and quite thoughtful about the human condition is not the easiest achievement. You're asking people to suspend not only their disbelief, but their ingrained assumptions about not only women, but the very nature of heroism.

Being heroic doesn't mean being perfect. For all of Buffy's physical strength, she's still emotionally vulnerable sometimes. She still needs her friends. She's still carrying a tremendous burden, unlike anyone else. She was chosen, which is not the same thing as getting offered a choice. And sometimes she doesn't like being special. The interplay of those sometimes conflicting states is what makes her so compelling, and why her interaction with other characters feels so real and true. Whether it's hanging out at The Bronze or wandering through a graveyard, talking about boyfriends, and casually staking vamps along the way.

As a woman, a feminist and a critic of pop culture, I'm fascinated by the intersection of what we watch to entertain us, and how it in turn influences us. The fact that a story about a little blonde girl fighting vampires resonates with so many people, explores so many themes, and manages to be both emotionally nuanced and legitimately fun, is an accomplishment very few things can claim. Being moved to laughter or tears is a testament to something that's well written, and when you look at the premise of *Buffy* (not to mention the name), it's probably not what a lot of people expected. That's horror for you: what looks like a simple story with monsters turns about to be about the complex nature of adolescence, the quest for meaning in our lives, and the way gender influences our idea of what a hero is.

It probably seems obvious, but as an editor, I love stories. But it's a little bit more than that. I intensely believe that stories have power. They can spark an idea, or a realization. They can, by just offering another perspective, change a person's mind. They can make us weep and cry and care. And they can connect us. That's powerful stuff. Buffy, as a story and a character, continues to impress me as one of the best examples of what storytelling can accomplish. At the end of the day, it's a story about a complex young woman trying to navigate life and figure out who she is. I think that's something every single one of us can relate to, young woman or not. And if we can do it with even half of Buffy's heart, then I think we've got the potential to change the world. Just like she has.

# My European Vacation:
# A Love Letter/Confession

**Kelly Hale** is the author of several short stories, a play, some overwrought poetry, a bunch of fan fiction, a co-authored TV tie-in novel of the *Doctor Who* variety, and her own book, *Erasing Sherlock* – first released in print by Mad Norwegian Press, and now available on Amazon Kindle. She lives in a crazy little place called Stumptown – jewel of the Pacific Northwest – where the streets are paved with espresso beans and the garbage recycles itself. She used to fantasize about doing the sex with cute vampires/timelords/vulcans etceteras. Now she fantasizes about making them a nice bowl of soup.

I fell madly in love with Mighty Mouse. He had muscles and a cape and he sang that song about saving the day. I imagined marrying him. I drew pictures of me in a long, long dress, carrying a bouquet, and wearing a princess crown and high heels. I was four at the time. The species of my future husband troubled me not. "Is he wearing a crown?" the adults would ask. "No," I would reply, "Those are his ears."

From Mighty Mouse to Spike? Not too far a stretch really. Over the course of the years, I fell in love with many a TV show and many a TV show character. My cohorts are part of the first TV generation. My first serious writing attempt was fan fiction for *Star Trek* – an elaborate, multi-chaptered adventure, shared with my one friend via hushed phone readings in the stairwell of my parents' basement. At school I would turn over the latest installment to her, tucked into a Peachy pocket folder. These stories were secret and no one else could ever know about them. They had to be secret because I still lived in the hope of being popular. Boys thought I was pretty. That figured keenly in my ambitions. Also in my fan fiction. For example:

> I'm Ensign Chekov's beautiful carefree sister that Captain Kirk falls in love with who *almost* dies tragically while sucking poison out of an alien snake bite wound on Kirk's chest but is miraculously saved by Doctor McCoy and decides she has to become a space nun and devote her life to helping victims of a horrible space disease on Omicron Ceti 3. Or some previously unused planet name.

Note the creative use of classic fanfic tropes and Mary Sue action figure. I was 12 when *Star Trek* first aired. But I had already obsessed over such diverse offerings as *The Monkees*, *The Man From Uncle*, *That Girl*, *Honey West*, *Hogan's Heroes*, *I Spy*, *F-Troop* and *Bonanza*. The sixties and early seventies were formative years for television viewing. Imports like *The Avengers* and *Space: 1999* during the summer months fed my obsessions until school and the new TV season began. When I was in high school, *Kung Fu* premiered. I wrote *Kung Fu* inspired hai ku for a poetry class. I wrote a "treatment" for it during study hall in which we meet a beautiful Chinese prostitute/secret assassin (me) in the *Kung Fu* flashback scenes who Kwai Chang Caine meets up with later in America. She overcomes her desire for vengeance against the emperor through the awesome power of his Shaolin priestly wisdom and some sexy kung fu fighting. *Kung Fu* was my last truly mad television passion until *Buffy the Vampire Slayer* came along 25 years later.

By the time Kwai Chang Caine was in the picture, I was fully committed to being a writer – a writer *or nothing* (and if retail sales counts as nothing, then count me successful). Expanding on those television fantasy surrogates of mine, I wondered what pressures in life would make them different from me, alien to me, yet familiar. What kinds of worlds they might come from? Of course, my interest in writing stories about television characters would not have been as strong without a solid background in *Grimm's Fairytales*, Laura Ingalls Wilder, Nancy Drew, Ursula K. Le Guin, Frank Herbert, Roger Zelazny, Jerzy Kosinski and Daphne du Maurier. If television was like a window onto other worlds, books were definitely the doors for me.

I guess what I'm doing here by way of this lengthy preamble is officially confessing to a long history of writing stories about television shows. Many years have been spent adamantly denying this, despite the fact that somewhere out there copies of *Enterprise, a magazine for Star Trek* fans, are floating around with the horrible fan fiction evidence inside (and some costume illustrations). It was easy not to reveal or share my secret. For years I didn't even know anyone else did it. I plugged away at the original work and all the while I was still "using."

As the years went by, I returned to it again and again. It kept me sane through the darkest times, entertained me while walking home with groceries, and kept boredom at bay during the off season at the costume rental shop where I worked. Writing *Star Trek* stories became my go-to outlet whenever my original fiction seemed stalled. I could always throw Kirk into some situation somewhere and see where he'd land (on his feet and smelling like a rose, usually). Or torture Spock (he suffered so stoically). But the stories I had submitted to *Enterprise* were light comedies of the Mary Sue variety. Anything serious or really interesting was used as grist for my original fiction.

In fact, bolstered by apparent encouragement and interest in my work, I cheerfully admitted – to the editor of *Zzyyvva!* (a serious literary journal of contemporary fiction) – that I wrote *Star Trek* stories whenever I was feeling blocked on the serious, arty stuff. To be clear, he *had* asked me about my "process." I never heard from him again, of course.

Fan fiction. My dirty little secret I didn't even have a word for. I made a solemn promise to myself I would not be sharing that information with *anyone ever again*. And then *Buffy* came along.

Ha, you were wondering when I was going to get to that, weren't you? *Buffy the Vampire Slayer* is the fandom that finally set me free. Fan fiction is the reason I got to see the International Arts and Crafts show at the Victoria and Albert Museum in London, had my first (and only) honest-to-God Devonshire cream tea in Exeter, enjoyed a real (and absolutely delicious) traditional English breakfast with fried bread and black pudding at Dart's Farm in Devon, and a Cornish pasty while gazing onto the darkest blue water in Penzance. I drank martinis in Harry's New-York Bar at 5 rue Daunou, and (lest you think this mostly about food) bought buttons from a stand in the Marche Paul-Bert. I climbed the steps to the Basilique du Sacre Coeur and looked out over all of Paris. Fans of *Buffy, Angel, Doctor Who* and fan fiction in general gave those experiences to me and fans shared them with me. How I got from shameful dirty secret to that miracle requires a little back story.

In 1997, I was in the middle of working on a novel when my hard drive crashed. All of my back-up disks were corrupted and I had only printed off about 60 pages of it. It was a very intense loss, and though I can't reasonably compare it with the loss of a child, the grief I experienced was real, intense and absolutely devastating. I was barely functioning, lost my appetite. I was prone to crying jags at work and long silences at home. It *felt* like the loss of a loved one. Or a limb. Or possibly a stillborn child whose potential would never be realized. Or maybe there is no comparing it. I lost a book in progress, a grief unto itself. But the reason I lost that book, the reason I have never confessed before is this: I was being unfaithful to my novel. At the moment my hard drive crashed, I was fantasizing about the eighth Doctor Who, and vaguely plotting a story about the same.

I'd been reading the TV-tie-in novels, you see, and liked them a lot. But the plots were really complicated and I didn't think I could ever pull one off, so I wrote snippets and bits and toyed idly with ideas that were far too angsty and relationship heavy for *Doctor Who* (keep in mind, this was 1997). That's what I was doing while my novel languished unattended. That's what I was doing! So, if not for an indulgent foray into the world of *Doctor Who*, my gorgeous novel about a malevolent ghost in antebellum Louisiana might still be alive (and published!) today. Little wonder I've been hesitant to admit my shame. I swore never to write fan fiction again. Fan fiction was bad, it detracted from serious writing; it was an immoral use of other people's characters – a strange attitude coming from someone who ended up writing *Erasing Sherlock* about Sherlock Holmes and a time-traveling maid, but hey, this is where *Buffy* comes in.

I was late coming to *Buffy*. My 12-year-old son tried to interest me in the show during the first season. This is the same son who, during the year he was eight, refused to watch *Buffy the Vampire Slayer* the movie because of a deep-seated fear that someone he knew would show up in the middle of the night floating outside his window and cracking wise. (He was also afraid that an alien would pop out of his stomach, having secretly watched *Alien* at a sleep-over even though I told him he wasn't old enough. Also that he would be stung by a bee and die horribly like that kid in *My Girl*. Also that he was going to hell for dreaming about kissing a girl, even though we weren't Christian.) At 12, he was full of sophisticated pop culture references and daft comedy. He was really good at getting out of trouble by making me laugh. But despite his insistence that the TV show was really funny and cool, I couldn't be bothered watching television. I was working on that Sherlock Holmes/time-traveling maid novel by that time and had no brain to spare for television (or housecleaning or proper parenting).

It wasn't until the third season of *Buffy* that I started watching regularly. "Faith, Hope, and Trick" was the episode that sucked me in. I don't even know why that one in particular. Maybe it was Faith's unabashed joy in the slaying. "Isn't it crazy how slaying just always makes you hungry and horny?" Or Mr. Trick's thoroughly modern vampire perspective on the curious lack of people of color in Sunnydale. I used to idly ponder the absence of Mexican-Americans in this southern California town, though considering the lack of awareness and constant denial of Sunnydale's white residents, it is perhaps a tribute to the good sense of minority citizens that they chose not to live there.

So, yeah, "Faith, Hope and Trick," a story jam-packed with new characters, new trouble, and new developments, still managed to bring on the funny and the drama. It was the first time I'd simply sat down and watched without doing something else at the same time. It was a revelation, this show. I was hooked. It wasn't until the sixth season that I started writing fan fiction for it though.

* * * *

On the morning of September 11, 2001, I discovered that several pages in a novel I'd co-written for the *Doctor Who* TV tie-in series (yes, I got to do that!) had been printed out of sequence. I logged onto the internet to dash off furious and hysterical emails to my co-author and the publishers when I noticed photos of a plane crashed into a building. It looked like something out of an action movie. I know we all thought that, those of us viewing from a distance. I sent my emails and then looked at the caption accompanying the photos. Then I went to the living room and turned on the television. No one on that terrible day had any idea how this event would ripple through the economy. I'd made plans to move to LA in October. I'd given notice at my job and cashed out my 401K and everything – that's how certain I was about my future success before 9/11. I couldn't have altered my plans to move to LA even if I'd wanted to. Too much was set in motion. But by the time I got there, the work I'd hoped for had disappeared. I found myself at Macy's applying for seasonal jobs with people who'd just been laid off from DreamWorks. The only person I knew in California was my brother. With no job and diminishing prospects, I had my computer, the Internet and email communications with a few friends. I had not taken the headlong plunge into fandom yet. I was still afraid of that place. That place was where the crazies lived.

See, my very first post to a *Doctor Who* newsgroup was also my very first experience being "flamed." When those two things go together, there's a good chance a person is going to run away and never come back. I was very tentative about getting involved with fandom of any sort. Instead, I escaped into reruns of *Buffy the Vampire Slayer*, lived for the promise of new episodes, and searched the Internet for fan fiction because *Buffy* was all and everything wonderful. On *Buffy*, evil did not win. Not ever. You might think it did, but eventually Buffy saved the day. She was like Mighty Mouse that way.

Here was something to ponder, to revel and exalt in, and, yes, laugh at – both for the cheesy monsters and the scintillating quips. Delightfully deep and totally fresh, *Buffy* (for all the sadness and gothic despair of its teenaged protagonists and their undead lovers) seemed a celebration of bright spirit, girl power and the wonder of being alive. *Buffy*, both the show and the girl, reminded me that people could get through the most awful things and still go on – still walk, talk, shop and sneeze. You don't have to sleep on a bed of bones, she told us. *Buffy* was a literal lifeline for me. And, as I soon discovered, many others. With the Internet I could feel part of a community, all of us reaching out with one thing in common: we loved that damned show.

* * * *

One night, I wrote a dark, tragic tale in which Spike narrates an incident in the distant past when Drusilla killed and turned a newborn baby. I posted it to fanfiction.net. Back in Portland, my 17-year-old son had become addicted to meth. Not many people know this. None of the people who praised my stories, whose stories I praised, knew how much I needed them. Stuck in LA with no money and no prospects, and no way to get back, I wrote and wrote, anxiously awaiting feedback, and read and read, leaving breathless reviews to the brilliant writers and words of advice to the amateurs. It was the only thing that kept me from completely losing my shit. My brother was drinking heavily again and wanted me out, even if that meant living in my car. Then, a miracle.

One of the first people whose stories I'd read and commented on (and vice versa), knowing a little about my situation, sent me $200. With that and a Chevron credit card, I packed up my belongings and returned to Portland. This was only the beginning of the generosity and friendship and spirit offered to me from people I knew only through their stories or their reviews of my stories.

My son realized that most of his friends were either dead or in jail and that he didn't want either of those things. I filed for bankruptcy. My friends in *Buffy* fandom sent me a DVD player and the first three season boxed sets.

When my sewing machine and serger were stolen – and with them my hopes to supplement my income – a friend in *Buffy* sent me a sewing machine she claimed never to use and was *still in the box.*

When my wages were garnished by the state for back taxes I hadn't even known I owed, I despaired of ever digging my way out of poverty, and wondered if I would soon be one of those shopping cart people. I took a deep, deep breath and turned to my friends in Buffy for encouragement and suggestions about how to stay positive about the future in the presence of a dismal now. They responded with the most amazing method for staying positive *ever*. A trip to England! I'm not kidding. I still can't believe enough people cared about me to contribute the small bits that added up to such a huge and wondrous once in a lifetime thing. That these people are still some of my closest friends is the best tribute to the power of the Whedonverse, to the richness of the stories we saw on television, and the kinds of people who were attracted to them. I know stay-at-home moms who write zombie fiction, I know pediatricians, freelance copy-editors, espresso baristas and McDonald's employees, published authors, educators, scientists, philosophers, computer programmers and a guy who works for Home Depot – all equal in the land of fan fiction and fandom.

The time of Buffy is gone. Sometimes, out of nowhere, I get this wave of longing, a wistful melancholy that we'll never have anything like it again. Nothing I've seen has matched up to the place it held in my life. Not even *Lost*, which I watch but have no urge to write fan fiction around or about, or the new *Doctor Who*, about which I'm mostly contented to let the stories unfold as they will. And though I might feel loss for the mad conversations, kerfuffles and squee that *Buffy the Vampire Slayer* generated in me, I don't need it the way I did back then, when a show like *Buffy* was brilliant and new, and my life was crap. Even then, I always knew the crap wouldn't last. It was just about finding a way to weather and get through it. I got through it with *Buffy* and *Angel* and *Firefly*. And all the wonderful people who loved it with me.

So this is my love letter to you. This is all the pictures I didn't take, and the postcards I didn't send, and the travel journals I didn't keep. This is me leaning out a window in a Paris hotel on a Sunday morning in May, listening to a dozen distinct church bells ringing out across the city, looking down at the row of scooters parked below, laughing in complete amazement at my good fortune.

Thank you. Thank you. Thank you.

# Romancing the Vampire and Other Shiny Bits

**Lyda Morehouse** leads a double life. By day, she's a mild mannered, award-winning science fiction novelist; by night, she's witchy, best-selling vampire romance writer Tate Hallaway. Lyda's *Archangel Protocol* won the Shamus for best paperback original featuring a private investigator, and her *Apocalypse Array* scored the Philip K. Dick special award for excellence (aka 2nd place). A prequel to these books, *Resurrection Code*, is due out from Mad Norwegian Press on the same day as *Whedonistas*. Tate's novels include the five book Garnet Lacey series, the young adult vampire princess of St. Paul series, and a new adult series called *Precinct 13* (an *X-Files*/*CSI* mash-up). You can find them both on the web: *www.lydamorehouse.com* or *www.tatehallaway.com*

> **Willow:** So you're feeling better about Angel?
> **Buffy:** Well, we talked, and then he ripped out the heart of a demon and fed it to me, and then we talked some more.
> **Willow:** See! That's how it should work!

Perhaps you've been to a bookstore in the last few days and wandered intentionally (or accidentally) through the science fiction/fantasy section. While there, you noticed a trend. Book after book with covers showing women – usually from the back and often scantily dressed in leather, possibly tattooed – holding a weapon of some sort (like a wooden stake), and looking out at a supernatural, urban scene. If you haven't noticed this phenomenon for yourself, you'll have to trust me[1].

Urban Fantasy/Paranormal Romance is the "it" thing in my genre right now. What exactly do I mean by "Urban Fantasy" or "Paranormal Romance"? Let me put this as succinctly as possible: think *Buffy the Vampire Slayer* only, as a book, okay? That's pretty much it. You've got a strong, sexy, spunky female lead, who may or may not have supernatural powers of her own, ala being "the Chosen One," and her vampire/werewolf/ghost/

---

1. Always a bad idea, so an informal survey of the *Romantic Times* Book Reviews shows 42 Paranormal Romance/Urban Fantasy titles reviewed for September 2010, not including Teen/YA or Fantasy titles, though some are listed as Paranormal. By comparison, in the same issue there were 26 Historical Romance, 12 Science Fiction/Fantasy, 29 Inspirational (Christian), 13 Romantic Suspense, and 10 Erotica titles reviewed.

incubus/golem/zombie boyfriend. Together they have wacky (though sometimes dark) adventures and romance together in a thoroughly modern world, often accompanied by a Scooby Gang made up of what we in the biz call quirky characters.

Though it would be unfair to say that Joss Whedon single-handedly created the Urban Fantasy craze in its current format, *Buffy* did a hell of a lot to popularize it.

So, Joss, if you're reading this, thanks for the job.

As Tate Hallaway I write Paranormal Romances and Urban Fantasy, and have done since the 2006 publication of *Tall, Dark & Dead*. Previously, I wrote Science Fiction, and yes, I'm still waiting for *Firefly* to do for that genre what *Buffy* did for this, but I'm not holding my breath, and I'll tell you why.

*Buffy* tapped something that Romance readers and writers were waiting for, I think.

The thing that Whedon hit, in my opinion, was sexual equality. And adding wry humor/metafictional self-awareness, but I'll get to that one in a moment. Let's stick first with the juicier bit: sex.

Buffy could kick Angel's ass, and I found that totally hot.

Though I'm sure Whedon's wasn't the first, my imagination was utterly captivated by the romantic dynamic presented in Slayer versus vampire on *Buffy*. Here was a romance that was on equal footing, for once, not only in terms of forceful personality, but also physical prowess and strength. This was a new thing for romance, because, frankly, it's kind of queer.

And, yes, by that I mean gay.

**Joyce:** Honey, a-are you sure you're a Vampire Slayer? I-I mean, have you tried not being a Slayer?

But seriously, you just didn't find that kind of physically equal hot outside of slash.

"Slash," for those of you just tuning in, is usually homoerotic fan fiction that got its name from the "/" in Kirk/Spock. I read some *Buffy* slash, but I never got much into it because I didn't find the idea of Xander/Angel terribly exciting, because for me what makes slash hot is this idea of physical equality... with raunchy sex.

Let me step back a pace, and set the scene of the early 1990s.

Though I usually don't admit it, I was reading sassy, modern, alpha female (almost!) leads in time-travel romances in those days. Sandra Hill[2] was a particular favorite of mine, because she combined smartass women with, well, time-traveling Vikings, and who doesn't like time-traveling

---

2. *The Last Viking* (LoveSpell, April 1998) and *The Outlaw Viking* (LoveSpell, August 1998) by Sandra Hill are examples.

Vikings, I ask you? Like Whedon, she also played the situation for laughs, but the Vikings were still hulking, massively weaponized warriors compared to heroines, who often had nothing more in their arsenal than a sharp tongue. That disparity left me kind of cold.

I wanted something... more.

Especially since I tried any number of other Time-travel Romance writers, including the very popular Diana Gabaldon's *Outlander*. Despite what most people think, Romance had mostly gotten away from bodice-ripping even by the late 1980s. Yet there's a very disturbing, not-hot for me at least, scene in *Outlander* in which the hero Jamie beats the heroine. Like, seriously slaps her around for bring uppity. It's not S&M sexual foreplay, either. It's very much I'm-putting-you-in-your-place-and-I'm-way-bigger-and-stronger-than-you gross. I think we're supposed to excuse him because he's from another century, but it has always stuck in my mind as an example of what traditional Romances really needed: a kick in the pants, and *not* that kind, and definitely not from that guy.

We needed a chick who wouldn't take that kind of crap. From anyone. Not even Godzilla. I mean, on the big screen we were finally getting gun-toting women like Ripley in *Alien* to root for, but, while they delightfully blew up the big bads, they rarely had any kind of sustained romance. In fact, in my opinion, early action heroines tended to be not only sexual non-starters, but also irritatingly maternal, defending cats or stowaway children[3]. Regardless, they almost never had time for boyfriends because they were too busy having stiff upper lips to use them to kiss anyone.

Then, along came *Buffy*.

**Buffy:** You never take me any place new.
**Angel:** What about that fire demon nest in the cave by the beach? I felt that was a nice change of pace.

Buffy's romance with Angel blew away the tropes of my genre. Suddenly, it wasn't all about the knight in shiny armor who rescues the helpless princess trapped in the tower. Buffy could bash the door down and let herself out, thank you very much. She didn't have to lean on Angel (or any other man) for the physical stuff. In fact, she was more often than not better at the punching bits than anyone else.

Okay, this was new and exciting for me. I'd been waiting for a woman like this for a long time. If anyone was going to do the spanking, it was going to be Buffy, and I liked that. A lot.

However, I think the thing that particularly appealed to the general

---

3. Just sayin' the writers even added a child-in-peril to the movie version of *Tank Girl*, how wrong is that?

Romance types was the idea that Buffy was *magically* strong. She wasn't sweaty and muscle-bound, like some kind of She-Hulk (who is still hot, but you know what I'm saying). She didn't have to have some horrible personal history (ala Tasha Yar on *Star Trek: The Next Generation*) or a glimpse into a nuclear future (ala Sarah Connor in *The Terminator*) to explain away her badassitude. She was "The Chosen One." It was like getting to be a princess... but of ass-whooping.

When she wasn't dusting vamps, Buffy was a girly-girl, a femme. She was a cheerleader. She complained about breaking a nail. Perhaps even more importantly, she could wear really cute outfits while round-housing oozingly evil monsters. This is very much what a lot of Urban Fantasy/Paranormal Romance heroines are like.

For example, MaryJanice Davidson's Betsy the Vampire Queen spends an inordinate amount of time fretting over her shoes. The heroine of my own Garnet Lacey series can be quite a loveable airhead when not channeling the fearful power of the dark goddess Lilith.

This is a fun fantasy for a lot of us. Even if I don't wear anything with higher heels than All-Star Converses, I can still appreciate the idea of an uber-femme superhero. It subverts the sharp-tongued, but physically incapable heroine of Gabaldon and others, and gives us a silly girl with the ability to put the hurt on the big bad.

Or her vampire boyfriend.

Now, if you want to, you could write a reverse of the creepy beating scene; Buffy could totally put Angel over her knee. I wouldn't want her to (okay, maybe in some het-slash, but not in canon), because one of the things that's fun about adding magical abilities into the romance is that now the boy can be as interesting as the girl. He can crawl out from behind that shiny armor and they can rescue Xander together.

This is really kind of subversive, particularly for popular Romance.

**Xander:** Cavalry's here. Cavalry's a frightened guy with a rock, but it's here.

Vampires had, of course, for a long time been associated with sexual subversion/perversion. Bram Stoker's *Dracula* abounds with thinly disguised taboo sexual images[4]. One of the earliest vampire short stories, "Camilla," is about the horrors of lesbianism. Lots of more scholarly and intelligent writers, like Pam Kessey, have written extensively about the connections between vampires and GLBT issues. But the Dracula/Camilla vampire represents a different kind of queerness than the one I'm extolling. The sexual-

---

4. See Chapter 9 "Sexual Symbolism" in *Dracula: The Novel & The Legend* by Clive Leatherdale (The Aquarian Press, Northhamptonshire) 1985.

ity of pre-Buffy vampires is supposed to scare you. That's why, pre-Buffy, most books about vampires (even the sexy ones) were all found in the horror section.

Thing is, vampires make nasty lovers, because, well, unless you're one of them, they eat you. Part of what makes vampires sexy, at least for me, is the fact that they are predators. They're a sort of ultimate alpha male (or female). They're immortal. They're strong, fast, and superhuman. It totally works for me, except for the whole being a snack part.

Anne Rice, who started the first of the vampire renaissances of my generation of writers, straddled the line between Horror and Romance. Her Romance was meant to be tragic, in my opinion, however. Louis in *Interview with a Vampire* was a Bryonic hero. He was totally gay, in a hot boy-on-boy-sploitation sort of way, but Lestat was not a fun boyfriend. When they tried to play house and adopt Claudia, the whole folly ends with one of the most horrifying scenes ever written. I still shudder when I think about it. Thus, this is not a relationship I would like to imagine myself in, for instance.

Also, Louis had to become what he feared/hated in order to be with his lover. Louis and Lestat had a physical/supernatural equality afterward, but Rice intended, I think, to unsettle the straight reader, and make him or her deeply uncomfortable, even horrified and disgusted.

Meanwhile, Angel and Buffy get to experience a moment of perfect happiness. Okay, so afterward everything went to Hell, quite literally. This moment is problematic for me, because it's easy to read as Buffy being punished for her sexuality, which then collapses my argument that Buffy and Angel represent a kind of queerish ideal. But I'm going to stick by it, because, while it might not be perfect, what Buffy did for Romance writers is give them a chance to play with power in a new, unique way. Which is to say, let the girls have as much as the boys.

Most of us never get past the HEA, anyway. (HEA, for those of you not versed in Romance tropes, stands for Happily Ever After, the fade to black once the prince has swept the princess off her feet and carried her up to the castle to snog.)

And, perhaps, too, what's more important is the idea of Buffy and Angel infected a whole battalion of writers that followed after. I'd wager that without even trying you could think of a novel or two featuring a tough heroine paired with a hot supernatural hero (not all of them vampires even). There's Laurell K. Hamilton, Charlaine Harris, MaryJanice Davidson, Lilith Saintcrow, all the way down to me. Joss Whedon gave us a very rich playground to explore, and, from the looks of things, we won't be done for some time to come.

But, I think *Buffy* (and, many other Whedon projects,) infused Romance with something else that keeps the genre bright and lively. That is: humor.

**Xander:** I laugh in the face of danger. Then I hide until it goes away.

Previously if you had a vampire in a movie or a book, s/he was more likely to bwah-ha-ha! than knee-slap. But *Buffy* changed all that. Even in the darkest moments, there was usually something that made me smile or laugh on *Buffy*.

This, in particular, I think fit very well with what was happening with Romance at the same time. Leisure Books launched a series called "a Wink & a Kiss" which specialized in Humorous Romance. I happened to be aware of it, because the first book in the series is *Bewitched Viking* by Sandra Hill (LoveSpell, June 1999), whose career I'd started following a few months earlier.

It took several more years until someone started combining humor and vampires in romantic literature, and though there were probably others before her, the first to make a huge splash was MaryJanice Davidson with *Undead & Unwed* (Berkley, 2004).

I think that humor has been critical in making the vampire an acceptable romantic partner. Through the Buffy-magic, you get sexual equality, but I think the *romance* starts with a bit of humor. It helps take the vampire away from his or her dark, brooding castle and puts her or him somewhere much more accessible. Not every Paranormal Romance since *Buffy* or Davidson has been funny, of course, though humor is something I personally look for. I also strive to have a bit in my own work. But, I've never been attracted to over-the-top slapstick in novels, so I try to follow the *Buffy* model.

There's one thing that I think is very specific to Whedon's humor, it's something I've dubbed "iconoclastic realism."

Let me see if I can explain what I mean. When given something so tired and old and laden with cultural baggage like vampires, Whedon manages to make moments fresh by thinking deeply within the box – so deep, in fact, that he comes out the other side. By that, I mean it's as if he asks himself, "What would really happen if a vampire walked into the room right now?", and then adds, "No, *really*."

**Buffy:** I don't want any trouble. I just want to be alone and quiet in a room with a chair and a fireplace and a tea cozy. I don't even know what a tea cozy is, but I want one.

The reason I think of this kind of humor as iconoclastic or metafictional is that usually fiction (particularly Speculative Fiction) is something we experience as somewhat distant from ourselves. It's often written in third person (he, she, etc.). It happens once upon a time in a magical enchanted forest or a long, long time ago in a galaxy far, far away. In the dark days before *Buffy*, creatures like vampires and werewolves were rarely[5] something you'd meet on a city bus or that might show up in school one day, for instance.

But Whedon put vampires on the bus.

Now, suddenly, with this mash-up of fantasy and hardcore reality, you can imagine being there. Everyone has gone to school or taken public transit, so it's familiar, even if the idea of a vampire still seems preposterous. The veil is lifted. You've crossed the Fourth Wall and walked on stage with the actors.

Because, what Whedon does quite brilliantly, in my opinion, is say what you're thinking. You're looking around thinking, "Seriously, a werewolf on the bus? How weird is that?", and then Willow says something almost exactly like that, only funnier, and the whole situation seems that much more impossibly possible. Like, if there really were witches and ghosts, that's just how it'd be.

Plus, Whedon's Buffy often examines clichés and tropes to the extreme until you can see the funny in it.

> **Spike:** We like to talk big. Vampires do. 'I'm going to destroy the world.' That's just tough guy talk. Strutting around with your friends over a pint of blood. The truth is, I like this world. You've got ... dog racing, Manchester United. And you've got people. Billions of people walking around like Happy Meals with legs. It's all right here.

In Speculative Fiction, the operative word is "speculative." Thus, I think it's important to really think through the consequences of whatever change you make to the future, or, as when writing Paranormal Romance or Urban Fantasy, the now. Whedon inspires me to keep looking at all sides of whatever fantastical monster I want to write about, so that I can find that angle of light that will feel real... or at least funny.

Or, with the best of luck, *really* funny.

---

5. Emma Bull and other fantasy writers in the 1980s gave us elves on motorcycles, but, for whatever reason, that early urban fantasy never broke out of the SF/F ghetto. Maybe it was the foreign-looking words like *pucca* or other slightly more obscure Irish fairy?

# An Interview with Juliet Landau

**Juliet Landau** co-starred in Tim Burton's *Ed Wood* as Loretta King, and starred opposite Whoopi Goldberg in New Line Cinema's *Theodore Rex*. She created the role of Drusilla on *Buffy the Vampire Slayer*, appearing on *Buffy* and *Angel* over the course of six seasons. Juliet directed the short documentary *Take Flight* about and for Gary Oldman, co-directed/ appeared in Godhead's *Hero* music video and co-wrote two issues of the Angel comic book about Drusilla. Her lead roles in Independents include: *Monster Mutt*, *The Yellow Wallpaper, Darkness Visible, Hack, Toolbox Murders, Repossessed, Carlo's Wake, Life Among the Cannibals, Ravager, Direct Hit, Citizens* and *Going Shopping*. TV guest appearances include: *Millennium, La Femme Nikita, Strong Medicine*, a starring role in the Lifetime movie *Reunion* and a project directed by Jake Scott for HBO. She has lent her voice to various characters on the popular animated series *Justice League Unlimited, Ben 10: Alien Force* and *Green Lantern*, as well as on *Bioshock 1* and *2, Star Wars: The Old Republic* and *Ben 10* video games. Animated features include: *Green Lantern: First Flight, Justice League Doom* and *Strange Flame*. Juliet has worked extensively in the theater, garnering outstanding reviews every time out.

**Q. You've been involved in a lot of creative mediums: dance, acting, singing, directing, writing, and voice-over work. How do each of these mediums fulfill you creatively? Is there a different creative approach required for such diverse output?**

A. I love being creative in all these avenues. They each involve different skills, but I think I approach all of my work in a similar way. I do a lot of rehearsal, preparation and research ahead of time. I really get immersed in the project and therefore feel a freedom to go with the flow on set, in the editing bay, while writing, on the stage or in the sound booth.

**Q. Do the different mediums inform one another in a specific way? We would guess that your dance background informed how you played Drusilla (i.e. how she moved), but does it inform your voice work, for instance?**

A. I definitely bring my dance background to the characters I play. Physicality is such a strong component of every role. I think with voice work, it does help to involve your body to some extent when you are recording. Musicality comes into play when working with different dialects. When writing, I play all of the characters. Certainly, co-writing the Dru comics felt like a natural extension of portraying her. . I have learned so much from the directors I have worked with. I take that experience with me into everything I do.

**Q. Why do you think *Buffy* resonated so deeply with viewers, and has retained such a stalwart fanbase?**

A. Joss is super-talented. The show was smart, funny, interesting and original. It used the metaphor of high school as a nightmare, utilizing dark forces to illustrate that allegory to the absolute extremes. Even though the show was fantastical, everything was rooted. Joss told me that he wrote the scene where Joyce found out that Buffy was the Slayer, as if she'd just found out that her daughter was gay. Joyce said things like, "Are you sure you're the Slayer?", and "Can you try not to be the Slayer?" Then there's the episode about the girl who felt ignored and invisible, then actually disappeared and became invisible. And the evil man who dated Joyce, played by John Ritter, who Buffy had to kill. It told real stories that people could relate to and had experienced, using this extraordinary paradigm.

**Q. Drusilla has turned into such an iconic character, did you have any inkling going into the role that the character would become so popular?**

A. I knew that she was a phenomenal character with tremendous depth and dimension, but I didn't think about it from the outside. I felt blessed and excited to play her.

**Q. What is your favorite memory of working on the *Buffy* set?**

A. I loved working with Joss. He had such a specific vision of the world he was creating, which made my job really easy. I loved the table reads we had in Season Two, where the cast, writers, producers and director all came together to read the episode. I loved rehearsing with James. Television shoots very quickly. Both James and I have a theater background, so we would get a jump on the scenes by meeting up and rehearsing. Every day was filled with creativity and joy.

**Q. James Marsters has said in interviews that he got cast as Spike because you liked him. He also called you fearless as a performer. Can you give us an example of a scene that, while shooting, best exemplifies your working relationship with him?**

A. That's so nice! That's a great word... "fearless." James and I had a wonderful acting chemistry right from the get-go. After I was cast, they paired me with the final choices for Spike. His audition included a scene from our introductory episode, "School Hard," in which we were talking to the Anointed One. We got caught up with each other as if we might kiss, then we rested our foreheads together and only eventually turned out, while talking to him. It not only made it into the episode, but they used it in the promos; our resting foreheads and then us turning out with this booming voiceover: "Evil has a few new faces... " It was pretty cool. That's how it was with our scenes. It was truly what they call moment-to-moment acting.

**Q. Your portrayal of Drusilla was a delightful combination of crazy and menacing childlike wonder. How much of that was stage direction and how much of it was your interpretation of the character? What did you access within yourself to play Drusilla?**

A. Joss said that he had Spike and Dru running around in his head for ten years. After he cast me, we got together for a meeting where he described everything he wanted in the character. He described Drusilla with all these opposing adjectives. He said that she was sweet but diabolical, childlike but sensual, delicate but powerful, sadistic but loving and gentle, Victorian but relevant... Dru had been tortured and was mentally unwell. She had an epic love affair that endured centuries. He gave me the keys and then really let me run with it. There came a point where Drusilla's illogic became very logical to me. I remember when we were working on the show, Joss would say something about Dru being crazy and I would say, "She's not crazy. She's just a bit touched!" Then Joss would say, "Yes, it shows that you feel that way. Don't change that." Now if I see a rerun, I think, "Wow, Dru is really crazy!" I loved that she was not only a character who had experienced a lot of pain and tragedy, but also had this sumptuous sensuality and sexuality.

**Q. You've had the opportunity to have even more input into Drusilla's character through your comics writing. Has the way that you think of Drusilla changed significantly since you began playing her?**

A. Joss filled me in on Dru's backstory in our initial creative meeting. There was such a clarity, that I knew what made her tick right from the inception. Of course, with getting to inhabit a character over the course of so many seasons, that knowledge deepened and broadened, but the underpinnings were there right from the start.

**Q. Joss Whedon seems to create an incredible sense of loyalty among people he's worked with; to what do you attribute that?**

A. He's brilliant and lovely and passionate and hard working. It's so much fun to work with him. He really is a wonder.

**Q. What did you take away from working with Joss? Has his working style affected your choices as a director and creator?**

A. Yes. He creates the best environment for everyone to thrive and do their job optimally. He is true to his vision. He's meticulous. He loves and enjoys what he does. He allows/ pushes people to do their best. I hope I am able to bring even a thimbleful of that to the projects I direct/ create.

**Q. One of your earliest roles was acting with Johnny Depp, in Tim Burton's *Ed Wood*. Can you tell us a bit about that experience? Given Burton and Depp's popularity at the time, was working on one of their films daunting?**

A. I loved working with Tim. There aren't enough words to describe his brilliance and Johnny Depp's, who is not only gifted, but also extremely giving. It was a dream set to be on. Tim has an ebullient spirit that is contagious. Everyone was excited and giving their 100%, collaborating as a team. *Gilbert Grape* was out at the time, and I decided to wait until after the shoot to see it. My character, Loretta King, meets Ed / Johnny in my first scene in the film, so I thought the less pre-conceived info I had, the better. As far as with Tim, I felt an ease from the moment I met him. We seemed to speak a similar language. I was doing night shoots on a film when casting director Vickie Thomas initially brought me in to audition on tape. When I got called back for Tim in person, I was in the waiting room looking over the script, preparing to audition again, when someone came out and said, "You won't be reading... Tim just wants to meet you." I went in and Tim immediately said, "I loved your audition!" And then we proceeded to have the most interesting stream of conscious discussion. We didn't talk about Loretta or the film. When I left, all I knew, was that I had had a wonderful time. When I was hired and went for my first hair and make-up test, the producer, Denise DiNovi, greeted me with, "Tim loved your audition. He made me watch it eight times!"

**Q. You've recently finished filming *The Yellow Wallpaper*. Can you tell us about that project?**

A. It is based on the story written by Charlotte Perkins Gilman in 1892. I play the title character, Charlotte. In feel, it is a bit like the Nicole Kidman movie *The Others*. Michael Moriarty and Veronica Cartwright, who I just worked with on another film, are in it.

**Q. The world has become a much smaller place thanks to social media. Actors, etc. can now interact with fans in real time. What is your take on this new availability? Do you think it is a good thing or bad thing?**

A. I think it is an incredible thing. I can have a direct dialogue with people without the middleman. The people who follow me and support my work are amazing. I recently released my Gary Oldman documentary, *Take Flight*, online as a pay-per-view streaming. I was able to promote it via Twitter, Facebook, MySpace, Model Mayhem, etc. I put together a promo campaign that timed out with the release, posting one promo every few days on YouTube, which led even more people to the *Take Flight* site. The promos included Christian Kane, Amy Acker, Michael Rosenbaum, Sam Anderson, Armin Shimerman, David J and Kat Von D. I have also recently released a series of behind-the-scenes sequences from different magazine photo shoots on YouTube. The response has been spectacular.

**Q. You're using your online store to microfinance your film *It's Raining Cats and Cats*. Can you tell us a bit about the film, and the funding model?**

A. I followed fellow *Buffy* alum Amber Benson's model. She raised the money for two of her feature films by selling autographed merchandise on a website. We met a few times to discuss how she did it. *It's Raining Cats and Cats* is a piece I wrote, and in which I will play seven different characters.

**Q. Is there anything that you yourself are "fannish" about?**

A. Getting a good part!

# I am Joss Whedon's Bitch

**Maria Lima** is a writing geek with one foot in the real world and the other in the make-believe. Her *Blood Lines* series (Pocket Books) is set in the Texas Hill Country – a fabulous place for things that go bump in the night. She loves to read, write and watch genre TV, and feels very lucky that people actually pay her to do at least one of these things. www.marialima.com

I've joked a great deal in the past that I was Joss Whedon's bitch. I even bought the fabulous ThinkGeek T-shirt that states: "Joss Whedon is My Master Now." But despite the amusement factor, one fact is pretty much true: Joss Whedon can write. His ideas, his treatment of genre television goes so far beyond traditional tropes and expectations that there are words invented to talk about his impact. (Ever been "Jossed"?)[1]

Though he's not the only person that has – and still does – yank my genre fiction chain, he's one of the top five that make it into the "OMG" group – as in "OMG, I wish I'd have thought of that first." The others? Tanya Huff, Fred Saberhagen, Charlaine Harris and Christopher Golden. There are a ton of other writers on my list, but these five are the epitome of the kind of writing I not only love, but that influence my own work for the better.

For the purposes of this essay, I'd like to concentrate on my Joss Whedon gateway drug, *Buffy the Vampire Slayer* (the TV show, not the movie). Not that I'm not totally a fan of *Firefly* and of *Dollhouse*, but I could write a novella on each one. *Buffy* lured me in with the first episode, then kept me as a slave to the Whedon Way for its entire seven seasons. I learned a lot of lessons about writing via the Scooby Gang, and I hope I put them to good use in my own work.

Somewhere around late elementary school, I discovered vampires – thanks to a voracious reading habit and a set of parents that allowed me free access to the many hundreds of books in the house. I don't remember when I first met the Count, but I know that I still have a battered *Dracula* paperback from the mid-70s, acquired shortly after diving into the delicious

---

1. Jossed (v.) . According to UrbanDictionary.com, this is "when a fanfiction writer's explanation of a certain event or exploration of a characters' motivations which previously is ambiguous, is then explained by the actual fandom, and contradicts the fanfiction writers story."

cheesiness that was *Dark Shadows* and the haunted domain of Collinwood. Saturdays often meant thrilling in delicious terror at Christopher Lee in *Dracula: Prince of Darkness*. Weekdays became rushing out of school to get home in time for Barnabas Collin's latest adventure. Barnabas, as played by Jonathan Frid, was the first (to me) sexy vampire. In college, I found Fred Saberhagen's fabulous series, beginning with *The Dracula Tapes*, followed by the unforgettable Frank Langella as the Transylvanian count in the 1979 movie. My roommate and I walked home after that movie, vowing that Langella was the Best. Dracula. EVAHR! (Of course, I still haven't forgiven the producers or whomever for trading Lucy for Mina – I mean *why*? I never actually got that.) He'd even beaten our previous favorite, Louis Jourdan, in the 1977 PBS movie. Then later that year, we discovered *The Rocky Horror Picture Show*. Frank N. Furter wasn't a traditional vampire, no doubt, but few can argue that Frank was a sexual vampire... and so bloody hot!

Little did I know that the future held so much more for us fans of the bloodsucking fiends. In fact, I don't think that there's ever been a dearth of vampire fiction available, whether in print or at the movies. Just do a key-word search on IMDb. You'll get nearly a thousand results for movies; some as early as 1896 and several listed as in production for release in 2010. John Polidori published *The Vampyre* in 1819.

Dudes. That's nearly two hundred years of bloodsuckers – whether fiendish, gruesome, horrific, terrifying, sexy or just plain fabulous. But it wasn't until a certain tiny blonde chick who redefined the word "perky" hit the screen that my take on the genre exploded.

I have to admit it: at first, I wasn't watching. I mean, really? Buffy? Who the heck would name a character some dumb valley girl name? It sounded ridiculous to me (thanks, years of conditioning!) so I didn't bother to try to tune in. Despite the assurances of many friends whose tastes I trust, I blew them off, thinking all along that I was winning in this friendly battle. Until 2001, when a very kindly enabler friend lugged 14 videotapes with her from New Jersey and put Buffy Seasons One through Five in my hands. I took the tapes, because you know, what the heck was I going to do? I figured I'd even humor her and watch a few episodes, so I could then legitimately say I did-n't like it.

It's a good thing I wasn't a published writer at the time, with deadlines and work to do after my regular job – I would've missed all those targets. I can't remember how long it took, but I watched every single one of those grainy, second-generation recordings as if they were crack and I was the world's newest addict. It was funny, snarky, sexy, and the show pulled no punches. People *died* – people I cared about – in the very first part of the show, even. My world had just turned upside down in the best way possible. I had to rethink my paradigms, relearn what I knew about writing.

I tried to keep up; Season Six had just begun to air while I was still scarfing down Season Four of the show. I sent frantic emails to my pals: how does Buffy have a sister? Willow is gay? They all laughed and told me to watch faster. So I did. I cranked up the old VCR and pretty much did nothing on weekends but watch episode after episode. *Whew!* A wild ride indeed. When I watched Buffy take that slo-mo swan dive off that rickety tower in "The Gift," I felt this amazing sense of rightness – this was a show about life and death and everything in between and after. Whether it was about high school or college or just being a grownup, the Whedon creative brain nailed it.

This Whedon guy not only had a clue as to what audiences wanted, he gave it to them in spades, and sometimes gave them things they didn't even know they wanted. It's been nearly nine years since that fateful weekend, and I, in turn, have helped hook several more folks into the Whedon madness. I've published my own books since then, silently thanking Joss and his brilliant writing team every time I take a risk, do something in a plot / character development that isn't "safe." Because, ultimately, that's probably the most valuable writing lesson I learned from watching Buffy – a lesson reiterated again and again through *Angel*, through *Firefly* and *Serenity*, through *Dollhouse* – the safe choice in writing may work, but it's boring. Good writing is about conflict and challenges. What can you, as the writer, throw into the mix to make it even tastier? Another death, an unexpected twist of plot that was actually hinted at long before? A new rival? What can we, as writers, do to subvert the expected and create a combination that not only entertains, but makes people think?

In *Buffy*, when Spike got his soul, I cheered the absolute genius of it: the dichotomy of the ultimate Bad!Boy seeking out his salvation, fully knowing the torment that awaited him, in contrast to the unasked for soul-bearing of Angel (which was in itself, fascinating). The delicious battles and mental anguish between the two vampires, between them and Buffy. Similarly, the amazing episode that was "Out of Gas" in *Firefly*, where we discover our characters' pasts. They're not what we thought, were they? Yet, at the same time, the characters' story arcs were consistent within themselves and though, often surprising, didn't appear out of thin air. No, the writing wasn't perfect, nor unblemished, but all of Whedon's shows shone above nearly everything else on TV at the time (and many things after). Joss Whedon and his writing team forged entirely new directions in television scripts, unapologetically developing flawed characters and hard-hitting storylines while delivering both with a trademark sense of humor.

As a writer, because of examples like *Buffy*, *Angel*, *Firefly* and *Dollhouse*, I ache to play with the genre conventions. Do I create my own angst and guilt-ridden vampire with a soul? Do I build a character whose cavalier attitude towards lesser humans is tempered by love? The idea behind a being who has cheated human death, who is in so many ways superior, and yet is vulnerable to so many mundane things tease the creator in me. How much can I change?

What differences can my vampires have but still be recognizably vampires? That's the beauty of the genre and the reason that keeps drawing me back to reading and writing vampires, werewolves, shapeshifters and other magical creatures. The possibilities are endless. This is what I learned the most – not to feel constricted or chained by genre past, but how to mold my own version, while still using the more recognizable traditions. My vampires still have fangs. My werewolves follow wolf pack behavior. My Sidhe still have the age-old conflicts between Seelie and Unseelie. The differences lie in bringing these tropes to the modern, twenty-first century world, with cell phones and the Internet and text messaging. How are these characters, these creations, relevant to modern audiences?

Using these conventions to explore our own human lives isn't a new trick, nor is it exclusively Joss Whedon's (*Star Trek*, anyone?), but Joss and his writers freshened it up, polished it to a shiny and very accessible new bauble for the audience. Turning genre tropes upside down and back-asswards is probably the primary hallmark of all of his work. See that cute vivacious blonde girl wearing a school uniform in the first episode – guess what? She's the monster. The other cute blonde? The other monster (to the vamps, anyway) – I mean, c'mon, she's a killer, right? When *Buffy* first aired, no one else had gone this far. No one had pulled out quite as many stops and let that train just roll on to its not-so-inevitable conclusion.

It's the kind of writing I both admire and aspire to. It's never stale. It never gets old. "Welcome to the Hellmouth" is just as watchable now as it was in 1997 – even though Buffy has to rely on a pager and not a cell phone. The first season of *Buffy* is just as relevant as the second season of *Dollhouse* – because underneath, the stories are still about people, about emotions and challenges and how we deal with our world. It's not about the trappings of technology or buried in stale tradition. It's all about life. That's why I still continue to be Joss Whedon's bitch even now.

# Going Dark

**Jackie Kessler** writes about demons, angels, the hapless humans who come between them, superheroes, the supervillains who pound those heroes into pudding, witches, ghosts, and the occasional Horseman of the Apocalypse. She wrote a two-part *Buffy*verse *Tales of the Vampires* comic called "Carpe Noctem" for Dark Horse Presents. Her work for teens is written under the byline Jackie Morse Kessler. For more about Jackie, visit her websites www.jackiekessler.com and www.jackiemorsekessler.com.

Growing up, I loved superheroes. I would wear my Wonder Woman Underoos and watch the *Super Friends* (it was the 1970s; don't judge me), and I'd spend Saturdays reading comic books about how the good guys fought the bad guys and always won. By the time I was 12, I was all about the X-Men – so much so, my folks got me *X-Men* #94-100 in mint condition for my bat mitzvah present. (I know, right? Best present *ever*.) My favorite hero, hands down, was Kitty Pryde. A brainy, Jewish teen with cool powers helped fight to save the world? Awesome! Small wonder, then, that I loved Willow Rosenberg on *Buffy the Vampire Slayer*. I guess I have a thing for brainy Jewish teen superheroes[1]. (Who knew I had a type?)

But what I discovered as I got older was that the heroes, while still fun to read about and watch on television, weren't nearly as much fun as the villains. Sure, the heroes get their names in the series titles, but the villains play the role of the Big Bad, which is infinitely cooler. And good-girl Willow giving way to mega-sorceress Dark Willow is coolest of all.

### Heroes And The Villains That Pound Them Into Pudding

Let's face it: heroes are stupid. I'm not talking about the Big And Dumb variety that tend to join groups like the Initiative. I mean the sort of stupid that allows heroes to get up every day and go hunt monsters and save the world, all without A) getting paid, B) getting thanked, or C) getting any guarantee there will be some sort of eternal reward at the end of the day[2].

---

1. Yes, I'm saying that the super – and supernatural – powered characters in the Buffyverse are superheroes, even before the "Twilight" story arc in *Buffy the Vampire Slayer* Season Eight via Dark Horse Comics. Xander and Andrew may disagree, but they're fictional characters, so that doesn't bother me.
2. Shanshu Prophecies not included.

If heroes really sat back and thought about just how much their situation sucked, they wouldn't go out there and do the job that only they could do. That's why they're heroes, after all. They're determined. They're focused. And even if they question why they're the ones who constantly have to put their lives on the line to save humanity, they always come back for more. Like I said, heroes are stupid.

Just look at Buffy Summers. She died. Twice. She had to send the man she loved to Hell. More than halfway through her tenure as the Slayer, she got saddled with a teenage sister and a dead mother. She's had her body stolen and been forced to sing show tunes. She's saved the world – a lot, as her tombstone points out – and didn't even have a date for the prom. Buffy's had a tough time of it. And yet, she keeps coming back for more. That's because she's stupid. Or, if you prefer, because she's a hero.

But the villains? They rock. Loudly. They plan. They scheme. They exist to make heroes' lives utterly miserable. Villains never lose sight of the important question: what's in it for them? Sure, they might get defeated along the way... but they take a piece of the hero with them[3]. I'm not talking about wannabes who think that robbing a bank means they're badass[4]. I mean *real* villains, the ones who know it's not necessarily about *killing* the hero (although that would be a bonus) but about *damaging* the hero. With any luck, permanently.

And that's why the best villains are former heroes. Sure, the whoops-no-soul former heroes rank up there (hat-tip, Angelus). But way better are the heroes who have fallen, and fallen hard – the ones who started completely driven to do the right thing and wound up devastated, destroyed and, barring major intervention, doomed. I'm talking about Faith, before she got on the redemption bandwagon in *Angel* Season One.

Most of all, I'm talking about Dark Willow.

### From Sidekick to Sorceress

Yes, that's right: everyone's favorite witch, Willow Rosenberg, is the perfect villain. No, it's not because she's a redhead, or Jewish, or a lesbian. It's not because she's a geek. It's because she allowed her phenomenal power to overwhelm her when her true love was killed before her eyes and then decided to hunt down and kill everyone involved[5].

Willow's come a long way, hasn't she? Remember when Willow was just a shy, sophomore brain, the sort of girl whose lot in life was to be nice and get rescued and maybe earn a place as a sidekick? But then computer teacher and local witch Jenny Calendar gets her neck snapped (again: hat-

---

3. Or maybe just their goldfish.
4. I'm looking at you, Trio.
5. Nothing like getting spattered with your lover's blood to really bring out the Dark in you.

tip, Angelus), so Willow steps up as the resident witch-in-training (and temporary computer teacher). Next thing you know, she's magically floating pencils and nearly burned at the stake (by her own mother) for witchcraft[6]. And then it's helllllllllo, Tara (both in terms of magic and nooky). Soon enough, Willow's power grows exponentially enough to seriously hurt a goddess and recover Tara's ravaged sanity. Not too shabby for a girl who started out as little more than vampire bait!

That being said, Willow Rosenberg was primed for going Dark. She'd mentioned to Buffy back in Season Three that doing magic was all about emotional control[7]. Well, by Season Six, Willow's emotions were a freaking mess. First, she lost her best friend during a fit of self-sacrifice. Then she had to help raise a former mystical object now trapped in the form of an overly emotional teenage girl. Oy. No wonder Willow was ready to try the Dark stuff to get Buffy back from the dead. Sure, she was all "Save Buffy From A Hell Dimension."[8] But frankly, raising Dawn with only Tara (and a Buffybot) while still fighting bad guys is probably enough to make anyone take desperate measures. (Of course Willow was still fighting the bad guys, even when Buffy was dead. Heroes are stupid, remember?)

So angsty Willow makes with the major Dark ritual, and boom: Buffy's back. Consequences ensue, of course. Cue more emotional angst... as well as Willow using magic to make things easier. No time to decorate for a party? No worries – one wave of the hand should do the trick. Arguing with your sweetheart? Again, no worries – just magic away the memory of the fight so that your sweetie is back to being her loving self again. Need a magic jump? Just pay a visit to your local warlock for a quick fix. By this point, Willow's emotional control has gone the way of the Master, post-Harvest. Sure, she recovers for a while as she proves to Tara that she can too stay away from magic for the sake of true luuuv. But Willow Rosenberg is a hero – so you know that the recovery can't last. Heroes have to suffer[9].

And so, goodbye, Tara. Hey, Dark Willow. Love what you've done with your hair.

## Evil Is Cool

Let's face it: Dark Willow is amazing. She's uninhibited. She's single-minded. She's got terrific fashion sense[10]. She's brutally honest and, barring that, just brutal. She can save people (bamf! – goodbye, bullet in Buffy's chest) and torture them (oh, the things she *did* with that bullet). Dark Willow doesn't give a damn about what's right and wrong. All that matters

---

6. Someone's gonna need lots of therapy.
7. "Plus, obviously, magic."
8. How many of those things are there in the Whedonverse, anyway?
9. It's in the handbook.
10. All the black means the bloodstains won't show.

to her is *what matters to her*, and the rest of the world can go take a flying leap. If her friends are on her side, groovy. If not, she'll smash them, and possibly mourn for them later. (Or not. Her call, completely.)

Dark Willow, in other words, is freaking *cool*.

What is it about villains that makes them so appealing, both to viewers and readers? Part of it is the clothing, which tends to be flattering and yet somehow quite practical[11]. And part of it is the outward appearance, which usually ranges on a scale from Extremely Attractive (say, Glory) to Worshipfully Beautiful (i.e., Jasmine). While there may be some skin issues at times – vampire forehead ridge comes to mind – the hair more than makes up for what cosmetics can't hide (product is your friend, whether alive, dead, undead or immortal). Sure, looking good seems to go hand in hand with villainy but the Villain Cool Factor is much more than dressing to kill.

What it comes down to is the *attitude*. Real villains don't worry about their image. Actually, real villains don't worry, period. They're too busy cracking heads to bother with navel gazing. Villains don't care about consequences. They don't waste precious energy on things like ethics or law or Right versus Wrong. Instead, all that drive goes into their attitude. That's why they tend to have such great one-liners.

Granted, clever dialogue is not a villain prerequisite; the Beast from *Angel* Season Four didn't pause in the midst of murder to crack wise, not even when he was slaughtering all the lawyers at Wolfram and Hart. And there are some notable heroes who are renowned for their banter (case in point, the entire Scooby gang). But let's face it: the best villains are the ones who captivate an audience with their witty repartee (yet again: hat-tip, Angelus).

Look at Dark Willow. Way more than a one-liner in black, Dark Willow doesn't pull her verbal punches. She says the stuff that we, the audience, have thought all along... the stuff that no one wants to say out loud. And not just the classics, like "Oh, Buffy. You really need to have every square inch of your ass kicked." No, Dark Willow tells it like it is: "Let me tell you something about Willow. She's a loser, and she always has been. People picked on Willow in junior high school, high school, up until college with her stupid mousy ways. And now, Willow's a junkie."

Ouch. Okay, the painfully honest approach was probably less about not lying to herself and more along the lines of hurting Buffy. That doesn't make the barb less painful.

Sure, the truth hurts. Along with that, Dark Willow does the one-liners brilliantly. Can you hear the phrase "Bored now" without getting a shiver up your spine? Who else could flay a human being alive, then turn to her horrified friends and say "One down"? (Ooh. Shivers!)

---

11. Even second-hand leather coats can be quite stylish on the right vampire.

## Other Former Do-Gooders

Credit where it's due: Willow isn't the only character in the Buffyverse to flip her white hat to black. You could write an entire thesis about Angel and Angelus, and whether his vampiric nature tainted his ability as a champion or vice versa. Ditto Spike and his I-Did-It-For-Love soul reclamation. But both of those characters started as evil (that's speaking chronologically, not episodically – Angelus was around way before Angel got cursed into existence). What about the ones who started out good and then became evil?

Let's see how many Black Hats these characters get for their evil actions.

- **Gotta Have Faith:** Vampire slayer Faith burst onto the scene in *Buffy the Vampire Slayer* Season Three, and she kicked ass. She was the darker side of Buffy Summers, the one who exclaimed in "Bad Girls" that life as a Slayer was extremely simple: "Want. Take. Have." One accidental staking of a human pushed Faith over to the Dark side, and she hooked up with that season's Big Bad and proceeded to kill, wreak havoc and, in general, make Buffy's life miserable. That Faith was five by five – until she sought redemption for her evil ways during *Angel* Season One. Alas. **Three and a half Black Hats out of five.**

- **Cordelia, You're Breaking My Heart:** Did this former Sunnydale cheerleader and queen bee go evil in Angel Season Four all of her own accord? Probably not. Was she possessed by the fallen High Power called Jasmine before, during, and/or after her own stint on a higher plane? Most likely. Did her actions nearly bring about the end of free will (and squick us out when she slept with teenage Connor)? Uh huh. Did she redeem herself in *Angel* Season Five when she helped Angel in "You're Welcome?" Yep. **Two Black Hats out of five.**

- **The Illyria Argument:** Some people may believe that Illyria counts as a former do-gooder because her body once belonged to Angel and company's very own pre-magic Willow, Fred Burkle. This might have been true if Fred's soul had survived the infection that transformed her into Illyria. But sadly, Fred was nothing more than a shell for the Old One, with sparks of Fred's memories as decoration. Sorry: no hat-switching here.

  That being said, Illyria was a walking Black Hat. The most horrific thing about Illyria wasn't her incredible power (which, for plot purposes, was tamped down drastically[12]). No, the thing that made Illyria so terrible, so upsetting to behold, was that she was parading around in Fred's

---

12. Can you imagine how boring the final battle would have been had Illyria retained her Old One power level? She would have demolished the Black Thorn with a little more than a thought. Yawn.

body. The constant reminder that Fred was obliterated to make way for Illyria was what gutted the heart out of the champions in *Angel* Season Five. And that earns her some Black Hat points.

Sure, the original Illyria – the Old One who predated almost everything – would have been a phenomenal villain, especially if her army had survived long enough for her to wage war against humanity[13]. But instead, Illyria wound up being stranded, lonely and misunderstood – and even helped Angel and company in their efforts against the Black Thorn. Have to take away some points there. **One and a half Black Hats out of five.**

- **Doing it Dark Willow Style:** Oh, Dark Willow, how art thou evil? Let us count the ways – by way of spiffy Evil Checklist!

  Force a dead Slayer out of Heaven and back to Earth via Dark magic? Check.

  Manipulate friends and lovers, including through memory magic? Check.

  Abuse power to the point of nearly killing a minor in her care? Check.

  Abuse even more power and destroy a warlock in the process? Check.

  Hunt, torture, and flay a human? Check, check, check.

  Attempt to slaughter two other humans, as well as anyone protecting them? Check.

  Nearly destroy the world? Check.

  As far as donning Black Hats goes, Dark Willow does it best. How many Black Hats? **Five out of five.**[14]

### The Things We Do For Love

Villains are like heroes in one major way: there must be some fatal weakness. Maybe it's something physical, like sunlight. Maybe it's intangible, like pride (if Angelus had actually listened to Spike, Buffy never would have made it past Season Two). Heroes must have a way to defeat the villains[15].

If the heroes didn't have a fighting chance, the story would go something like this: "There was a Slayer. The monster killed her. The end." Which is neat if you're the bad guy, but rather boring for the audience.

So even though Dark Willow is a fabulous villain – and, according to me, she's also the best Big Bad that Buffy and company ever had to fight – she has an Achilles' Heel. We saw it way before Evil Willow from "The Wish" and "Dopplegangland" ever made an appearance in *Buffy* Season Three.

---

13. Although one wonders why a being of Illyria's might actually needed an army to make with the devastation.

14. Which is nothing like five by five.

15. Or they must have a way to leave the parallel universe in which vampires rule or the Hell dimension into which they had been banished.

Willow Rosenberg's weakness is she needs to be loved.

Not just any love would do, not for a fatal weakness. It has to be Fairy Tale Love, the sort that makes hearts beat faster and makes sunlight a little brighter. It has to be true love, the sort that makes you feel like anything is possible (say, like taking on a Hell goddess). For Willow, that love was Tara. Her connection with Tara allowed her magic to blossom, and then love followed suit. Forget Buffy 'n' Angel or Buffy 'n' Riley or Buffy 'n' Spike: Tara and Willow were the power couple of the series. They showed that no matter what, love conquered all.

So of course, they had to be ripped apart – first by Willow's addiction to magic, and then, once it looked like Willow had that under control, bam! Fatal gunshot. No backsies fatal. Heroes have to suffer, remember? Only in this case, the suffering immediately led to a murderous rage that spawned Dark Willow.

Think about that: Willow loved Tara so much that without her, she went Dark, tortured and flayed a human, and nearly destroyed the world. All Buffy did after she lost Angel at the end of Season Two was run away and become a waitress.

Willow's love for Tara was the real deal – so much so, it defined Willow, shaped her and nearly destroyed her. Like Dark Willow says when she and Buffy confront each other in Season Six, "The only thing Willow was ever good for – the only thing I had going for me – were the moments, just moments, when Tara would look at me and I was wonderful." Ah, *l'amour.* Definitely not for the weak of heart.

But just as love shattered Willow into Dark Willow, it was also love that brought Willow Rosenberg back to herself. Not romantic love, but a true love all the same: the love that Xander Harris has for his lifelong best friend. Dark Willow was literally about to destroy the world in "Grave" when he showed up. As he says, even though she's about to do something "apocalyptically evil and stupid," he still wants to be with her because she's Willow: "The first day of kindergarten you cried because you broke the yellow crayon and you were too afraid to tell anyone. You've come pretty far; ending the world, not a terrific notion, but the thing is, yeah. I love you. I loved crayon-breaky Willow, and I love scary, veiny Willow. So if I'm going out, it's here. You wanna kill the world, well then start with me. I've earned that."

He had me at "crayon-breaky Willow."

And at the end of the day, it's the guy with no powers to speak of who's able to reach the Big Bad and remind her of her humanity. Xander's love for Willow – this pure, unquestionable love – brings her back from the brink. Willow Rosenberg needed to be loved. It's her weakness... and, ultimately, her strength.

*Adieu*, Dark Willow.

For now.

## What Tomorrow Will Bring

So Dark Willow was defeated by being loved, and thus by remembering her own humanity. Big deal. That was then – specifically, that was *Buffy* Season Six. By Season Eight, things have changed. If you haven't read the "Time of Your Life" story arc, do so. Go on. I'll wait.

There now. The future is looking mighty Dark, isn't it? Pardon me while I gleefully rub my hands.

So go ahead and root for the good guys if you want to. Me, I'm in it for the Big Bad. It's all too clear that Dark Willow is going to return.

And I can't wait to discover why.

# Joss Giveth

**Jaala Robinson** lives on a Hellmouth (sometimes referred to as "Texas"). She is neither a Slayer, nor does she possess any magical abilities. As such, she's often tucked into a corner with her laptop and her cat, hiding from the demon hordes. In her spare time, she likes to ponder on what Buffy would do.

In high school, I went through fairly typical pre-teen drama and angst. ("Woe is me. I'm an adolescent.") As a form of escapism, I devised my own fictional world full of awesome, mainly female, heroic characters. At the time, this was purely wish-fulfillment on my part: something I could day-dream about in my moments of spare time. I didn't think too much on the whys or reasons. I just did what any creative teen with an overly active imagination would do: I created my own stories.

Looking back, I see a frustrated young girl looking around to see what I could become. I had to forge my own role models, while growing increasingly disillusioned with what the media was presenting as female heroes. I was just coming into an awareness of how men seemed to dominate... everything. Every story. Every trope. Every archetype. Media kept teasing me with glimpses of wonderful women, but then it would refuse to actually do anything substantial with them. I corrected this, if only in my own head.

My little fictional universe had everything: female war heroes, calculated female politicians, Machiavellian female dictators, brutal female CEOs. The women were strong, flawed, talented, respected, feared, and, most importantly, they were central to the narrative that unfolded in my head. Women weren't an afterthought thrown in an attempt to appease the female audience. They *were* the story.

Sometimes a particular female character from a TV show or movie would inspire me. Usually, she was underused in whatever story she'd originally appeared in. So I'd give her a home in my own stories, fleshing out and giving her an integral role in whatever plots were going on at the time.

These unwritten stories were my escape from the real world. More than that, they showed my absolute *yearning* for heroic women who made differences in their world, and stood on their own apart from any men. When I say "yearning," I mean soul-wrenching *need*. It's not like me wishing there were more jeans that fit me perfectly (though that would be nifty). No, this was central to my life, to who I was.

Joss Whedon changed things for me. He gave me a show (or three) that I could relate to and get horribly emotionally invested in. More importantly, he gave me female heroes that might as well have come straight from my own overactive imagination. It felt as though my wishing for it, for years on end, finally had made it happen.

*Buffy the Vampire Slayer* came out during a time when TV didn't throw us many strong female characters. Women were only a focus so long as they affected men, and they had little bearing on any actual plot or story being told. In the years preceding *Buffy*'s appearance on our screens, we were given action/adventure shows such as *Sliders, The Sentinel* and *Stargate SG-1*. Some of these attempted to give us noteworthy and well-developed female characters; most of which fell short due to inattention from the writers later in the series. *Xena: Warrior Princess*, starting a year earlier than *Buffy*, had tested the waters of a more female-dominated form of storytelling in syndication, but Buffy delivered on network TV.

*Buffy* is perhaps deceptive at first glance. Before watching it, I thought it would be some teen vampire romance story. I wasn't interested in vampires, romance, or teenagers. Three strikes against it are hard to get around. Of course, my initial impression was completely wrong; it launched a passionate obsession.

The vampires, the romance, the teen-ness are incidental to the real point of the show: *Buffy* focuses on a girl in a way that's rarely seen in TV and movies. She develops during seven seasons, consistently saves the day, and has the entire plot revolving around her, and she *is not a man*.

There's a trend in action movies for the female love interest (ostensibly upgraded to "lead") to get her own bad guy for the big finale. Usually, it's another woman, not as threatening as the main bad guy, stuck in there to give the woman something to do while the man handles the *important* stuff. That way, the movie can be praised for having a strong female character, despite the fact that she's completely extraneous to the story and is only important in her romance with the male lead. The best example of this is in *The Mummy Returns*. The main bad guy, with whom Brendan Fraser's character has the big finale showdown, is the Scorpion King, while Rachel Weisz's Evelyn is left fighting the secondary – female – baddie, only to achieve ultimate victory when she's shown to be better at loving her man than her designated nemesis.

Female characters with actual influence on the plot are a rarity outside of romantic comedies (which fall into the category of "chick stuff"). For most of TV outside of the designated female zone, the women are depicted as supporting pillars for the men. The men *do*. The women help. The female character does things that the man tells her to or she has things done *to* her. She's not supposed to affect the plot in any meaningful way because that's the man's job. Her story, her development and her purpose are all secondary to his. She's an afterthought. See such testosterone-heavy shows as *Supernatural* or *24*. *Supernatural*, in particular, has made attempts to introduce female characters, but they haven't made much of a dent in the male domination of the show.

*Buffy* bucks this trend: instead of being an afterthought, a woman *is* the thought. She's the foremost instigator. When Buffy makes a decision, the entire shape of the story changes. And I'm not talking about like when the female lead of an adventure series accidentally trips the secret doo-dad that releases the Big Bad a la Willie in *Indiana Jones and the Temple of Doom*. No, this is a woman making purposeful decisions and taking control of the story. The story follows her.

TV producers like to play it safe. They like their white male leads because it's been proven to work in the past. Feminism is sometimes boiled down to its simplest concept, which is that women are people. Unfortunately, not many TV shows abide by this concept. Women on TV are women first, people second.

Trying something different – like the revolutionary idea of a woman leading an action/ adventure show – is risky and undesirable.

Joss Whedon takes that risk in his works, though, because he knows that there are stories to tell involving women that are more than just love triangles, marrying men, and having babies. His women are interesting people fully capable of carrying a genre show all by themselves. Artists always seem to want to explore "the human condition," whatever that means. Pretentiousness aside, it seems that "the human condition" usually means "the man's condition." Women are still the "other" (those mysterious, otherworldly creatures who have wombs and sometimes bleed). Our condition is either unimportant or distinctly separate from the other humans. Joss includes women in his definition of human.

There are moments in each of Joss's shows that epitomize, to me, his dedication to giving women stories of their own. Moments that stand out as powerful, affirming, and inspiring.

I hit one of those moments at the end of *Buffy*'s second season. Buffy is fighting Angelus, and he's successful in knocking the sword from her. She's backed into a corner, and he's taunting her – as Angelus tends to do. He says, "Now that's everything, huh? No weapons. No friends. No hope. Take all that away and what's left?"

When he brings his sword down (and let's stop to marvel at the phallic imagery here), she catches the blade between her hands and replies, "Me."

*Buffy* isn't the only series of Joss's to have such moments of feminist awesomeness. *Angel* steps up to the plate in "Billy." Cordelia pays a visit to Lilah, who had been beaten as a result of the title character's – Billy's – misogynistic powers. Cordelia's encouraging words to Lilah, who has been beaten up as a result of Billy's influence, resonate strongly: "It's not the pain. It's the helplessness. The certainty that there is nothing you can do to stop it, that your life can be thrown away in an instant by someone else. He doesn't care. He'll beat you down until you stay down because he doesn't even *think* of you as alive. No woman should ever have to go through that, and no woman strong enough to wear the mantle of 'vicious bitch' would ever put up with it."

These are the moments I *dreamed* about for women when I was younger. These moments, and the many, many more sprinkled liberally throughout Joss' shows, encapsulate why his work is so important to me.

Here's the trick (and the beauty) of Joss's characterization: he has characters in fantastic situations. By all means, his shows would fall under the "escapist" category to most outside observers. However, in the midst of these plots that involve vampires and brain-wipes, the women he populates his series with are more familiar to me than that token "chick" you'd find in any other show, in an effort to show diversity.

In those other shows you have a cast full of men. The Hero, the Scientist, the Rebel, and then you have the Woman. She probably doesn't resemble any actual woman. Instead, she has to embody and represent the media ideal of what Woman is. So she's sexy, smart (but not as smart as the guys), strong (but not as strong as the guys), and often boring (because any semblance of a personality would be taxing the supposed demographic). Your more interesting token chicks are forced into the background and never given any opportunity to display their awesomeness.

For instance, *Men in Black* teased us with a morbid medical examiner, played by Linda Fiorentino, who remained largely underused. Even though she ends the film by becoming Will Smith's new partner, she is absolutely absent from the sequel.

Joss doesn't abide by that nonsense. His shows have girls and women that could come straight from the real world. Willow is so like me, right down to the darker streak that leads to the badness at the end of the sixth season (I've never flayed anybody alive, though, nor have I attempted to end the world). I've known many Cordelias. Buffy isn't just a character for me. She's an actual person living in a fictional world.

I think that's the appeal. We've had a ton of history to work out stories for men as heroes. Now we're to the point where we can take the basic archetypes and work at detailed characterization. Instead of just having a Hero, we subvert the Hero to show his dark underbelly. It's fun! Women, though, are still relatively new to the hero game in television. There's not the tomes and tomes of precedent to rely on. We write what we know, but if we've only known women as love interests in TV and movies, how are we to write something else?

The obvious answer is to write women as they are in the real world, but this apparently escapes many writers.

See, there's this mummy hand-type loop that the TV executives that hire writers get stuck in. It frustrates me to the point of... not watching much TV. It's used as a way to justify the lack of representation for women by shrugging and offering up that, "That's just the way it is." It's couched in capitalist terms and lays all the blame on "the market" or "the audience." TV execs don't want programs that aren't "marketable." It's all about numbers, they say, and there's an established audience for shows that feature men. Of course there are! The whole history of TV has primarily been about men!

They use this as an argument against putting a woman in a leading role. Fact is, when they do decide to take a risk on a female-led show, they're hesitant to spend as much money on it as they would for a more conventional, male-featured series. Less money equals less promotion, which means less people even knowing about it. Look at *Dollhouse*, which got the unenviable Friday night timeslot and promotional ads that are cringe-worthy to the max. ("Oooh ... I'm your doll, baby. Who do *you* want me to be?") *Dollhouse* can easily be read through a feminist lens, though you wouldn't be able to tell just by looking at Fox's ads.

They fumble these "experimental" shows, in other words. And the subsequent failure of the show (often due to mishandling by the execs) is then blamed on the fact that it starred a woman, and is then used to justify *not* featuring women more.

See? Mummy hand-type loop. Somewhere, Buffy is crying in frustration (or stomping on Giles's glasses).

Joss alternately gets praised and criticized by feminists for his shows. As one of the only outspoken feminist TV producers, this is to be expected. No piece of entertainment is going to be flawless, and Joss surely has his weak spots. What resonates for me – and what keeps me firmly on Joss' defense – is that the dude started his TV career writing about a high school girl fighting vampires. Just putting aside the cool factor inherent in this, his first work is almost guaranteed to be at least feminist-friendly for several reasons:

1. The protagonist was a female hero. Buffy acted as the focal point for the entire show. Most shows featuring women are in the romance or sitcom genre. *Buffy* is a sci-fi/ fantasy, action/ adventure genre show that features a woman – a rarity.

2. The cast featured an equal male to female ratio. Of course, this varies by season as characters come and go. However, when you average everything out, the number of regular characters is equal across gender.

3. The show-runner was passionate about his feminist ideals. Even though Joss may not be the Perfect Feminist, he made more of an attempt than most show-runners will to keep the show from devolving into simplistic hot girl eye-candy for men.

After successfully getting such a show on the air (and running for seven seasons) a lot of show-runners might feel it easier to turn to more conventional storytelling. Joss, though, didn't. He continually gave us interesting and unique female characters, and his work shows an increasing amount of self-reflection as well as social commentary (especially looking at *Dr. Horrible's Sing-Along Blog* and *Dollhouse*) on gender dynamics.

Joss continues to be passionate about feminism and female representation on television, creating something of a safe place in the TV realm for fans like me. Sure, other shows may be treating their female characters horribly and encouraging stereotypes but this guy? This Joss fellow right over here? He's got my back. I know he respects women and that he'll incorporate female characters into his show as best he can.

Movies and TV give boys a book full of snapshots of their sex being strong. Being powerful. Being awesome personified. They're overflowing with heroes. Hell, I'm getting *bored* with heroic men. I've seen them all before. Yawn.

My book o' snapshots is a lot smaller, and it had been populated primarily by my own creations until I wandered across Whedon's work. Suddenly, the pages are full of Buffy swinging a scythe, or Zoe gearing up to rescue Mal, or Willow taking on a hellgod by herself. Each image gives me inspiration. It gives me another alternative of what's possible for *me*. And if it's providing that for me, a woman in her mid-20s, I can only imagine what it's doing for younger girls actively looking for role models.

During my formative years, I created my own strong women heroes. I made up what I wanted to see: a variety of different types of women. Anything that went beyond the standard Love Interest or Token Chick (often melded together). I loved these characters that I had created. And yet, they were little more than ephemeral teases. They didn't really exist. I couldn't pop them in my DVD player and rewatch their Moments of Awesome. Nobody else knew about them.

With Joss's writing, though, I find I don't need that fictional set of characters anymore. Joss has given me the type of women I'd wanted so many years ago. Actual, really-on-the-screen awesome women doing awesome things. Lesbian witch with a dark edge? Willow. Manipulative businesswoman? Lilah. Quirky, yet genius, engineer? Kaylee. I could go on, but a comprehensive list detailing the sheer awesomeness of each of Joss's female characters would require its own book.

Joss has served up the female characters I've long desired. He's given substance to my imagination, and has fueled my fervent hope that others will follow suit. To dream of something that doesn't exist is a misery. To have that dream made flesh, even for a short time, gives me more than just a warm fuzzy feeling. It gives me affirmation that my former fantasies of strong and complex women *weren't* the delusional imaginings of a girl unhappy with the world around her. Those fantasies became real and are now part of the public consciousness. Everybody has the opportunity to enjoy the power of these amazing women. Even better, people want *more*. I look forward to the sure-to-be-awesome female characters of the future and I thank Joss for his part in paving the path.

# The Kindness of Monsters

**Sarah Monette** wanted to be an author when she grew up, and now she is. She lives and writes in a 104-year-old house in the Upper Midwest with four cats and one husband. She writes both novels and short stories, and sometimes does both with Elizabeth Bear. Her next book, *The Goblin Emperor*, will be published by Tor Books under the pen name Katherine Addison. Visit her online at sarahmonette.com

Endings are hard.

I say this both as a writer and as a reader – or, in *Angel*'s case, a watcher. If the maker of fiction has done his, her, or their job well, the audience does not want the fiction to end. But no story can continue indefinitely without becoming just that: no story. Thus, you have to make the ending worth the audience's disappointment that there will be no more story, and it's a very hard thing to do. It's terrifyingly easy for everything to go wrong in the last chapter: you turn in a flawless performance and then fall flat on your face.

*Angel* sticks the dismount.

I have to confess, I was never a fan of *Angel* – although I was and am very fond of Angel the character. I love Angel not because he's the brooding Byronic vampire hero, but because of the guy under that facade, the one who's not too bright but doing the best he can, the one who asks Gunn perplexedly, "They talk about me in the chatty rooms?" The real Angel is the one who gets turned into a puppet – *and* who perseveres to defeat the forces of evil and get his own body back. For me, the moment that defines Angel is the moment in "Becoming," when he tells Whistler earnestly, "I want to *learn* from you, but I don't want to dress like you."

Angel is the first sign of ambiguity in the universe shared by *Buffy the Vampire Slayer* and *Angel*, the first hint that things aren't going to be as simple and clear-cut as the main characters want them to be. Not all vampires are evil, and although Seasons One and Two of *Buffy* go to considerable trouble to establish Angel as a unique exception, at the same time, he opens the door. After all, Buffy's supposed to be unique, too, but the series keeps producing more Slayers (Kendra, Faith, and then the plethora of junior Slayers in Season Seven), and if a Slayer can do evil, like Faith in Season Three, why can't a vampire do good? What *actually* separates the monsters from the heroes?

This question is one that Joss Whedon and his writers keep coming back to: what makes a monster a monster, and does it have to stay that way? We have Angel and his problematically slippery soul; we have Oz, who is surely the *nicest* werewolf in the history of lycanthropy; and we have Spike. Even on his first appearance, Spike upsets everything we think we understand about vampires – he's a monster, but he's also devoted to Drusilla and takes care of her in a way that is the absolute antithesis of the self-centered greed for power and pain we have been taught to expect. It's true that Spike and Dru share the upside-down morality of Gomez and Morticia from *The Addams Family*, but that doesn't make their love for each other any less real.

Monsters can love. That's the first real blow against the simple schematic of humans versus demons. Even without a soul, Spike loves Drusilla. Moreover, monsters can be self-aware. When Angel loses his soul in Season Two, as Angelus he revels in his evil. And Spike can look at that same evil and decide he wants no part of it. His reasons are predominantly selfish, but the important thing is that he can and does choose. There's no fatalism in this universe. Buffy may be fated to die at the end of Season One, but Xander knows CPR. Just because you're a soulless demon doesn't mean you can't do your part to save the world.

Free will, of course, makes everything harder, and one thing we see throughout both *Buffy* and *Angel* is the monsters struggling with their own nature. It's a pattern, a theme that Whedon returns to over and over again: the monster trying to learn to be human. Angel has been wrestling with this for most of a century, careening from rat-eating wreck to a somewhat bumbling Batman; Anya, trapped as a teenage girl, has to figure out high school and emotions and social interactions (which she never does quite get a grip on). One of the most memorable and poignant expressions of this theme, in fact, is Anya's monologue in "The Body," as a formerly immortal creature contemplates death and discovers just how horrible and unfair it is and how much it hurts. It's clear that the existence of a demon doesn't have space for grief, or for feeling pain on someone else's behalf, and Anya's bewilderment shows both how alien human existence is to demons and that she has found something good in it. She couldn't be this hurt and bewildered over the death of someone she didn't care about.

Joss Whedon's monsters can learn to feel compassion. At the end of "Fool for Love," Spike, in a fury of wounded *amour propre*, storms off to murder Buffy. But when he reaches her house, he finds her distraught... and he forgets about his anger. He does his awkward best to comfort her. And from that point on, through the rest of Season Five and into Season Six (up to "Seeing Red"), Spike tries and tries and tries to help Buffy, to be what Buffy needs. He may be a terrible babysitter for Dawn at the beginning of Season Six, but he's doing his best. He may do absolutely the wrong thing, as in "Dead Things," because he's still working with that upside-down morality, but he does it because he wants, desperately, to help. He tries and fails, just as Anya tries and fails. Whedon suggests, both here and in *Firefly*, that compassion is one of the most important human traits – what makes the Reavers terrible, aside from the whole killing-raping-eating-not-necessarily-in-that-order thing, is that not only do they have no compassion, but in turning their victims into themselves (as vampires also do), they destroy compassion in the world around them. But Whedon also shows that compassion is difficult, that even the best intentions don't mean you'll do the right thing. And those failures are the most painful to watch: Giles' betrayal of Buffy in "Helpless"; the mistake Willow makes in bringing Buffy back from the dead; Spike, throughout Season Six, trying to reach Buffy and always failing. The human condition is that we try to reach out to each other, and more often than not we fail; Whedon uses his monsters and their struggles to learn to be human as a way to highlight that, to make it a theme that we return to again and again.

Which brings us to the finale of *Angel*: "Not Fade Away." And although, as I said, Angel was always my favorite part of *Angel*, he's not what I want to talk about. In the finale's general excellence, the part that remains vividly in my mind is Wesley's death and Illyria's response to it.

I was a hard sell for Illyria because I was extremely fond of both Fred and Wesley. I was delighted by their relationship in Season Five, thrilled by the way that two adults, both damaged and prickly, were finally finding each other – and doing it *as adults*, not in any of the cheap TV romance ways that only work if you accept that everyone is emotionally the age of Romeo and Juliet.

So I was Not Happy when Fred was killed.

And you may imagine the profound ambivalence with which I discovered that Illyria was a really interesting character. I give tremendous credit to Amy Acker for this, because what makes Illyria convincing is her body language and her delivery. She is exiled god as feral cat. I was almost annoyed at being fascinated by her, by her anger, her amorality, her impatience – and by her reluctant dependence on and growing tolerance of Wesley. (I hesitate to use the word "affection," because – as with feral cats – it's not really what's at stake. And, as anyone who has experience with feral cats can tell you, tolerance is not merely a small concession on the cat's part; it is a profound upheaval.)

We learn that Illyria has all of Fred's memories and access to her personality; she can "be" Fred, and – as she proves with Fred's parents – she can do it flawlessly. There isn't a hint that the creature inhabiting Fred's semblance isn't Winifred Burkle. Wesley finds this well nigh unendurable, and he forbids Illyria ever to do it again. She is baffled by his fury – it's no secret to her that he wants Fred back more than anything else in the world – but she agrees.

All of which sets up the scene in the finale. Wesley is delirious, dying, and Illyria makes the choice to come to him as Fred. Again, she's pitch-perfect, and Wesley is no longer coherent enough to remember that she isn't Fred. She comforts him, says exactly the things he needs Fred to say. He dies at peace, and Illyria discards Fred as an uncomfortable and no longer needed mask.

This scene made me cry. That's hard to do – no other Joss Whedon death scene has done it, although parts of "The Body" come close – and the reason it succeeds is this thematic bone that Whedon keeps gnawing on and gnawing on: the question of monsters and humanity and compassion.

Yes, the script is excellent. And again, I have to praise Amy Acker and Alexis Denisof, who make every second of the script work. But I think the key is something that at first seems like a weakness: an ambivalence inherent in the scene itself. What Illyria is doing – counterfeiting Fred – is exactly what Wesley told her never to do. If Wesley were in his right mind, he would, as his reaction to her earlier performance of Fred shows, find it abhorrent and vile.

But Wesley isn't in his right mind. He doesn't know. And Illyria's right: this is the closure he needs to die peacefully. *But* the audience isn't in Wesley's altered reality. We know this isn't Fred. We know this is Illyria, counterfeiting emotions she doesn't understand and has no use for. We're alienated from Wesley, but rather than reducing the scene's emotional punch, it increases it. We aren't just watching someone die with their lover as a helpless witness (Willow and Tara, Zoe and Wash, and any number of other examples, all the way back to Angelus leaving Jenny Calendar's body in Giles's bed – and, of course, Wesley and Fred, only a few episodes earlier). We're watching someone who understands neither love nor death transcending herself and her limitations in perhaps the first altruistic act of her existence: a monster trying to be human *and getting it right*.

That's the beauty of this scene: it's the payoff for so many failures, so many times that Angel and Anya and Spike have tried and failed, so many times that the *human* characters have tried and failed, that it achieves an extraordinary grace. *It is possible*, this scene says. *You can learn how to care. You can learn how to reach out without hurting.*

Wesley would tell Illyria she is wrong, and perhaps ethically, she is. But if the peace she brings him is wrong, I'm not sure any of us would want to be right.

# Shelve Under Television, Young Adult

**Jody Wurl** lives and works as a public librarian in the Midwest. In her free time she reads (a lot), explores television and film, dabbles in artistic expression and manages to keep her home from collapsing under the weight of many bookshelves. She also volunteers for library associations and science fiction conventions, and gets confused when there's no one wearing corsets at library cons, and no free advance reader copies available at science fiction cons.

### So It Begins

In 1997, I was getting my Masters degree in library science, beginning my journey in a profession laden with stereotypes of repressed rigid women. How could I resist a show that included a hot male librarian, a research-loving teen, and a complex young heroine with serious problems? I rushed home from my grad school classes on Tuesday evenings so I could watch the newest episode of *Buffy.*

Giles was a revelation. His bad boy Ripper past ("Band Candy," anyone?) and folk-singing mojo (I am pretty wild for "Where the Wild Things Are") were some of his more surprising layers, but his intelligent and respectful support of Buffy and the Scooby Gang still warms my heart. What a mensch! I treasure my copy of the journal of the American Library Association, *American Libraries*, where he poses on the cover in his virile tweedy glory. (Thank you, Tony Head.) My profession was reinventing itself for the twenty-first century; his presence on the cover seemed like an omen that our efforts paid off, and that I had chosen a cool career.

I used my newly honed librarian research skills to find out who created this fun and fascinating show: Joss Whedon. Here was a man who had assembled a creative team with an obvious respect for young adults, and, even more importantly, women, *and* wrapped those elements in some of the best dialogue and story arcs to ever appear on the small screen. I fell hard. He totally had me at a character named "Buffy." What is not to love?

During its run between 1997 and 2003, *Buffy* competed with hour-long dramas featuring teen characters like *Beverly Hills, 90210, 7th Heaven* and *Dawson's Creek*; sitcoms like *Moesha, Sabrina, the Teenage Witch* and *Clueless*; and shows featuring women like *Ally McBeal* and *Charmed*. At the time, I was also considering what to do with my Masters degree. Working with teens in a public library setting has a lot of momentum in the library world thanks to the Young Adult Library Association (YALSA). I wanted to be part of the wave that helped transform service to this underserved demographic. I've always filtered my pop culture consumption through a feminist lens; now I was doing so through the lens of someone who wanted to work with teens.

When I look back at these programs, many of the teen and female characters seemed like flat stereotypes who didn't evolve, and, in some cases, were deliberately kept in stasis to keep the show's premise going. In the Whedonverse, though, characters adapted and changed in reaction to their world. Teens earned the respect of their enemies as well as their allies; women were given strong and challenging voices; characters you cared about died.

I found myself following Whedon's work across the airwaves as he launched new shows such as *Angel* and *Firefly*[1]. I even watched the works of the other writers, directors and producers from the Mutant Enemy creative team. I'm especially grateful that Joss's televised stories continued in the versatile format of comics. Withdrawal got ugly when the televised shows ended; I know friends and family are thankful that I have additional ways to get my Whedon fix. I read his comic-book work – *Fray* (his story about a future Slayer who later appeared in the *Buffy* comic), and his run on *Runaways*. I also made a special date for myself to read his run of *Astonishing X-Men* when I learned that Kitty Pryde was one of his inspirations for Buffy Summers.

### By the Book

I realized that Joss Whedon's work and its fan community help me with two major aspects of my job: connecting people with books and supporting teens as they develop into adults. It's easier to connect books with librarianship, so I'll begin my self-analysis there.

Being a fan girl takes time and energy: all those hours to read graphic novels and watch shows add up. As I completed my degree, and I graduated in 1999, I realized that my obsession with the Whedonverse supported my job. I love doing what is called Readers Advisory in the library world, helping people find books they might enjoy. Librarians have five "laws" about these skills, posited by Dr. Shiyali Ranganathan. The third law, describing reader's advisory, says: "Every book its reader." As professionals, most of us do everything in our power to connect our patrons to "their" books. I'm lucky enough to work with colleagues who recognize the value

---

1. I tried *Dollhouse*, but that was one show that failed to connect with me. It is dark stuff, a true dystopia. I think I needed more "hope" in my life while it was on, but as a Whedon fan I now feel a little bit of guilt that I did not contribute to the numbers to keep the show on the air.

of comics and graphic novels as works of art and literature, as well as a format that appeals to people reluctant to read a text-heavy tome. We have created a large comics collection in my library system, with lists of recommended titles to help people discover it. Ergo, reading Whedon's and other fine creators' comics totally supports my goal of being a good readers' adviser. But I can take this self-gratifying logic *even further*.

Vampires, werewolves, and demons in stories, rare in 1997, are ubiquitous now, especially in books. The potent mix of supernatural love, action and suspense, and beautiful young beings in *Buffy* and *Angel* launched a major trend in Urban Fantasy books that has been building momentum for the past decade. Add sexy fashion and great music, and I observed the leading edge of a cultural phenomenon. The shock waves continue to ripple outward, especially in young adult literature. I sit back with some smugness knowing that my love of Whedon's work had me tracking Urban Fantasy, especially for teens, well ahead of the curve.

I attend a number of Science Fiction, Fantasy, and comics conventions in my quest to become fluent in pop culture and genre literature. In 2005, I made a point of attending San Diego Comic-Con, mostly because the film *Serenity* was being promoted. I really wanted to breathe the same air as Joss and his cast and crew. I think, in my heart of hearts, I hoped that genius was catching.

A funnier, warmer, more committed group of people have never graced the dais of Hall H. Nathan Fillion doing his Wonder Woman impersonation and Joss' response to a fan's question "Who is your favorite Harry Potter character?" – "Hermione, of course" – are memories I treasure for that tiny bit of insight into what makes Whedon's creative teams tick. I will forever mourn the fact that Alan Tudyk (the actor I have had a crush on since I first saw him playing with dinosaur action figures) was doing a show on Broadway, and was the only one who couldn't be there. I made my sister Paula pinch me to reassure me that I was really in the same room with the people who made River, Kaylee, Zoe, Inara, Jayne, Mal, Simon and Book live and breathe.

In addition to my Whedon fix, I also attended some established and up-and-coming author and comics creator panels, and saw presentations on films and television shows that became trend setters with young audiences, thus justifying the trip as *actually working*. I should clarify: I go to Speculative Fiction conventions as a labor of love. Sadly, they're not recognized as official job development opportunities. But I'm happy to pay my own way, because I love my job. I love supporting the arts, connecting library patrons with artists, and providing a space for patrons to build communities, all of which happen in public libraries. Conventions fuel that passion. Library mission 2005 accomplished. W00t!

I only go to Comic-Con every few years, but I attend a number of

Midwest fan conventions regularly. A very cool synergy exists between my fan and library communities. My continuing mission is to explore strange new authors and to seek out new life-changing discussions with my fellow fans. As a librarian I collect information (as well as books) so I can share it. What I learn from the fan community I bring to work as blogs, book lists and programs for my library patrons. I share what I learn about publishing trends, pop culture and great books from library publications and colleagues by volunteering for panels at conventions and seeking out conversations with my fellow fans.

I connect two rich traditions: if fandom and librarianship met through a personals ad, they'd find that they're a pretty awesome match. Librarianship is the perfect profession for a fan; people like libraries but authors *love* them. You always have something to talk about that can help prevent you from gushing your way into uncomfortable "oh my god, did I just squee at this person I really admire" situations. Win!

## Watch and Learn

Reading comics is clearly within the scope of my job; but watching season after season of television? Comics, film, and television give storytellers a modern voice. Since I accept the visual format of comics as a powerful medium to share stories, it would be hypocritical of me to exclude television. As hard as it is to admit as a book lover, television provides more of a common denominator to discuss stories and characters. Odds are greater that I may have watched the same TV show than read the same book as someone I meet.

Television gives me a better grasp of current popular culture than books; I understand what people are looking for when they come to the library, as I have a shared cultural touch point when I talk to them. In the public library world, when you work directly with patrons, you have three focal points of service: adult, children (K-18), and teen (specializing in 12-18). I have worked all three but I now specialize in working with teens. It is part of my job description to be aware of cultural trends that affect the tastes and attitudes of young adults. To put it bluntly, television helps prevent me from looking stupid in front of the teens I work with.

I've learned a lot through my work about ways to support young people as they explore their paths to adulthood. I marvel at Whedon's instinctive grasp – and that of his creative teams – on how to empower the young characters in his stories, the same methods used in my work. Treat them like the adults they are becoming. Have high expectations and assume they will rise to the occasion. Respect their opinions. Yes, they may not have much experience but their fresh perspectives and passion may change the world, or at least a little corner of it. If you provide this kind of support to adolescents, they develop the tools needed to become healthy, caring, responsible adults.

In the Whedonverse, this teen empowerment seems to be part of the standard package. We have Buffy and her Scooby Gang of Willow, Xander, Dawn, Anya, Tara, Cordelia and Oz, as well as a legion of Slayers past and present. On *Firefly*, we have the inimitable River Tam. The comic *Fray* is all about future Slayer Melaka Fray and her twin brother Harth, living in a dystopian world which is invaded once again by vampires centuries after Buffy's epic triumph. And in the comic *Runaways*, a group of teens run away from home and band together to fight on the side of good when they discover their parents are super villains.

I hate to play favorites, but I must confess I found River's journey the most powerful. Absentee parents and a loving but self-absorbed brother did not give her much emotional support during her first 14 years of life. Unfortunately, going away to the Alliance-funded Academy gave her every right to own the descriptor "tortured genius" at the ripe old age of 17. Although Simon rescued her from the Academy and its experiments, she was damaged and vulnerable, and found it hard to connect and communicate with other people. Luckily she found herself with people fighting their own personal demons, who had some sympathy for what bedeviled her.

I suspect teens may relate to River. Working with teens, I've observed a lot of benign neglect in families (as well as criminal negligence in a few rare cases). Feeling alone in a crowd is common; sometimes one can feel alone in a family. River experiences both neglect and loneliness, and these feelings of alienation seem to be part and parcel of surviving adolescence.

I've read in various places that Whedon believes strongly in "found" families (the people who choose to include you as an important part of their lives) – a theme that often runs through his work. I love this notion; it happened to me when I discovered my core group of friends in my teens and early twenties. These are people I grew up and out with, who've seen me at my best and worst and still name me friend. I think many young people cobble together a family of choice during this time so they have the support they need on their voyages of self discovery.

This belief in found or chosen families comes across strongly with the crew of *Serenity*. Although the adults are fighting to survive and have little energy to coddle River, they accept her as part of the crew and support Simon in his quest to heal her. But they can't quite embrace her as a full member of their dysfunctional family since she's too damaged to pull her own weight, until the episode "Objects in Space." River's disassociation spirals out of control and the crew faces hard decisions; she's a danger to others as well as herself. Jubal Early, bounty hunter and evil incarnate, enters the picture and takes away River's support. Forced to rely on herself, she magnificently rises to the occasion and saves her crew mates. She starts to recognize her own inner strength and earns the respect of the people who now acknowledge her role as part of their family. Sadly, *Firefly* went off the air, but the next time we see River almost makes up for it. In the feature film *Serenity*, she starts kicking ass and taking names, literally[2].

Throughout the film she continues to grow, transforming into an equal partner in her chosen family as she takes on a new role as Mal's co-pilot. Once again, Whedon and his creative team empowered a young woman to make a difference, and that can make all the difference for us as well.

Stories have the power to educate and to inspire. It's easy to put yourself in the shoes of a sympathetic character, and echoes of that experience follow you in your daily life. By putting myself in River's shoes, I can acknowledge that as damaging as life can be, it also teaches me the skills to survive. And more importantly, I carry the example of her heroism forward. If River can overcome psychotic breaks with reality to defeat an evil corporation driving an empire, I can stand up against injustice in my world with the tools available to me. Feeling one person can make a difference is, after all, the first step to actually causing change. If Whedon's work makes me feel this strongly, I know it can inspire young people with far more in common with his teen characters. I'm doing what I can to point the teens in my life toward his work.

### Cultural Artifacts

Librarians by nature archive stories and knowledge in a plethora of formats. Our ultimate goal is to keep these cultural artifacts safe and remind people they exist so we can share them and help these artifacts "live" again.

I am writing this essay in 2010. I sat down to do the math and realized that today's 13-year-old teens were born the year that the *Buffy the Vampire Slayer* television show premiered in 1997, and they were only seven years old when it went off the air in 2003. If you would like to feel old with me, here is a time line of Whedon's other television shows: *Angel* (1999-2004), *Firefly* (2002-2003), and *Dollhouse* (2009-2010). At least teens today had a shot at discovering his work in *Dollhouse*.

One thing I have learned the hard way is that teens rarely go backward to hunt for treasures.. Mostly they focus on what is happening now, right in front of them. I fear that some of Joss Whedon's older creations are sliding off the cultural radar of a whole new generation of adolescents who would benefit from his storytelling. My hope is that the readers of this book will share these works with generations to come. Everyone needs stories that help us discover the power of identity, respect and relationships, but especially people who are at the crossroads of childhood and adulthood.

I recently bonded with one of my teen volunteers over *Buffy* and *Angel*.

---

2. May I just say the scene where River is triggered remains one of the most outstanding pieces of fight choreography I have ever seen? Summer Glau's River embodies deadly poetry in motion.

It turns out her mother knows a friend of mine in the fan community who introduced her to these shows. We shared something important in that moment: we had a story that inspired and excited us in common. We knew that we were members of the same tribe.

Although I don't have children myself, I'm fortunate enough to be an aunt. I've already indoctrinated my two oldest nieces into the Whedonverse and plan on sharing these stories with the rest of my nieces and nephews when they're old enough.

Whether teens eventually identify themselves with the tribe of fandom or not, I know these young people I care about have been exposed to some pretty amazing role models by experiencing Whedon's work. These stories need to be shared so that teens can grow up knowing that girls can be powerful, boys can be sensitive, and that young people can save the world.

I'll leave you with this quote from Whedon himself. "I'd rather make a show 100 people need to see, than a show that 1000 people want to see." I think he succeeds in this goal. Don't you?

# The Browncoat Connection

Growing up a product of the Texas suburbs, **Dae S. Low** discovered her life in the glorious city of Portland, Oregon, where she resides today. Having dabbled in writing during her college years, she revisited storytelling by way of fan fiction, mostly in the Whedonverse. Dae credits her mother, Lana Bryan, as her influence, and thanks her for the patience and open-mindedness she exhibited while editing Dae's fanfic (even the "naughty" stories). The Browncoat Connection is Dae's first attempt at a more personal story.

On a warm early spring afternoon, a dozen or so folks make their way to the top of Powell Butte Park in Portland. The incline is slight, but the mood is heavy. Powell Butte lends itself to hikers and cyclists, fathers and sons who see each other only every other weekend, scout troops who bag and tag every insect and plant leaf in hopes of earning that one special badge. These somber dozen or so folks, I among them, march forward to a special place, to stand at the high point of the park. We spontaneously form a circle around the directional compass built into the ground with old railroad ties, helpfully informing us that it is 70 miles to Mt. Hood, 30 miles to Forest Park, 50 miles to somewhere that has been eroded away by time and rain. In our circle, we tell stories. We laugh, then weep openly. There is prayer and song. We are remembering a friend. But not just a friend.

A Browncoat.

In its purest form, the definition of a Browncoat is "a fan of the television show *Firefly.*" On a more personal level, I define Browncoats simply as "my friends." However, nothing is really that simple, is it? I mean, just because you watched the DVDs once, found Kaylee irresistibly cute in her pink shindig dress, and were sufficiently creeped out by Jubal Early, does that make you a Browncoat? And even if you are an avid fan, with a handmade Kaylee dress and authentic Mal six-shooter, does that automatically mean that I'm going to like you and call you my BFF on Facebook?

No. Probably not.

But the Browncoats in my town, even the ones that on the surface I don't have that much in common with, are my friends. I can even go a bit further than that, I think. These are the folks who I see at least once a month, almost without fail. They have woven their way into seemingly every part of my life. We have become one big, loving, laughing, fighting, dysfunctional

Browncoat family.

I would be a completely different person without them. I would not have found my voice.

Six years ago, I was living on the surface. I had a stable job, a nice roommate, a car that got me places, and a wonderful sister who I was proud to call my best friend. Each day I busied myself with work and food and traffic and cubicle-sitting and couch-sitting and more food. I was just existing. Looking down I could see my feet touching the ground, but I saw no footprint. I knew that I mattered and that I was a special unique flower, but where was the proof?

I was good at my job, that I knew. But other than that, who was I? I looked around and saw nothing that reflected me. I lived in a house that my roommate owned and a bedroom that was filled with crap I had collected over many years. This collection, if given to Goodwill, would not have been missed.

I had two groups of friends. A small group that I worked with, and those I saw at game night once a month. I wondered if I was friendly with my coworkers simply because our cubicles were next to each other. And my game night friends? Well, it was my sister who took me to my first game night, so weren't they really her friends?

Now, I'm not saying that I didn't really like my friends. Of course I did. But it felt like they were friends of convenience. "Hey you! You're nearby and seem like a nice person. Wanna be friends?"

One day in the late fall of 2004, I was feeling icky so I stayed home from work. As I expected, there was nothing on 120 channels of television at 2 o'clock in the afternoon on a Wednesday. But wait! An episode of *Buffy the Vampire Slayer*? I'd never seen the show, but had heard good things. Snuggling with my cat and TheraFlu, I began my venture into the world of Joss Whedon.

In just three months, I had watched every episode of *Buffy* and was close to the end of *Angel*. For some reason, there was a delay in getting the next *Angel* disc. Being on a Joss Whedon high, I did some research and found out about a recently cancelled show called *Firefly*. A quick trip to the video store, and less than 48 hours later, I was in deeper than I could ever imagine.

In the worlds that Whedon had created, I found my reflection. Each universe incorporated characters with richness, full lives, flaws, and an overall need to connect with other people. Buffy became a great Slayer because of the help from her friends. Angel would be a shell of a vampire if not for the humans and demons that surrounded him. Mal's love for his ship alone couldn't keep her in the air; his love for his crew kept them all flying.

Immersed in these 'verses, I became even more desperate to find that kind of connection. Not just people my sister hung around with, or people

I sat next to in the office, but my own friends. A Google search for *Firefly* and "Portland" resulted in the Portland Browncoats, folks who chatted online and got together once a month for "shindigs." I read that they were planning to attend as many of the pre-screenings of the upcoming film *Serenity* as possible.

Too shy to join them at the screenings, I lurked in the discussion group for a few months to see what folks had to say and to figure out if these people were... you know... sane. Eventually, I summoned the courage to comment on a few threads of conversation; I remember feeling elated when someone commented on my comment. Here I was talking with like-minded folks who seemed intelligent, relevant and thoughtful. Folks with whom I could connect.

As the *Serenity* premiere approached, I knew that many of these Browncoats were planning a viewing party. But I hadn't met any of them yet. And I was shy. Oh, boy, was I shy! I had been chatting with these folks online for the past several months, but actually interacting with them face to face was daunting!

What if I wasn't as smart as I came across online? What if I thought I was funny, but they didn't? What if they were really crazy? What if they thought *I* was crazy?

At the theater with my sister and some friends from work, I saw many folks in costume or wearing *Firefly* T-shirts and buttons. Still too shy to approach, I watched them from a distance thinking, "That must be the Browncoats. They're all dressed up and talking about favorite quotes and episodes. Can I connect to this kind of insanity?"

It was another month before that question was answered. I went to my first shindig in November of 2005. I was scared out of my mind, but forced myself to go – in search of that connection.

I was terrified of ending up in a corner with my beer. Being too shy to talk to anyone. Or worse, no one even noticing I was there. Luckily, my first shindig was at a Sara's home. She was prolific online, so I felt like I knew her.

I had rehearsed what I was going to say when she answered the door. "Hi, Sara! I'm Dae. It's so great to finally meet you. What a lovely home you have! It's so great of you to have all of us over like this. Where can I put this bottle of wine?"

I was ready! Bring it on!

I forgot the bottle of wine. Then I got lost. When I finally found the house, I was shaking as I approached the door. My script was repeating over and over in my head. ("Hi, Sara! I'm Dae... Hi, Sara! I'm Dae... Hi, Sara! I'm Dae...")

The door opened.

It wasn't Sara.

Crap.

After the introductions (it was Sara's husband Alex who answered the door), I got *the* question.

"How did you find *Firefly*?"

To this day, this question is asked of every person at their first shindig.

All of these folks, about a dozen at *my* first shindig, seemed so excited just to be there, among other folk with whom they could talk to about this strange and passionate love for *Firefly*. And they seemed genuinely excited to have me there.

As the evening progressed, discussions revolved around our favorite episodes; the best quotes; the most dramatic, most tragic, funniest part of the movie. Which character do you most relate to? And just like that, you're sharing a connection. Everyone was smiling and talking. No one was left in the corner, nursing a beer and thinking, "Ten more minutes and I can leave. Ten more minutes is long enough, right?"

When the party was breaking up, we crammed into cars and drove to the nearest theater. *Serenity* was still playing!

I got home at 2 a.m. on a strange kind of high. These people *were* my kind of crazy!

I couldn't get enough of them. I attended every shindig, every *Serenity* viewing party. I even had a *Firefly* viewing party of my own. Whenever a gathering event was posted online, I was among the first to say, "I'll be there!"

After awhile I found myself chatting more and more with Elizabeth. She had been the first to grab my attention in the online discussion group. When we met at that first shindig, we connected pretty quickly. We had honest to goodness things in common. She was the biggest *Buffy* fan ever, and I loved talking with her about the characters and the writing.

In the spring of 2006, a local theater brew pub started showing two episodes of *Buffy* every Tuesday night. Elizabeth and I never missed a Tuesday.

In short order, we were inseparable. We attended all Browncoat functions together. We would hang out at each other's homes and watch the TV shows and movies we enjoyed. It got to the point that we just did everything together.

It was kinda awesome.

The Browncoats, now officially the "PDX Browncoats" with our very own website and online forum, became my go-to people. Any question asked, found an answer: where is the best place to go on a first date? Where do I find yarn to make a Jayne Hat? What's the cheapest burrito place in town? What do I buy my cousin for her wedding? I'm moving! Who can help?

We were our own little community, spread all over the city and the suburbs, with different ages, jobs, family statuses, and interests, save for one. *Firefly*.

The following story has approached legend among the PDX Browncoats: Near the end of *Serenity*'s second run in theaters, a group of Browncoats were driving home from yet another viewing (far into the double digits by now). A random thought was voiced aloud by The One True b!X (not his real name, of course, but very seldom referred to as anything but b!X).

He said, "I wonder if there is a way we keep *Serenity* in theaters longer."

That thought transformed into, "Maybe we can get a theater to show it for charity." Then, "Maybe we can get other cities involved."

Within 90 seconds, b!X started a worldwide phenomenon, now an annual event called Can't Stop the Serenity (as of this writing, in the middle of its fifth year).

Our group was good at having parties. We could pull off a shindig at the drop of a Jayne hat. Pick a place. Add Browncoats (and usually beer). Shake. Shindig!

Putting on a charity event, though, was a little more daunting. That first year, we didn't have a clue what we were doing, nor what we were getting into. But that doesn't stop Browncoats.

We found a theater, got permission to show the movie, got the word out the event was happening, found a way to come up with all the upfront costs, figured out what to charge people, then sat back and prayed people would show up.

On June 23, 2006, Browncoats came out in force. Not just as the audience; the folks who attended monthly shindigs and posted on our forum showed up to take tickets, sell t-shirts and raffle tickets, give out raffle prizes, programs and information about Equality Now (the charity for which we were raising the money), and entertain the line.

And, boy, did we have a line! It went around the block! Our very first charity event sold out the theater.

The PDX Browncoats had accomplished something real, even if we didn't get an evil television corporation to bring back the show that brought us together. Together, a group of geeks put together an event that raised money for a worthy worldwide nonprofit organization. Not only that, but we influenced similar Browncoat groups around the world to do the same. That first summer, 41 cities in five countries hosted their own event. As a whole, the Browncoats raised almost $66,000 for Equality Now ($7,000 of that from Portland alone).

This was something new to us. We weren't just a fan group anymore. We got things done. Not only did we raise money in 2006, but we have every year since, and started doing more. We volunteer at the food bank and had a fundraiser for Haiti after the January 2010 earthquake.

And me? I am in the thick of it. The first year, I gave out will-call tickets and then moved on to assisting in shindig planning. Eventually, I became the coordinator for merchandise sold at Can't Stop the Serenity and other events like OryCon and Game Storm. I am currently the Shindig Coordinator and a member of the PDX Browncoats Work Group, the committee of six who orchestrate all the events.

The PDX Browncoats are my guys. I am part of a society that understands me. They don't think I'm strange for watching a lot of television, and writing fanfic about it. Nor do they find it unusual that I'm as much a fan of television writers as actors.

I never thought that I would be so *comfortable* around people. Finding a connection with one other person, let alone dozens, was extraordinary for me.

These folks broke through a shell that I had lived in for years, poking my head out to make sure my surroundings were safe, then retreating where it was warm and cozy and I didn't have to challenge myself or share anything personal.

When I met the Browncoats, no one pointed and laughed. No one said, "Look at her, all exposed and vulnerable! Let's poke her with sharp words until she shivers and runs back inside!" They embraced me and said, "Oh my God, I feel the same way! Hold my hand and we'll figure out this craziness together." No matter what was happening in my life, the Browncoats were always right beside me, to help me through any challenge. This is my family. I am home.

Eventually, through the Browncoats I found love.

At the 2008 Can't Stop the Serenity event, fellow Browncoat Chandler paired up with a friend of his. They were in costume as the creepy "blue-hand men" from *Firefly*. Arin played his part well, being very menacing in his suit and blue hands. He and Chandler won Best Costume that evening, and only after that did he break character and socialize.

Arin and I talked all night at the after-party. He gave me his phone number, but it took another month and a half for me to call him. It may have taken a while to get that first date to happen (more than two months after we first met), but by the fourth date, I was hooked.

That's when things started getting complicated for me.

I had spent the last several years finding my place in the world. Finding out that I didn't have to be shy, that I could be a part of something big and important. The Browncoats had become my life.

Arin was a Browncoat too, but he wasn't as involved as I was.

Before we had met, I had committed to coordinate the upcoming 2009 Browncoat Ball. Browncoats from around the world gather in a different city each year at a weekend event centered around the Browncoats themselves, as opposed to conventions that focus on celebrities and vendors.

As the host city of the 2009 Ball, Portland had a very large and very expensive event to plan. This was quite different than our annual Can't Stop the Serenity event, since it was all weekend and people were coming from all over the country. Coordination involved event spaces, food, activities, transportation, hotel rooms, money and a crazy amount of time.

Balancing my commitment to the Browncoats and my budding relationship with Arin was a challenge. However, we found that meeting the challenge strengthened our commitment to each other.

The weekend of the Browncoat Ball was executed nearly flawlessly. Arin choose the night of the Ball itself, with everyone in their finest finery, in front of my Browncoat family (and my real family – mother, step-father, sister and sister-in-law in attendance) to propose. On one knee, with the ring, right there on the dance floor stage, with everyone watching and cheering him on.

Yeah. It was pretty much perfect.

I can't say that Arin and I still don't have tiffs about the time I spend with my Browncoats, but I like to think I've found a balance. Arin still considers himself a Browncoat and comes to most of the shindigs with me and attends many of the events. There will come a time, perhaps soon, that I take a break from the planning aspect of the Browncoats. But the Browncoats, my PDX Browncoats, will always be there.

The PDX Browncoats do our best to look out for one another. As I've mentioned before, we've found each other homes and jobs, and comfort and support in times of need.

But there have been times when we have failed in that support.

Since 2006, Kay was very active in our community. She was passionate about animals and politics. We loved her company; she spoke her mind, and her presence lit up a room.

About a year ago, we began seeing less and less of her. Every once and a while someone would ask, "Hey, have you seen Kay?" and folks would struggle to recall the last shindig she attended.

Finally, in the spring, after one such conversation, the search for Kay was kicked up when a non-Browncoat friend of hers contacted us, asking the same question.

When we finally found out what happened, we were just a week too late. Kay had passed away as the result of an illness she had concealed from us.

Her death hit us hard.

Within a few days, we arranged a memorial for the Browncoats, to grieve and remember. It was that occasion that found us at the top of Powell Butte Park on that warm early spring afternoon.

We talked informally, sharing stories of Kay. The first time we met, the time she won the prize because she was only one in a room of hundreds who knew the full Firefly class ("midbulk transport, standard radion-accelerator core, classcode 03-K64 Firefly"), personal stories of joy and sorrow. The gathering broke up later that evening, we vowed to not let anyone else fall through the cracks.

This community of the PDX Browncoats, this family, will be a part of my life for years to come. We have a connection that we can't shake. A group of fans that found each other on the internet, commiserating over a television show that few people had heard of, and had no chance of being brought back, somehow believe that we can do the impossible. We can keep a failed show in the foremost of anyone's mind who can hear us. We organize events to raise money for international charities, without knowing how. We open our doors and embrace anyone who thinks they are too shy, scared, or geeky to join a social organization.

I want every fan out there to find the closest Browncoat group and go to their very first shindig. Make that connection. When a group of folks realize that they are not alone in the world, they can accomplish what they thought impossible.

Together we are mighty.

# Late to the Party: What *Buffy* Never Taught Me About Being a Girl

**Racheline Maltese** is a performer and storyteller focused on themes of sex, gender, desire and mourning. Her training includes a journalism degree from The George Washington University, as well as acting and directing coursework at the Atlantic Theater Company Acting School (New York City) and the National Institute of Dramatic Art (Sydney, Australia). She wrote *The Book of Harry Potter Trifles, Trivias and Particularities* (Sterling and Ross, 2007) and also works as an independent scholar focused on pop culture topics through her affiliation with The Society of Friends of the Text. She lives in New York City with her partner.

Joyce died last night.

Ten years after "The Body" first aired, I am finally getting around to watching both *Buffy the Vampire Slayer* and *Angel*. It's a strange experience, this after-the-fact immersion, especially when I was resistant to the programs for so long. A bit like finally being persuaded to delve into *Harry Potter* sometime around the release of the fourth book. I've fallen, and I've fallen hard.

I haven't fallen alone, just late. A lot of people are eager to talk about my sudden interest in the shows. I'm fannish by nature and the thought of doing this without anyone to obsess to about any number of trivialities (Giles and his tweed; the way Angel and Buffy are a lot more interesting as a couple once they break up; and whether Xander is a typical guy or an offensive guy) would be pretty appalling. But everyone, it seems, still cares about these shows.

I'm relieved, even if it often feels like a test. Everyone I know is a fan, and they want to know who I love (Wesley), who I hate (Faith) and when I've cried (I haven't, yet), and sometimes I worry I'm not doing it quite right because I'm neither the age nor living in the moment in time for which these shows were originally intended. As such, the things in them that grip me are often minor plot points, political issues or desires for fan fiction all my searching on Google still can't meet. (Why is there not more Cordelia/Wesley/Angel? They are so cute together, at least in Season One. I wonder if I write it, will anyone care?)

These thoughts are probably pretty typical of anyone entering a dead fandom (or in this case, what hopefully seems to be at least a partially undead fandom, all puns intended), but aside from the general strangeness there, experiencing *Buffy* and *Angel* for the first time ten years too late is peculiar for me, because these shows were my partner's first fandom.

That's actually one of the reasons I'm finally watching them. While she and I met through fandom, we mostly don't play in the same sandboxes. I've no taste for the anime she loves, and no matter how much information she's absorbed about *Doctor Who* through osmosis, she still has no interest in watching it, even if she does make regular jokes about Daleks and probably knows the astrological signs of the entire Series One *Torchwood* team.

I thought, perhaps, *Buffy* and *Angel* could be a common ground. Besides, I needed to see "The Body" for a bit of scholarship I've been working on. It seemed silly both to view that single episode without context and to forgo the opportunity to explore these shows she loved as a teenager. They must, I quickly decided, hold some secret clues not only to who she was then, but to who she is now. Besides, there was the way she beamed at me when I suggested maybe we start watching together. I knew I was in for the whole thing then whether I liked the show or not.

It only took a few episodes for me to become convinced that somewhere, amidst the graveyards, schools and old hotels, the secret to why she likes me might possibly be hiding. And I'm afraid, just a little bit, that that secret's name is Spike. Actually, it's more than that. Right now, I'm afraid *I am* Spike.

While I can assure you I'm not an undead stalker with a mannequin fetish, the facts are also that my bark *is* worse than my bite, that I love junk food, and that I have a long and dubious past involving bad poetry, crazy goth girls, and relationship entanglements that are probably best left unexplained. I also swagger, and sometimes, in response with a smile and a kiss, my partner tells me I'm a smug bastard.

No matter how often our friends tell me that I can't be Spike – moral compass, lack of fake British accent, better taste in clothes, and unlikely to have ever dated someone named Harmony (although, how great is Harm as a nickname?) – I remain unconvinced in a sea of bad and paranoid logic. *Buffy* fans think Spike is hot, girlfriend is a *Buffy* fan who puts up with my pretentiousness and ego... therefore, it must be about Spike.

So my friends spend a lot of time laughing at me. And you can't tell me that isn't a Spike-like quality too. As such, I remain concerned.

More seriously though, what's strange about this, of course, is that I'm a woman in a relationship with a woman, and it's not, by and large, the female characters that interest me in the *Buffy*verse. Nope, not even Willow and Tara, even if I was once a bisexual, redheaded Wiccan college student too (although in the 90s, who wasn't?).

At first glance, this experience of just not quite connecting with a show's female characters isn't particularly surprising for me. I have a long history of identifying with fictional men; just ask me about Severus Snape or Jack

Harkness sometime. But the more I think about it in the context of *Buffy* and *Angel*, where there are so many more great, kick-ass and diverse female characters than in most other pop-culture hits, the more this feels a little strange to me. Here, there are all these powerful women to identify with, and yet somehow I still can't.

There are a lot of places it's tempting to place the blame for this, of course, including the broader fandom culture that often seems to be about women, even queer women, not just valuing male characters over female characters, but holding female and male characters to very different and equally unacceptable standards. We love, it seems, male characters for their flaws, and yet vilify female characters for the same. And if that dynamic doesn't work for a particular property, let's not forget the way female characters, even those in the hands of male writers, are often called Mary Sues when they are "too perfect." When it comes to women in TV and in fandom, it often seems they can't be good and they can't be bad, and, perhaps more importantly, they can't win.

I've been playing in fandom long enough to know that my own internalized misogyny probably often comes into play when it comes to which characters I respond to. And, to be fair, that internalized misogyny comes, not just from some of the quirks seemingly inherent in fannish culture, but from the mere fact that I live in the world where non-fictional women too find themselves held to double standards when it comes to power, flaws, emotion and leadership. Certainly, those double standards are also overtly acknowledged in *Buffy* and *Angel*, even if not always successfully.

At the end of "Into the Woods," for example, Xander has a long and – to my mind – somewhat appalling monologue to Buffy about how Riley was the Best Boyfriend Ever and it was All Buffy's Fault that he was leaving her. While Buffy certainly didn't have her head 100% in that relationship, both because of her role as the Slayer and because of the ongoing specter of her history with Angel, Xander's criticism somehow managed to blame her for the fact that her boyfriend was essentially cheating on her with vampire prostitutes (a topic I may have initially addressed on the Internet in language far more crass, accompanied by rampant and excessive capitalization along with a bucket of exclamation points).

It wasn't the message I expected from a show everyone has spent a lot of time telling me was the most feminist program they'd ever seen, and the episode certainly made me angry. With a certain degree of hindsight though, I can say that far too much of what made me irate while watching the episode was its realism in the way the bulk of the relationship burden was placed on Buffy. It was, at least in Xander's eyes, her job to do, not 50% of the work in the relationship, but 75% of it. Or more. What hurt, in watching, wasn't that someone felt like this; that was expected. But how readily Buffy, who is so exceptional in so many ways, proved to be so ordinary in others: she believed Xander, without question.

Among other things, it is these moments of troubled realism that make *Buffy the Vampire Slayer* and *Angel* so successful in my eyes. But they are also, I suspect, part of what keeps me at a distance from the female characters. It's not that I don't want to be that girl who is so tough but still has self-esteem issues. It's that I don't know how to be that girl. In fact, I've never been very good at being a girl at all, and nothing has brought that home to me recently quite as clearly as *Buffy* has.

Because am I tough and still plagued with self-esteem issues? You bet. It's just the girl part of the equation that can make things a little weird for me. The best way to put it would be to say that I'm gender non-conforming. That doesn't mean I'm a tomboy who likes to climb trees and play sports; I'm not really a sports sort of person. It's more a sense that my internal identification and other people's reaction to what they see don't tend to match up. I like my curvy body, but I also prefer to wear suits and to be addressed by strangers as "sir."

I suppose this means you could say I'm butch, but that's a little bit like saying Wesley Wyndham-Pryce is butch. It's not untrue, but it's definitely mostly besides the point. And so, through that lens, I suppose it's reasonable that I don't particularly see myself in any of the women of Buffy they're all so girly. There are skirts, high heels, color-coordinated sweater sets, earrings, and even eye-shadow for every slaying occasion! These are skills all seemingly more arcane to me than demonology, witchcraft or martial arts.

To be clear here, I mean girly as a compliment. I see these skills as difficult, critical to living in the world, obviously pleasurable and well beyond my ken. Anyone, I believe, can learn to fight, or stand up in the face of fear (two central messages in the character arcs in both *Buffy* and *Angel* – look at all the people who rise out of seeming mundanity and fear to do what needs to be done). But to do that and continue to present to the world a face that's comfortable, expected and pleasing? Oh so much harder. And, even more than that, to be so strong and ferocious and yet still partake in simple pleasures like shopping or having dinner with friends? It's that that seems like the hardest skill in the world to me, and it's one *Buffy* celebrates.

All of which gets us back to my partner and my Spike paranoia. My partner is girly. Now, she looks at me sideways when I say this, but when I say she is girly, I mean it in the mode that the women of *Buffy* are. Sure, she doesn't like high heels and doesn't often wear makeup, but she takes up 2/3rds of the closet space in our house and owns more pairs of earrings than I can count. More importantly, she keeps a pick-axe under the sink, because she's an archaeologist. About once a year she goes to some isolated location for ten to 12 weeks and does hard, physical labor in the name of discovering the past. And if I'm occasionally chivalrous towards her – opening a door, guiding her into a room with my hand at the small of her back – it's not because she needs me to be, but because she lets me, because she's *indulging* me. That's a *Buffy* woman through and through.

Which means that in considering these characters in which I can't quite find myself, I should probably should stop asking my girlfriend if I'm Spike. ("Have you ever used effulgent in a poem?" she asked last week as we revisited this topic yet again as we cooked dinner, forcing me to confess I could not confidently answer "No.") Instead, I should start asking her if she sees herself in those women the way I see them in her. Did she want to grow up to be a Slayer or a witch or a seer? Is this part of how she became an archaeologist? Or a woman who loves jewelry? Or both?

Even more than that, however, when confronted with the women of *Buffy* and *Angel*, I find I have to ask myself what impact this show would have had on me had I watched it as it aired. Or, perhaps more importantly since I was not a teenager when it originally aired, if I had been able to watch it at the same age my girlfriend did.

What would I think of women, I wonder? And would I feel differently about the fact that my body and the way people react to it tells me I am one, even if my brain and my heart and fashion preferences often tell me differently?

Temporal what-ifs, are, of course, impossible to answer conclusively. Might Buffy have had a huge impact on how I see myself, women and the world? Absolutely. Maybe I would have learned that I could be strong and wear a dress or have all the men I know take me seriously no matter how traditional (or not) my beauty is. But maybe I am just the way I am, and instead of having been compelled by Cordelia's fashion sense, my hypothetical teen self would have simply gravitated towards suits and ties 15 years earlier than I did.

Even if questions of time are inherently unanswerable, they seem as fundamentally central to my experience of *Buffy* and *Angel* as gender must necessarily be. If I can ask if my partner became an archaeologist because of *Buffy*, do I not also have to ask if I've become an archaeologist of this show's fandom past – again, in that desperate attempt to find fan fiction about pairings only I seem to care for (can't anyone point me to some good Giles/Willow?) – because of my partner?

And, because television is, in some ways, the recollected narrative of true things that never happened, isn't it incumbent upon me to decide if Joyce died ten years ago, last night, or over and over again every time one more person discovers, or perhaps even re-watches, these shows?

These aren't questions I know the answer to, any more than I know who I would have been if my fandom life had occurred in a different order. But they are questions that matter. Clever stories remind us of this over and over again; they remind us that even though a thing isn't real, that doesn't necessarily mean that it isn't true.

There's truth, after all, in the immediate aftermath of Joyce's death, whether you believe she died never, once, or continues to over and over again, just as there's truth in the suspicion a lot of *Buffy* fans have that they may just be a little bit Spike too (how relieved was I to discover my affliction is apparently a common one?). Similarly, there is truth, no matter how personal, in my sense that in addition to being a woman, I am also a man, just as surely as there is truth in the story that there was once a girl named Buffy who could kill vampires.

And, actually, she's still out there; she's just waiting for next viewer, the next – dare I say it – *watcher*, like me, to figure it out. And the one after that. And the one after that. And the one... well, you get the idea.

Stories, unlike vampires, never die.

# How an Atheist and His Demons Created a Shepherd

**Meredith McGrath** is an ordained minister of the Evangelical Lutheran Church in America and is currently serving the Good Shepherd congregation within the community of La Crosse, Wisconsin. She primarily delivers oral biblical meta (a.k.a. sermons). Whenever possible, she peppers them with pop-culture references. Her personal favorite was opening a sermon with the classic gem other pastors only joke about using: "Mawidge. Mawidge is what bwings us togewer todway." Meredith completes graduate degrees in ten-year intervals (1997 Master of Science in College Student Personnel, Western Illinois University and 2007 Master of Divinity, Luther Seminary), so is open to suggestions for 2017.

Joss Whedon made me a shepherd. Well, it's all not *solely* due to Joss; that would be more than a mite touched in the head.

Before Joss, I considered three different paths – a doctorate in higher education, a law degree, or seminary. All three pulled at me, and it seemed wise to know for sure what I wanted before choosing among those very different paths. And then Joss and his demons arrived – the right catalyst, lifting up the right questions at the right moment in time, leading to clarity about that call.

The spring of 1997 stands distinct in my mind. A "thousand year flood" in Grand Forks, North Dakota, and East Grand Forks, Minnesota, ripped homes from foundations and "relocated" them, filling nearly every basement in those communities on the plain, including those of grandparents on both sides of the family. Freezers bobbed like apples in a basin. In the slush of mud and ice water, everything from furniture to picture albums was bloated beyond rescue, eventually hauled out to the curb. It was a time of devastating loss.

That same spring, I graduated with a Master of Science degree in College Student Personnel – the degree necessary to work in the student services side of university life. While I, like my classmates, had been job hunting all semester, nothing had panned out by the time of graduation. So I did what so many 20-something graduates do: I moved back into my parents' home.

Sadly, what I cannot claim is that the spring of 1997 was when I discovered *Buffy*. While it's possible that the large town in which my grad school was located didn't carry it, the more likely truth is that I intentionally ignored this strangely-titled midseason replacement. My discovery of *Buffy the Vampire Slayer* was entropy, or perhaps serendipity.

It was summer, and I was in the cool of my parents' basement family room, curled up in the comfy brown rocker with an Irish-themed cross-stitch project in my lap. The television was on, my show of choice being *7th Heaven*. I've always had a soft spot for family-friendly fare with a bit of faith life woven into it, in the tradition of *Little House on the Prairie*. Later I would fall in love with *Joan of Arcadia*.

When the top of the hour arrived, I was engrossed enough in the counted cross-stitch that the next show came on and I didn't bother turning the channel. I gave cursory attention to the boy in a letterman's jacket and a girl in a Catholic schoolgirl skirt who were climbing into a school building after dark. Her words and body language were broadcasting uncertainty and fear. It was clear where this was going. He was going to attack this girl, or something lurking inside was going to attack both of them. There would be screaming and some sort of *eee eee eee* knife-wielding slasher music. There's a predictable order to the television universe, after all.

That's what didn't happen. Sweet schoolgirl Darla vamped out and sank her fangs into the neck of that boy. Then the raucous *Buffy the Vampire Slayer* theme song broke in. I had the simultaneous thoughts of "Ooh, vampires!" and "Huh. That was different."

So I tuned in the next week and the week after. By the time the episode "Angel" aired, I was hooked. That kiss between Buffy and Angel had me aflutter, but when she walked away and I saw the burned imprint of that cross on Angel's chest that's when my pulse really raced. More than one person was seared with a cross that day. I had been introduced to the mind of Joss Whedon and unbeknownst to me, my life had just been changed. My vocational journey was about to get a whole lot more convoluted. In the next few years Joss Whedon schooled me, culminating in the epiphany that it wasn't a PhD or a law degree that I should seek, but a Master of Divinity.

Over the next five years and three different career moves within the field of college student personnel, there were three questions I had about the community I would live in if I accepted a job offer. Did it have a) an ELCA (Evangelical Lutheran Church in America) congregation, b) a quality public radio station, and c) a channel that carried *Buffy the Vampire Slayer* and *Angel*. So how exactly did the *Buffy*verse prepare me for my eventual spiritual vocation?

## Good versus Evil

My profession involved meeting with and sanctioning college students who violated the university's student code of conduct. The ongoing fight on the shows between good and evil resonated. I dealt with the "evils" of excessive alcohol use, but also with more serious issues up to and including the real evils of sexual assault. It was, at times, exhausting work, where the simple delineation of having "won" or "lost" didn't fit.

Occasionally I went home and cried in frustration after a hearing board was (in my opinion) too lenient in their sanctions. At least one time, I had tears of relief that they could be lenient and reverse my harsher, if consistent, original penalty that I had no desire to enforce. Like Buffy in "Lie to Me," I wished for that old worldview in which it was easy to tell right from wrong and to have the assurance that in the end, good does triumph over evil.

"Earshot" was the reminder that even when personally life "suck[s] beyond the telling of it," it neither gives one permission to harm others nor to give up on helping others. That episode and so many others constantly had me reexamining the questions, "How am I called to help others? Am I living out that call?"

### She is the Chosen One

When one begins the process of seeking ordination, one is asked multiple times to explain one's sense of God's call to the vocation of ordained ministry. In my case, there was not only an interest in hearing the call story, but the question of "Why now? Why in your thirties, why with years in another career, why do you feel called?" I would observe that contrary to what I was hearing so many voices in the world saying (that it's an anything-goes world in which people need a harsh reminder that they are sinful creatures), what I was called to do was offer a word of grace.

My experiences taught me that everyone suffers in some way; often we have no idea of the pain others bear. People are quite adept at beating themselves up over their faults and shortcomings, so they don't need more of that from me or anyone. The thing they need because they don't hear about it nearly enough is God's loving grace. As Giles said in "I Only Have Eyes for You," "To forgive is an act of compassion, Buffy. It's not done because people deserve it. It's done because they need it."

I also observed that at 22, when I was about to graduate from college, the idea of going into the ministry had crossed my mind, but right on its heels was me asking, "What do I know about life and the world? How could I possibly provide the ministry people need?" Which, on the one hand, was true. My life experience was pretty limited. On the other hand, if looking at the age spread in seminary is any indicator, that thought of not being prepared enough doesn't seem to enter the mind of a man of similar age, education and life experience.

It's a bit of a head shaker. My parents were fairly egalitarian. Their attitude for both myself and my brother was that whatever we wanted to achieve, we could, if we were willing to put in the hard work. My first job after college was running a building of 250 college students and a staff of 24

– some of whom were only a year younger than myself. I'd been willing to jump into that, yet I'd not been confident that I could be a good pastor. While I'd known lots of different male pastors of varying ages, I'd known exactly one woman – and she'd been old enough that her children were my age. At 22, I didn't have a woman with a call to whom I could relate. However, in the years that followed, I had several strong female clergy who were mentors and role models. I also had Buffy.

I realize Buffy is not a pastor (that comes later, with Shepherd Book). What Buffy has in common with pastors, priests, ministers, rabbis, imams, shepherds and other spiritual leaders is a call story. Buffy, a teenage girl more interested in boys, popularity and lollipops than anything altruistic, is chosen by a power beyond herself to stand against the vampires and demons. And ready or not, she must answer that call.

I watched her struggle with her status as the Chosen One, with how the power she now had and the responsibility it carried meant letting go of the powers she'd known: popularity, manipulating perception, and feminine wiles. At times she was ambivalent about the trade-off, only to have moments of realizing that her call wasn't a burden that had been placed on her shoulders, but had become an integrated part of her identity. She matured into the role and claimed it in all its complexity.

Knowing that Buffy was chosen first and then grew into the call was reassuring to me. Ironically, her struggle with being called as a vampire slayer, with feeling prepared (or not), with what it meant to build a broader community to face the demons and darkness, felt much truer to me as a pastoral call story than Lucy Camden's on *7th Heaven* in its later seasons: women seminary students, including myself, could not bear to watch the latter show. Yet there were multiple rabid fans of *Buffy* in my seminary community – most of them women. As Joss mentioned during his acceptance speech for an Equality Now award, the world still needs more strong female characters. Particularly, in my opinion, stories of women with a call. Imagine what might have been different if Buffy had existed in 1987 or 1977, for that matter.

## Works Righteousness Versus Grace

When it comes to redemption stories and religious themes, Angel's story resonated for me. Since the return of his soul, one of Angel's deepest urges was to atone, leading to his version of ashes and sackcloth: living in alleys and subsisting on rats. In Los Angeles, he takes atoning to a more active place: helping the hopeless. An irony, given Angel's hopelessness about his own redemption. In his opinion, nothing can make up for the atrocities of his past.

Then at the end of *Angel* Season One, along comes the Shanshu Prophecy. Angel interprets it to mean that if he does enough good, he will become human again. It immediately pinged me as a classic works righteousness storyline – that although one has sinned, if one does enough good, one can then earn salvation. Or in Angel's case, Shanshu.

In this theological storyline, there is no place for flexibility or creativity, only rules that provide measurable results. At its extreme, nothing matters but a one-to-one relationship between the individual and their Power That Is. Relationships with others decrease as the individual's obsession with their own needs increase. They ask, "What is in this relationship for me?" Relationships with others, particularly those whom one has just met or who are not of like mind, are viewed as messy, time consuming, and at certain times requiring more than they give. (There is one exception to this, which I will outline later.)

When people fixate on doing good works for their own salvific needs, a sense of their own entitlement clouds judgment. They believe they deserve for the world to fall into place. The people whom they are "helping" become nothing more than numbers to be tallied. In "Judgment," Angel Investigations slipped into that pattern. The humanity of individuals didn't matter; the quicker they solved what they perceived to be the problem, the quicker Angel got credit and could move on to the next case. To meet those quotas as quickly as possible, corners were cut and the ends justified the means. As is nearly inevitable with a works-righteousness mindset, when one does the "right" things for the wrong reasons, it all falls apart.

When Angel literally throws away the tally board at the end of "Judgment," he is figuratively throwing out the notion that he can earn through his own choices and actions a right to Shanshu. The entire Angel Investigations team rededicates themselves to helping the hopeless because it is the right thing to do, period. As Wesley so nicely summarizes, "Of course. We shouldn't be keeping score. We're not running a race – we're doing a job – one soul at a time."

Given my from-the-cradle Lutheran sensibilities, I was downright giddy by the resolution to that story arc. Angel's epiphany paralleled Martin Luther's own: salvation is a gift and gifts cannot be earned. (No matter how many times a parent may threaten that Santa won't come if the child doesn't behave.) When perspective changes from self-control and entitlement to a gift freely given, everything changes. In changing one's understanding of the individual relationship with God, what perhaps changes the most is one's relationship with others. One has time to care for others, attend to the need of the other when one isn't spending one's time worrying about making points with God. (Which, as I write this, may in part explain why I like atheists so much. At least in my circle of friends and fandom, they not only get the ideals of social justice, they live them.) From that point on, Angel again approaches his 'missions' in a more relational way. People matter. Their needs are addressed effectively without obsessing on efficiency.

The question of motivation for "why we do what we do" also played out in Season Two episode "Epiphany," when Wolfram and Hart's Holland Manners takes Angel on a little tour that ends at the home office of the Senior Partners. Angel expects it to be a horrible, torturous place similar to the hell dimension he opened with Alcatha, except the last stop is this world as it is. At first Angel is horrified. Is this world Hell? If so, then what's the point?

There are a fair number of religious people in various Christian denominations who don't see the world as Hell, or as Heaven. It's a way station at best. What matters is saving souls for the next life. (This can be another aspect of works righteousness: if one doesn't do everything one can to save others – as in getting others to accept Jesus Christ as their personal Lord and Savior – then one will have fallen short in the eyes of God on Judgment Day.)

But if all one worries about is saving souls, then there is no point in fighting for social justice, reform, basic human rights, etc., as this world is not the world that matters. The pithy explanation that a seminary professor gave me about this particular theological perspective was this: why polish the brass on the *Titanic* if it's about to sink?

That could have been the view Angel took after Manners's tour. But he didn't. Angel realized that this was the world he inhabited and up until his last figurative breath, he was going to fight to make it a better world. That's pretty close to the "Kingdom of God is here!" theological perspective. As the Wesleyan tradition says:

> Do all the good you can,
> By all the means you can,
> In all the ways you can,
> In all the places you can,
> At all the times you can,
> To all the people you can,
> As long as ever you can.

Angel's resiliency in the face of disappointment, be it in himself or in the world, has also been a comfort and encouragement for me.

These storylines occurred at the same time I discovered the online fandom community. Each week, we'd analyze everything, from the over-arching themes to the "throwaway" lines (not that we believed for a moment that there was such a thing in the Jossverse). Within that eclectic community I was one of the theological voices, trying to express from my lay person perspective (benefiting from years in Sunday School and decades of worshiping from the pews, but lacking formal training) what this wacky gift of grace thing is. While the community was appreciative of the perspective, I was aware of the limits of my theological depth and vocabulary.

The conversation threads that came from that story arc were a reminder to me of just how many folks view faith as a thing one has to earn – that while God is omnipotent, that love doesn't trump fairness. There exists a deep belief, alien to me from my tradition with grace at the center of it, that "If I work really hard at being good, then maybe God will find me acceptable."

This is another sharp edge to the sword of works righteousness. If one doesn't go the direction of entitlement and certainty, one usually goes the direction of hopelessness. Like Angel at his broody, brutal self-assessment best, failure is the one constant. The perception is that they are too broken for anyone, particularly God, to find lovable and forgivable.

At the same time these themes and conversations were playing out in my fannish life, I was experiencing them professionally. Again, for the most part, this was tied to my work with sexual assault survivors. For many, the assault had not only shattered their trust in other human beings as well as their own character-judging skills, but it had also put their relationship with God into question.

After living the first 18 or so years of their lives as good girls and therefore desirable to God, to then experience a sexual violation *though it was not their fault* put into question whether they were still worthy of God or if they had been rejected. Particularly for those who came from religious traditions that teach a very narrow range of acceptable, moral behavior, there was a deep need to hear from others that God is loving and compassionate. That it has never been about works, but about grace.

Like Angel in "Amends," they struggled to believe they had value and worth that transcended the failures (perceived or real) of their lives. Unlike Buffy, as an employee in a public school I really couldn't be the voice of reassurance that grace abounds – and I didn't have magic snow backing me up either! It wasn't long after the dovetailing of these fannish conversations and my work experiences that I picked up the phone, called the local seminary, and scheduled a visit to tour and pick up the requisite paperwork.

### From the Other Side of the Looking Glass

One might imagine that going into seminary would mean the end to my obsession with demons and slayers and watchers. (Oh my!) Quite the contrary. Having the Jossverse and its fandom as a lens through which to consider ideas only deepened my experience.

While I had an English degree, training in developmental theory and a love of critical thinking that predated finding fandom, there is nothing like an intense online fannish discussion about whether or not Spike intentionally sought out his soul to prepare one for theology classes. Not only was I comfortable in needing to support my arguments with specific details from canon, but I was also familiar with the reality that people viewing the exact same source text could have completely different interpretations of every-thing from the character's motives to the authorial intent. All this, while nurturing friendships across a spectrum of opinions and preferred character interrelationships. A number of my classmates did not have such a prepara-tion, and some struggled mightily with the concept of the passages in the Bible having more than one interpretation.

For example, when my Hebrew professor framed the story of Jonah as being the comic book of the Old Testament, I was all ears. He pointed out the hyperbole, the larger-than-life events, the humor in it. Jonah, spit out of that whale, must be covered in goo best left undescribed. Without stopping to clean up, he starts walking through the baking hot wilderness to make a crazy-sounding proclamation.

He went on to talk in great detail about other aspects of this comic book of the Bible. I'm not sure if there was a more nuanced point he was making, but what I heard was two-fold. The story of Jonah was not meant to be taken literally, but that didn't mean it didn't hold truth. For some of my classmates, the concept that the Bible was not literally true was more than a little head-splody. Yet for me this opened up all sorts of delightful possibili-ties in thinking about authorial intent as well as what the story still has to offer to us now.

I even more deeply enjoyed the chocolate-with-peanut-butter mix of seminary and Jossverse when the Shanshu Prophecy came back into play in *Angel* Season Five. Even more nummy theological layers! I found that the Shanshu sounded rather like the Christian doctrine of eternal life. While there are endless understandings of what happens after death, doctrinally the Christian belief is that there will be a "resurrection of the dead and life everlasting." No zombies without souls nor disembodied souls floating in the ether, but one's life and self is restored, body and soul. Isn't that Angel's desire – to be human, his body and soul rejoined? Which is a delightful irony – the immortal creature whose desire for mortality looks an awful lot like eternal life.

What does it mean that Angel signed away his right to the Shanshu Prophecy in order to join the Black Thorn? Perhaps not much at all. In the moment, I yelled at my television: "No, Angel, no!" However, as I reflected upon it, I questioned if it held any meaning at all. Could Angel really sign it away? First there is the question of how prophecy works. It's not like we've ever seen anyone in the *Buffy*verse sign up to be the receiver of prophecy. In fact, whenever anyone tries to avoid or change prophecy, it comes back to bite them and still comes to fruition on its own terms.

Secondly, following the theological overtones that have already been present in the Shanshu Prophecy with it being more like a gift (of grace) than an end-of-year bonus for making quota, can a gift be signed away? The biblical parable of the man with two sons – a.k.a. the Prodigal Son (Matthew

15:11-32) – would suggest it cannot. The plot of the story as it pertains to Angel is that a son asks for his inheritance while his father is still alive. The father grants it, the son goes off and spends it all – foolishly by the standards of some. Not unlike Angel spending his right to the Shanshu Prophecy "foolishly" on entrance to the Black Thorn.

We don't see within canon the result of Angel's action; however, the parable ends with the son trying to return to the father with hopes of being a hired hand, for clearly he is no longer a son. But the father doesn't see the situation from that perspective. Instead of viewing his son as disinherited since he already took his share, he still views him as his son with all the rights of a son. Might not the Powers That Be, who've never worked with the same sense of logic as the world's logic, take a similar attitude?

This ties in with Martin Luther's understanding of faith-filled contradiction. This concept may be more familiar via the Sarah McLachlan song, *Prayer of St. Francis*, which played during the final scenes of *Buffy* Season Six: "For it is in giving that we receive. And it's in pardoning that we are pardoned. And it's in dying that we are born to eternal life." It's contradiction. It is in the opposite of expectation that an answer is found. Similarly, when Angel truly and completely stops fighting for the Shanshu – not trying to gather up good deeds, not racing against Spike for the Holy Grail, and not even having hope left upon signing it away – it is closer than ever before. Perhaps it is only in fully letting go that he is finally prepared to receive it.

Did Joss have a working knowledge of these various theological ideas? Hard telling. My lens of interpretation may be seeing layers he wasn't intentionally creating. He and the shows' writers are incredibly well read, but Joss also appears to be one of those persons who has an intuitive sense of the truth of life.

In the opposite of expectation, an answer is found. Perhaps that best explains the relationship between Joss Whedon, creator of fantastical worlds – two of which involve demons, magic, and things that go bump in the night – and people of faith, particularly pastor types. I've lost track of how many ordained folks I know who are fans of Joss's work. Perhaps what draws us to these unlikely 'verses is the same thing that I imagine draws Joss to create them – seeing a complex and often broken world, and wanting to make meaning of it in a way that inspires hope.

# Older and Far Away

Pepper Espinoza has been writing and publishing Erotic Romance since 2005. She grew up in Utah and lives there now, where the landscape and history provide a great deal of inspiration for her work. Besides writing, she enjoys playing video games, watching movies and going to concerts. Vivien Dean returned to writing in 2005, and has published with Liquid Silver Books, Samhain Publishing, and Amber Quill Press. She currently resides in northern California with her husband and two children. Writing under the name "Jamie Craig," their first novel, *Chasing Silver*, was published by Juno Books in December 2007. Since then, they have published eight titles with Samhain Publishing, four titles with Liquid Silver Books, and over three dozen with Amber Quill Press, including two best-selling series. Their Urban Fantasies *Mosaic Moon* and *Dominion* were two of the six 2008 EPPIE Finalists. www.jamie-craig.com.

When we were approached to write an essay for this book, we knew we had a unique perspective to offer. And when I say *we*, I don't mean the royal *we*. I mean myself and my collaborator, Vivien Dean. Some people might know us best under our shared pseudonym, Jamie Craig. We've been writing together, both in fandom and professionally, for four years now, and we plan to continue the collaboration for many years to come. The origin story of Jamie Craig is really a story about the power of the Whedon fandom. If the online fandom for *Buffy the Vampire Slayer* didn't exist, then Jamie Craig would not exist either. Neither would Pepper Espinoza or Vivien Dean.

For both Vivien and I, it began in 2002. I was living in Upland, California at the time and attending the University of La Verne. Only 19, recently married, and literally hundreds of miles from my home or family, I needed something to not only fill my days but to sustain me. My husband was working long hours, and we had no money, no friends and no lives. I was alone a lot, especially during the endless summer without air conditioning or relief. On the other side of the planet, in Essex, England, Vivien found herself in a similar predicament. While her husband worked out of the house, she was left at home, pregnant, with a one-year-old daughter and no car. *Buffy* hooked us both in the summer between Season Five and Season Six, giving much needed entertainment and a respite from the other stresses in our lives. Soon after that, the fandom provided a much needed creative outlet, not to mention a means of social networking.

Vivien and I didn't formally meet each other in 2002, though we were aware of each other. Well, I wasn't just aware of her. I was a huge fan of hers. She wrote amazing fan fiction as Eurydice72. It was always proofread and edited, posted on a regular schedule, and she always replied graciously to comments left on her work. She never let me down as a reader. When I opened up a story of hers, I knew that I could trust her. Sometimes I do wonder how different things would have been for us if I had simply emailed her once to tell her how much I admired her. But I never did. As much as I longed to be part of that community, I was shy and had a difficult time reaching out to people. She was reading my fan fiction as well. I still remember how deeply honored I felt when she nominated one of my stories for an award on a fan fiction site.

I say honored because it was, and still is, a big deal to me to be recognized by my peers. When I see professional writers rant about the evils of fan fiction, I always think they're missing out on something pretty amazing and important. Fandom and fan fiction isn't just about mucking around in somebody else's toy box, making a mess of all their things, and then merrily skipping on to the next kid's treasured possessions. The fandom was always about so much more than that.

Vivien and I didn't meet in 2003 or 2004.

After *Angel* ended its run in 2004, I left the fandom[1]. I wanted to focus on my own writing career, and quite frankly, I was too heartbroken by the *Angel* series finale and too annoyed by the *Buffy the Vampire Slayer* series finale to find much pleasure in the fandom. Plus, I thought I had a pretty good run. I'd spent the previous three years writing fanfic after fanfic, I had met dozens of wonderful people, attended several fan conventions, and – thanks to the support and encouragement I received in fandom – I felt like I was ready to have a real career as an author.

I graduated with a degree in English with an emphasis in Creative Writing in 2005. I had not been accepted into any graduate programs, and I stood at a crossroads in my life. I could go find a real job like everybody else I knew. My husband certainly would have supported that plan. Or I could take advantage of the fact that I had no children or dependents to feed and spend the year writing. I chose to write, knowing full well that it could have very serious consequences for myself and my husband if I made the wrong decision. But I felt confident and determined.

I began investigating a new type of publisher. I knew I wanted to write Romance, but not the series Romance that Harlequin publishes. I wanted to

1. For my purposes, when I speak about fandom, I'm talking specifically about the corner of the online Whedonverse I'm most familiar with – fans of Spike/Buffy who wrote and read fanfic. The culture of fandom tends to be the same regardless of the corner of fandom you're hanging out in.

enjoy the same sort of creative freedom I had in fandom, but I wanted to reach a larger audience and make a career of it at the same time. To that end, e-publishers seemed like the most logical place to go after fandom.

E-publishing, or digital-first publishing as it's now coming to be known, is a very strange little niche. When the first Erotic Romance e-publisher, Ellora's Cave, was founded a decade ago, there was no market for e-books, and there were very few writers. The appeal of e-publishing was in the potential. Separated from the New York Romance publishers, there was far more leniency. Far more choices. An author wasn't restrained by limitations set by the publisher in order to keep the market happy. E-publishing has a very low overhead, and if a book fails, the consequences are less dire for the author's career or the publisher's bottom line. It is my firm opinion that e-publishing works best when it's providing something that readers can't, or won't, find in bookstores. Digitally published Romances that follow all the conventions set by publishers like Harlequin tend to not do as well as books that genuinely explore new territory. The biggest selling sub-genres of Romance in e-publishing are either kink or gay – another parallel to the fandom community, where writers pushed the envelope on sexual explicitness and embraced fiction with GLBT characters. Is it any wonder that fanfic readers and writers felt so comfortable with this new style of publishing?

E-publishing, like fandom, is always growing. More and more people are being introduced to this new, digital world. Digital media is a strongly democratizing force. The traditional "old media" gatekeepers are being abandoned or knocked down one by one. That is why New York publishers will tell you that publishing, as a business, is floundering, and why bookstores are currently in serious trouble, while digital first publishers continue to flourish, increasing profits annually. Some would argue that gatekeepers are necessary – that's why they exist – and losing them now would damn us to an endless onslaught of dreck. But the power of digital media is that it connects creators with consumers, giving people the chance to speak while providing a space for a market to form and grow. Fandom has existed for decades, in one form or another, but online fandom has taken the basic concept of community and the exchange of interests to a new level, just as digital publishing has allowed various literature genres to continue in new and interesting ways.

While I was investigating established e-publishers (not that there were many at the time, and they hadn't been established for very long), other fanfic writers were considering starting their own – which eventually became Linden Bay Romance, which in turn spawned one of the most popular distributors for e-published Erotic Romance, All Romance Ebooks. One of the original owners, someone Vivien knew well from the fandom, approached her about writing an original novel for them. She accepted, and that one novel turned into four titles with Linden Bay. Other fanfic authors joined the Linden Bay team, too. My career took me a different route, though, and I published my first novels with Liquid Silver Books and Whiskey Creek Press before expanding to places like Samhain and Amber Quill Press.

There's a widely accepted bit of wisdom that says every person must write one million words of crap before they start getting to the good stuff. I spent three years writing in the Whedonverse fandoms, and I know for a fact if I total up all my fics, it would be well over a million words. I knew I could write a novel because at that point, I had written several novels. My years in fandom were a time of unparalleled creativity. The community that naturally formed around the love of the Spike/Buffy relationship created a constant feedback loop. Joss Whedon served as the source of our inspiration, as we all took great pleasure in playing in his sandbox, but we also inspired each other. I positively devoured fan fiction, consuming it at an amazing rate, regardless of the quality. In turn, I was inspired to write more of my own. Every single word pushed me closer to my goal of being a *good* writer. Then I would chat about the show, about fan fiction, about my favorite characters, and that would inevitably inspire more idea or "plot bunnies." I have never experienced anything like it before, and while I do still dabble in various fandoms, I have never experienced anything so immersive or powerful. In fact, there are still echoes of those years in my writing, and I can say without equivocation that it was certainly the most instructive time of my life. I don't think people will discuss my work after I'm dead, but if they *did*, they would be obligated to acknowledge the incalculable influence of *Buffy the Vampire Slayer* and its fandom.

I thought I was completely done with fandom in 2005, but fandom wasn't done with me. Not quite. A good friend, who publishes under the name Phillipa Grey-Gerou and happened to be a good friend of Vivien's, invited me to participate in an online *Buffy*verse role-playing game. They needed more players to round out the cast, and informed me that I could write Wesley Wyndham-Pryce, who was, and still is, my favorite *Buffy*verse character. I adore him to an almost unhealthy degree, and my friends were all aware of that. The real selling point was learning that Vivien would be writing Spike. We might not have been friends, but I respected her as an author, and I adored the way she wrote Spike – always in character, always snarky, always fun. I told her I would love to participate. For the longest time, we never interacted with each other in the game. The storyline simply didn't require Wesley and Spike interacting with each other. Wesley spent most of his time with Faith. And then a series of strange events led to Vivien taking over Faith from another player. The first time we wrote together, it really did feel like kismet. We had genuine chemistry, and due to the years we spent reading each other's work, we trusted each other. We had a good understanding of what we were each capable of, we had an expectation for quality that we both lived up to, and we had *fun*. I can't stress that enough. I had never had so much fun writing before. I think it was the most fun I ever had with clothes on.

Shortly after we began writing together in the RPG, we decided to write a novel together. Given our previous publishing experience, we were confident that we could do it. We finished after two weeks of constant work, and both of us were surprised by how good it actually was. We found a new print publisher searching for books with strong heroines, and she loved our manuscript and offered a contract. At that point, *Jamie Craig* didn't exist, but our editor suggested it would be better if we published under a single name. My husband's name is Jaime, and hers is Craig. *Chasing Silver* ultimately wasn't the first book we published, but it is the one that set us on our career path and the one responsible for creating a new entity in our lives.

One thing I've learned over the past eight years is that a writer *needs* a community. Writing itself can be a very lonely, if not isolating, enterprise, but that just heightens the need to be surrounded by a very good community. You see this need (or desire) manifest itself in different ways. Some people join a weekly writers group, other people either take or teach creative writing courses. There are professional organizations for authors or aspiring authors, like the Romance Writers of America or the Science Fiction and Fantasy Writers of America, with each group supporting smaller, regional chapters. Authors form communities through reading and reviewing each other's work, through conventions, through correspondence.

Because of that need, I maintained the connections I had made while in fandom. Even though we'd all moved on to other television shows, movies and interests, we were still friends. We still supported each other. We still read each other's work and offered feedback and criticism. We still turned to each other when we needed help or a shoulder to cry on.

Fandom continues to touch my life in funny, strange little ways. I recently attended the Romantic Times Booklovers Convention in Columbus, Ohio, where I met not one but two former fan fiction writers. Not only did we play in the same fandom for a few years, but we read and enjoyed each other's fanfic. While we were all there with our professional hats on, there was something a little bit exhilarating about falling back into the old language, the old references, the old jokes and arguments. No matter your age, your background, your beliefs or where you were from, you could easily enter the fandom as long as you understood the common language – *Buffy the Vampire Slayer*. The community never really goes away, it just changes and the various threads evolve in different ways. My corner evolved towards e-publishing.

Vivien and I do all our writing online. She is my best friend in the world, and one of the few people I know I can count on. We see each other in the flesh four or five times a year, but the 99% of our communication and creativity happens over chat. We still write every single book like we wrote our first role-playing scenarios – a paragraph at a time with each of us writing specific characters. *Buffy* has infused our writing and our language, and sometimes I know the decisions I make for my characters are, for better or worse, inspired by Joss Whedon himself. On the one hand, our regular participation in fandom seems like it was a lifetime ago. On the other hand, no matter how many years pass, it's always going to seem like it's right there, just on the edges of my life.

I was once looking up information about a band I like, Okkervil River. I found an interview with the lead singer, Will Sheff, and something he said has always stuck with me. "I have felt a sense of fandom for things that I have loved that is so intense that it starts to bleed into spirituality, bleed into sexuality, and bleed into all kinds of areas of your life that love ... " He was talking about rock albums, but I think it beautifully expresses what any fandom can mean to a person. It's certainly an accurate description of how I feel about the Whedonverse.

As I'm writing this, I'm engaged in a very heated discussion on a message board about whether *Buffy the Vampire Slayer* vampires were really evil or if they all could have been redeemed like Spike. Why do I allow myself to get pulled into these debates? Because that question, and a million others that Joss Whedon raised, still matter to me. We probably won't reach a point where we all agree with each other, but that's all right. The question will linger with me, slithering through my brain like a snake, and sooner or later, an idea will form. A plot bunny will take shape. Maybe a year from now, we'll have a book that explores that particular question of the nature of good and evil. Either way, I don't think we will ever fully divest ourselves of what binds to fandom, and I don't think either of us would want to.

# Why Joss Is More Important Than His 'Verse

**Teresa Jusino** was born the same day Skylab fell. Coincidence? She doesn't think so. She is a freelance writer in New York City who is a regular contributor to websites like Tor.com, ChinaShop Magazine, Pink Raygun, and Newsarama. In addition to her geeky online scribblings, she also writes prose fiction and screenplays. Teresa is the author of a chapbook of short stories called *On the Ground Floor*, and her fiction has appeared in the sci-fi magazine *Crossed Genres*. She is also the last member of WilPower: The Official Wil Wheaton Fan Club. Visit her at The Teresa Jusino Experience: www.teresajusino.wordpress.com.

I didn't realize how big a Joss Whedon fan I was until I was across a table from him, meeting him for the first time. Until that moment, I knew I liked his *creations*. I was a fan of *Buffy, Angel, Firefly, Doctor Horrible's Sing-Along Blog*, and I was, at that time, looking forward to *Dollhouse*. But when I finally had the chance to speak with him at a *Dollhouse* promotional event in New York City, I was flooded with unexpected emotion, and it was about more than mere television. It was about *him*.

But first, my Whedon history.

When I heard they were making a television show based on that silly movie about a cheerleader who kills vampires that I only went to see because Luke Perry was in it, and it was going to star that girl from *All My Children* and *Swan's Crossing* fercryingoutloud, because they couldn't even get Kristy Swanson, I raised a skeptical eyebrow. I was a senior in high school, after all, and I had taste. I watched the first episode and thought, "Yeah, *that'll* get cancelled in a month," and I didn't watch it again. After all, if I wanted to watch teenagers running amok in California, I could always tune in to watch Tiffany Amber-Thiessen wreak havoc on *Beverly Hills, 90210*. Sure, there were no vampires, but those characters were in high school, like, *forever*, so they were *kind of* immortal.

Then, I was a drama student at New York University, and as part of my training I had to take a directing class. My teacher, Jim, who to this day is still one of the best and most intelligent teachers I've ever had (and, now that I think about it, reminds me a bit of Giles), would come into class every week and before starting would ask "Who watched *Buffy* last night?" Hands were raised, and the faithful in this little cult would talk about the episode that had aired the night before. At first, I had no idea what they were talking about, but when I asked Jim, and he told me that he was referring to that show about the cheerleader and the vampires, I couldn't believe it! First, *that show was still on?* And second, *Jim* watches *Buffy?* Jim, *Shakespeare and Aristotle enthusiast,* watches this show? When I asked him why someone of his intelligence and taste would watch a teeny-bopper show about vampires, he immediately jumped to its defense. "Oh, no, Teresa! It's one of the smartest shows on television right now! You have to give it a chance!" I must have made some kind of Doubt Face, because he smiled and shook his head. "You just have to watch it," he said. "I think you'd really, really like it."

Apparently, Jim knew me better than I did, which is the way of wise teachers. I, however, thought I knew best, and continued to ignore the show for years. It wasn't until 2001, when I graduated college, that I was forced to give *Buffy* a chance – I was living with my friend Dayna in my first apartment, and she was obsessed with the show. I knew better than to try to talk to her on Tuesday nights. At first, I'd leave the room when it was on, but as choice bits of dialogue made their way to me, I'd find myself stopping in front of the television once in a while before moving on. That progressed to leaning against the wall in the living room for longer stretches. That progressed to actually sitting down. Eventually, I knew enough about the characters and their stories to get something out of it, and I started to enjoy it.

And then came "Once More With Feeling." And my life was forever changed. Because it was then that I thought, "This guy. Is. A. Genius."

By the time Buffy and Spike kissed during the Coda, I was a *Buffy* convert. I made it a point to watch every *Buffy* episode I'd missed however I could. I started watching *Angel*, and while I never liked the show as much, I still thought it was great. Especially when Fred came on the scene!

But I still wasn't a Joss fan. Not yet. I was a fan of the *Buffy*verse. Not the same thing.

Then one day, I was flipping through an issue of *Entertainment Weekly* that discussed new TV shows that season, and I saw a cast portrait featuring some really attractive people – and one really hot guy in a long, brown coat – and noticed that this show, something called *Firefly*, was by the same guy who created *Buffy*. I was intrigued. However, it seemed different. A western in space? As I do with many shows, I didn't watch it when it first aired, waiting instead until a friend or a good review recommended it to me. Sadly, I didn't have the luxury of time to discover it that I had with *Buffy*. It was canceled shortly after it began. I forgot about the show. Years passed, and while I was still a fan of the *Buffy*verse, I wasn't a Joss fan.

Not yet.

Looking back, it's interesting how reluctant I was to watch *Buffy* in the first place. For the record, I didn't watch *The X-Files* when it first aired either. Both were shows that should've been right up my geeky alley, especially considering the fact that I grew up reading Ray Bradbury, watching *Star Trek* and *Star Trek: The Next Generation* and writing my own *TNG* scripts in a spiral notebook. I even sent a petition on loose-leaf with 50 signatures on it to Barry Diller at FOX when I was ten years old, because I'd heard that *Alien Nation* was being canceled. However, something shifted as I entered my teens and early twenties; something that I wasn't conscious of at the time, but seems crystal-clear to me now.

I was trying to *not* be a geek.

Growing up an overweight Hispanic girl on Long Island, I already had several things working against me. Whereas I spent my elementary school years in Queens, surrounded by Hispanics to the point that it was the norm, there were far fewer when I moved to Elmont, NY. While my junior high and high school had a high minority population – in fact, it was 51% "minority" – they were Black (lots of Haitians and Jamaicans) or Indian. There were Hispanics, of course, but I wasn't *surrounded* the way I'd been in elementary school, and so I spoke less and less Spanish. Being overweighis never a good thing, especially when you're young. I was called "Hungry, Hungry Hippo" on occasion, and I have a vivid memory of a boy named Anthony throwing calculators and pencils at me in my 8th grade math class. There was also the fact that I was a Smart Girl which, when you're in middle school or junior high, you try to hide so as not to risk being thought of as a know-it-all. Even when you start asserting yourself in high school, class discussions are generally dominated by the boys who insist on rambling on and on about their opinions even when you know they didn't do the reading assignment the night before.

So, I was a smart Hispanic fat girl. That's already a recipe for social disaster, and I think that in my attempts to fit in, as is the way of many teenagers, I tried to steer clear of things that would make me even more of an outcast. Once *Star Trek: The Next Generation* went off the air, I didn't watch *Deep Space Nine* or *Voyager*, turning instead to shows like *Beverly Hills, 90210* or *Melrose Place*. I think the only semi-fantasy show I allowed myself was *Lois & Clark: The New Adventures of Superman,* and that's because Dean Cain was just undeniably hot. I tried wearing trendier clothing, though I was never really good at that. I tried wearing make-up, though I was never really good at that, either. I had lots of friends in high school, but I was always on the fringes of every clique, never in the thick of one. Despite my not being good at being trendy, or not going to any high school parties that weren't all-girl slumber parties, I was also denying myself the kinds of stories that made me happy, because I didn't want to seem different. So, even when I was amongst geeks, I tried to look like I thought that one kid's wizard and dragon shirt was stupid (even though I kinda thought it was cool); or I'd not admit that I really wanted to keep playing this new role-playing game I was taught, called *Vampire: The Masquerade,* even as the other geeks were ready to call it a night. My friend, Heather, would draw characters from *X-Men*, and I would admire her artistic talent without daring to ask too much about the stories or the characters, because I didn't want to be one of Those People. Again, it wasn't a conscious decision, but when I think about it now, I remember feeling that in the pit of my stomach. The feeling that I shouldn't let myself enjoy that kind of thing. Not if I want to be "normal."

And so I think my reluctance to watch *Buffy* was a holdover from that. I didn't want to watch a show about vampires, because then I'd be one of those people who watches shows about vampires.

One of the things that made *Buffy* special, though, was that it was a geeky show with a non-geek at its center. Buffy was cool. She'd been a cheerleader. She was gorgeous. If she weren't the Slayer, she would've been the most popular girl in school (sorry, Cordelia!). Buffy made it okay for the geeky and the non-geeky to blend. Buffy introduced me to the idea that a girl could be cool *and* be into vampires. Hell, Buffy *dated* vampires. Twice! But more importantly, as cool as Buffy was, she had friends like Willow and Xander – who themselves were social misfits, but were kind to her, and so she repaid their kindness with kindness. Buffy, unlike Cordelia, never acted like social standing was more important than having quality people in your life. Buffy showed that being cool means being inclusive.

In 2004, as I was preparing to celebrate my 26th birthday, I met my friend Adam, who made the mistake of introducing me to comics (where had they *been* all my life?!) as well as all the *Star Trek* I'd missed since *TNG* (why did no one tell me that *Deep Space Nine* was so awesome?!). He was also a fan of the *Buffy*verse, and like me, had never seen that *Firefly* show. So he put it on his Netflix queue, and we watched it. And we were both blown away. Neither of us could believe that a show this creative, well-written and well-acted had been canceled! He bought me the *Firefly* DVD boxed set for my birthday, and we watched it all the time. When *Serenity* came out in 2005, we each went to see it multiple times, making it a point to bring newbies with us each time.

And is it any wonder I fell so hard for this show? If *Buffy* impressed me, because it was a show that was, in part, about embracing diversity, *Firefly* sparked my imagination, because it was a show *about* the misfits and outcasts. It was entirely devoted to a spaceship that housed fugitives, war veterans on the losing side of history, a prostitute, a girl who is as passionate about machines as she is about men, a mentally ill girl, and a priest with a questionable past. And you *believed* that this Amazonian looking woman and this slightly skittish, dorky pilot would totally be in love, despite people not "getting them" at first glance, because *Firefly* gave us a world in which even outcasts could get their due and find happiness. And did I mention that there were two black leads, one of whom was a Hispanic woman? Did I also mention that the characters spoke English and Chinese, and that the design of the show was influenced by myriad cultures? It was a show about out-siders, for outsiders. So, if *Buffy* planted the seeds of my geek resurgence, *Firefly* watered them.

And then, there's *Dr. Horrible's Sing-Along Blog*, and here is where my admiration for Joss the man begins.

*Dr. Horrible* was born out of protest, as Joss came up with the idea dur-ing the most recent Writers Guild of America strike. As a writer myself, I sympathized with the writers' demands, and did what I could to support the effort. After all, it's always annoyed me that writers seem to be the red-headed stepchildren in Hollywood. If studio executives are the administra-tion, and actors and directors are the jocks and cheerleaders, writers are the geeky kids that no one wants to hang out with. It's an acceptable joke that no one really cares what the writers have to say, that their stories are going to be ruined or changed by higher-ups anyway, that they're the bottom of the food chain. Why was that the case, when without them Hollywood would have no stories to tell; no productions in which to include actors, directors, crew? So I bombarded everyone I know with emails asking them to write to television executives and advertisers. I covered the strike on my blog, and I took to the streets with the Writers Guild of America in NYC, handing out flyers to passersby asking them to support the cause. When I heard a couple of weeks later that Joss Whedon, the man that had created three shows I really loved, had created a new project for the web – pretty much to show the television industry that they could be circumvented and that people would watch anyway – I was so excited! And when I saw the finished product, I was floored, both by the quality of the product itself and by its subsequent success. I thought Neil Patrick Harris was amazing, and I was introduced to an actress I'd never heard of named Felicia Day, who has since become one of my heroines. And who knew Nathan Fillion, the hot guy in the brown coat from *Firefly*, could sing?

But more than anything else, I was impressed by the writing, the music and the idea that a villain could tell his story without judgment. As usual, Joss was going deeper than anyone else would, all in the name of giving voice to a misfit, an outcast. The entire project was a statement against the admin-istration for catering to the jocks and cheerleaders without giving the geeky kids their due. It was astonishing. It was inspiring.

While following news about his projects and the strike, I was aware that Joss was a huge supporter of an organization called Equality Now, a not-for-profit that exists to raise awareness and fight against inequality and oppres-sion of women in all its forms. Joss's support of an organization like that came as no surprise. After all, he was already known for creating powerful roles for women, and surely a creator like that *must* think highly of women in order to write them so well. What I didn't know was just how deeply committed he is, and what I loved most was that he worked to inspire his fans to action. It wasn't enough to just throw money at the organization, or do the odd charity event, but he would post blogs on Whedonesque, the popular Whedon fandom blog, encouraging his fans to take action; posts like the one entitled "Let's Watch a Girl Get Beaten to Death," in which he describes the beating ("honor killing") of a young woman named Dua Khalil which was subsequently filmed on several camera phones for posterity, and eventually aired on CNN. In that post, after expressing his horror and examining why the entire world might believe it okay to think women are inferior, he passionately tells readers to do something. Anything. Not just for the cause of women, but for any cause.

And this is where the power of Joss Whedon truly lies. His body of work seems entirely about inclusion, about giving minorities, misfits and outcasts of all stripes a voice. Hell, even *Alien Resurrection* asks us to sympathize with a heroine who is now part alien, forcing us to re-think our feelings about The Enemy. And, of course, he was asked to write a powerful, complex female lead. By giving minorities, misfits, and outcasts a voice, Joss shows us that they *matter*. And by showing us that they matter, he allows them to think the most preposterous thought of all: that they can do anything.

And so, they do.

Whedon fans don't just mobilize to bring attention to canceled TV series, though it was their enthusiastic DVD purchases and campaigning that encouraged Universal Studios to finance the *Serenity* movie. They mobilize to change the world.

Joss's "Let's Watch a Girl..." post inspired a fan-edited anthology called *Nothing But Red*, which includes fiction and non-fiction contributions, and the proceeds of which go to support Equality Now. His efforts for the organization also inspired "Can't Stop the Serenity" screenings for Equality Now all across the country. Whedon fans make Jayne hats to raise funds. They have *Buffy* theme parties. They promote awareness. They do something. They do a lot of little somethings, and it all adds up to a large impact in the name of making the world safe for difference. They do it, because minorities, misfits, and outcasts matter, and it isn't enough for men like Joss to stand up for us. We have to stand up for ourselves.

And so Joss the Man is more important than any one thing he's created. Don't get me wrong. Joss is an amazing storyteller, and I could go on and on about how each of his works is full of creative merit, about how he's a genius, about how brilliant an idea it was to make the commentary track on the *Dr. Horrible* DVD a *whole other musical!* But the truth is, Joss is more important than his 'verse. It's important that he, as a creator, exists in Hollywood, not only to create characters and stories that inspire us, but to inspire us through his own actions. He's a hell of a writer, but he's an even better human being.

So I'd decided to go to that *Dollhouse* event because I was curious about his new show, but as I approached Joss's signing table, all I could think was how grateful I was that he, as a person, existed. Grateful, because as long as there are people like him in television and film, there's hope. Hope that there is at least one person in the craziness of Hollywood who is speaking for me, and for all the other people who, for whatever reason, don't quite fit. There is at least one person who genuinely values the stories and views of the minorities, the misfits, the outcasts, not because they're *en vogue*, and not as a punchline, but because they matter. That there is someone who sees that without those stories and views, the television landscape would be incomplete. And so I told him all of this in a nervous flood of words. That I respected him not only for his writing talent, which I hope to emulate, but that I admire him as a human being, and that I love how he inspires action from his fans by his own example. He blushed to the tops of his ears, stammered a little, and said, "Wow... Thank you... now I'm really shy!"

Then I asked Joss a very, very important question: *Is your brother Zack single?*

It was the *Commentary! The Musical* rap that piqued my interest. Then I Google searched for a photo and discovered that Zack Whedon's actually pretty damn cute. He's my age, a writer on *Fringe* and works in comics? A crush was born.

Anyway, Joss chuckled, then looked confused, then answered "Well... he does have a girlfriend... [conspiratorially] *but he hasn't popped the question yet, so ...*"

I said, "Well, you tell him that there's someone who's fallen in love with him entirely because of the rap song he does in *Commentary! The Musical.*"

And Joss said, "I *know*! It was *me*!"

So not only is Joss Whedon a gifted writer who has created worlds full of amazing stories and brilliant characters; not only is he someone who works to provide a voice for the voiceless; but he is also someone who will pimp out his own brother just to make someone feel good.

Now *that* is a quality human being.

# Let's Go to Work

**Catherynne M. Valente** is the author of over a dozen works of fiction and poetry, including *Palimpsest*, the *Orphan's Tales* series, *The Habitation of the Blessed* and *The Girl Who Circumnavigated Fairyland in a Ship of Own Making*. She is the winner of the Tiptree Award, the Andre Norton Award, the Mythopoeic Award, the Lambda Award, the Rhysling Award and the Million Writers Award. She was a finalist for the World Fantasy Award in 2007 and 2009, and the Locus and Hugo Awards in 2010. She lives on an island off the coast of Maine with her partner, two dogs and an enormous cat.

These days, it's almost a Cartesian axiom: I am a geeky postmodern girl, therefore I love *Buffy the Vampire Slayer*.

Of course I loved *Buffy*. She's only a couple of years younger than I am (depending on the continuity) and she had this whole high school experience that I had, too, though with fewer vampires. Not none – no one gets through life without falling under the spell of someone who just needs you to feed themselves. No one gets out of this fully sanguinated. But I had a close-knit circle that frayed as age and culture clash took hold, a feeling of standing on the brink of something, of trying so hard to hold on to everything, always, in the terribly bright California sun. I have always been baffled at people's attachment to *Sex in the City*, the endless are you a Carrie or a Miranda – but I was so terribly attached, and I can tell you without shame that I was a Willow, and for awhile, in the long, dreamlike desert between the end of college and the beginning of life, I had demons, and I had trials, and I had *Buffy*.

But for all that, I am not here to talk to you about that show. The fact is, I was just off the bubble of being able to watch the show in high school, with a high schooler's concerns and fears. *Buffy* was always cloaked in this strange golden nostalgia for a youth I almost but didn't quite have, for battles that seemed easy to call, easy to pick out the big bads, easy to root for the blonde in the middle of all those storms. Buffy, even when she goes to college, is a show for the young, the being educated, not the 20-something soul cast ashore on the crags of jobs and partners and compromises and the endless bleeding out of adult life. I love Buffy – but I'm not her. She was Chosen, she was special, no matter where she went and who she became when the camera was off, she was always that beautiful paladin girl standing in the light, with a mission and power that she only ever really lost for one episode. Instead, I want to talk about *Angel*.

Not the character. I never cared much for him – his story was always one of masculinity misused and misruled, a person who could never wholly be a person, older than most of the others, but naive and broad-chested and thick-skulled as any child learning how to be a man. I want to talk about the show, which was also about all those things, so terribly, terribly concerned with masculinity, in an explicit way few other television shows really are, the male animus played out in Wesley, Angel, Lorne, Spike. But sometime around Season Four, Angel finally hit on a metaphor as powerful as High School is Hell had been for Buffy. It wasn't as easy a metaphor, but for those of us watching as lost 20-somethings, it hit home with a kind of echoing din.

Can you work for the devil and still be righteous?

The most obvious iteration of this idea arrived in the form of Wolfram and Hart, and Our Heroes taking the reins of that wicked corporation to change it from the inside – as all corrupted folk once intended. I don't think we were ever meant to believe they could; it's only that the classic Faustian bargain requires believing you can control the worse side of your own nature and that of the infernal machines, that you can keep your soul and still dance with the devil. But it's there in the Jasmine arc, too, where the overt comparison to organized religion asks the question with a slightly different twist: if dancing with the devil brings happiness, does it matter that it's the devil doing that quick step? And maybe it's there throughout the whole series – after all, Angel is the devil, and all these people come to work for him, and are corrupted to his world in their turn, becoming other than they were, for better and worse. Corruption is sometimes just change. And sometimes it means having your whole body hollowed out and replaced with something terrible, as seemed to be the case with the women of *Angel*, over and over again.

The question is deathly important in this culture that says: you're worthless if you don't make money, but making the kind of money that makes you not-worthless usually means doing some pretty dire things for faceless entities out of the dark, hungry systems with a million mouths, petty awful hells that would like to believe themselves the whole earth. In high school, it's easy to say: that one is a demon and demons will never, ever be any good. That one is a vampire who only wants me for my body. But in the working world, everything is harder to see. That one will use me for the blood and sweat I can offer, but will give measure in return. This one is soulless and cruel and will destroy me, but I was assigned to his project by HR so what the hell am I supposed to do about it? The office is hell – but it's the hell you know, a hell that feeds and clothes you, a hell that becomes day by day indistinguishable from a pleasant middle class living. And for awhile, before it got cancelled, *Angel* was about how to navigate that and still be a righteous man. And yes – I say man, because to be a woman on *Angel* was a wholly different narrative ribbon, from the first episode when a blonde damsel had to be saved to erase the taste of *Buffy* from our mouths. Women were lost, like Fred, or Girl Fridays, like Cordy, fairy tale girls, twisted and set on their ears, yes, but still damsels in whatever dress. However snarky Cordelia was or smart Fred might be, they all needed to be saved, and they all ended up as vessels for higher and genderless powers – in part because the virtues and problems in traditional masculinity and/ or its deconstruction shows up most clearly when placed beside archetypal female behavior. Strong, yes. Also dead. And their paladins forever mourning them. *Buffy* and *Angel* were always mirrors this way, the one concerned with a feminine universe constantly besieged with sexually coded, penetrative or patriarchal (vampire or Watcher) threats, the other concerned with a masculine universe menaced with the loss of physical and spiritual integrity – to be invaded by the spirit of another, to lose the cohesion of the body or the mind.

And of course, in that binaried world of traditional gender roles, the Office is the purview of the Most Male, the jungle where he competes (no accident, I think, that Spike appeared at the same time, to be the younger, ambitious *All About Eve* sort of riposte to Angel's old man's *richesse*) for dominance and mates, where he does or does not become alpha. And that is hell, too. To become king of it, or to escape, or to never have played the game – Angel puts up answers to all of these: Angel, the collaborator, Spike, the iconoclast, Wesley, the lover and intellectual, and Lorne who just chose to play his own field.

But back in the real world, there are office girls, too, trying to figure out what it means to be locked into a palace of glass and metal every day, what that means for them, trying to sort out their own story in all those narratives meant for men. And I was like that, trying to decide whether to be an artist or to be safe, if I could be safe and still be whole, be myself. *Angel* became wholly its own show as *Buffy* waned, and for viewers of my age, high school slipped further and further away, becoming like a fairy tale, a collection of stories that everyone more or less shares, but no longer as vital and present as the decisions you make in your 20s that affect everything else you will become. As I have done all my life, I looked at male archetypes and saw myself, needing the lessons that in previous generations only men were allowed to learn.

And what was *Angel*'s answer to all this? I'm not sure it ever got to give one, given its cancellation. You could call it nihilistic and not go wrong: yes, you'll lose your soul and destroy what you love, but you can go down swinging. Sometimes the networks will swing their own axe, and all you can do is stand tall and beautiful as they cut you down. But I prefer to see it as a message of integration: Illyria could merge with Fred enough to love and grieve,

Spike and Angel could redeem their pathological champion complex with regards to Buffy, chasing her blonde ponytail through a dark club and never catching her – as if they could ever catch her. Wesley could be loved by the ghost of Fred in just as strange and controlling a way as he loved her. Everyone gets what they want. Everyone dies. Everyone is lost, everyone is found. Yes, the world is always bigger than you, hell is always stronger. HR will assign you demons and your 401k is run by vampires. All these things are true just as it is true that high school is hell. But you still have to live in that world, every day. You never graduate. The big snake and the prom were the easy parts. You must try to be a champion, though you'll never really manage it – that terrible, overused word – and never take the easy ways out constantly presented in the forms of Jasmine, Lilah and Lindsay, Darla, the ever-present Shanshu prophecy, promising a kind of reason and folkloric logic that the real world just never plays out: be good enough and you get your reward. In the end, *Angel* said gently: *kids, it just ain't so.*

And me? Well, *Angel* ended, *Firefly* got cancelled, the war started just about the time when Buffy was telling us we were all Slayers, and I dropped out of grad school. I couldn't find a job even in hell. But *Doctor Who* came back from the dead, and I moved to Japan, where I got lost for a few years, just like a certain waifish physicist I used to know. And just like her, I was saved by monsters – I started writing fairy tales and dark things on the walls of a cave, and eventually found the light again. But the funny thing is, there's never a point where I don't have to navigate the waters *Angel* was trying to chart – do I sell out when someone is buying, do I give up my soul and my voice for the chance at comfort, do I believe cynical old men when they tell me that this is the way the world is, and if I want to change it, I have to become part of the system first?

Or do I pick up a sword and head out to a dark alley where a hopeless battle awaits – hopeless, but forever worth fighting?

# Something to Sing About

**Jenn Reese** is a writer, martial artist and geek. Her first novel, *Jade Tiger*, is an action-adventure kung fu romance... with tigers. (And a pretty big homage to Bruce Lee.) Her next book, forthcoming from Candlewick in 2012, begins an action-adventure series for kids set in a future where humans have bioengineered themselves into mythological creatures. It includes plenty of fight scenes and lots of weapons... none of which are named "Mr. Pointy."

I've never written a personal essay or memoir before. Frankly, I find the concept more than a little terrifying. Expose my inner self for strangers? Publicly admit weakness? Talk about all the powerful ways in which *Buffy the Vampire Slayer* – a mere TV show! – has affected my life?

Yet... a statue of "Buffy Summers: End of Days" sits on my desk. She's wielding her axe from "Chosen," ready to slay whatever needs to be slain. A constant challenge for me to do the same.

As I stare at my computer and try to muster my strength, I can hear her voice in my head. "Seize the moment," she says, echoing her words to Willow in the pilot episode, "because tomorrow, you might be dead."

Well, here I go – seizing away.

> "Shoot me. Stuff me. Mount me."
>
> —Xander, "The Pack"

I started watching *Buffy the Vampire Slayer* in its first season, but I didn't fall in love until episode six, "The Pack." When Xander is possessed by an evil hyena spirit, he's not the goofy, affable dork we'd come to know and love. He's dangerous. He's cruel. He not only wants to hurt his friends, he revels in it.

Xander speaks some horrible truths to Buffy and Willow – truths completely unfiltered by kindness, friendship or love. The sort of things we wouldn't say to our worst enemies, let alone the members of our created family. But that's not the part that won me over.

After the hyena spirit is gone, Xander tells his friends that he can't remember anything about the experience. And that's how most TV shows would end. Cue knowing look between Buffy and Willow. Cue laugh track.

Cue Xander saying, "What? What did I do?" Roll credits.

But Joss Whedon is no ordinary writer, and *Buffy* was no ordinary show. He doesn't give Xander the easy out. He doesn't wipe away the memory. Xander has to soldier on with the knowledge of what he did and what he said for the rest of his life. (Or, at least, for six more seasons and a couple of comic books.)

Real life is like that, too. None of us have the gift of selective memory loss. Our tragedies and failures are ours to keep.

Mistakes, sadness, and regret litter the lives of Whedon's characters, just as they litter our own. But... are they really litter? Where would we be without those missteps, without the remembered pain of accidentally hurting ourselves and others? Without heartbreak? Would we have changed at all during our lives? Would we have learned anything?

One thing's for sure – we'd probably be in love with a very different, far inferior TV show.

> "Now this is not going to be pretty. We're talking violence, strong language, adult content..."
> —Buffy, "Welcome to the Hellmouth"

From 1997 to 2003, while Buffy and the Scooby Gang were going through their journey, I was going through my own. When *Buffy* first aired, I lived in Maryland with my first husband, two cats and a job that didn't inspire me. I had no sense of what I wanted from my life, except that I wanted something more. Something different. *Anything* different.

I started to write short stories. Stories with mythological creatures and aliens and fantastical technology. They were mostly terrible, but I managed to sell a few. In 1999, I got accepted to the six-week Clarion Writers' Workshop in East Lansing, Michigan. While Buffy and her pals were blowing up Sunnydale High, I was heading to an experience that, as I wrote in my journal at the time, I had simple hopes for. I just wanted it to change my life.

While I was at Clarion, the network finally aired episode eighteen of Season Three, "Earshot," which it had previously pulled from the lineup because of the Columbine High School Massacre. One of my Clarion classmates bought a VCR and taped the show so we could all gather around a tiny, 13-inch TV and watch it together. We bonded over *Buffy* that night, and over the echoes of Columbine's heartache. It's one of my fondest memories of the six weeks at the workshop.

> "This is just too much. I mean, yesterday my life's like, "Uh-oh, pop quiz." Today it's "Rain of toads.""
> —Xander, "The Harvest"

A few months after Clarion, I got my wish for a changed life – just not in any of the ways I'd expected. I asked my husband for a divorce. I packed up my cat and my computer and prepared to drive across the country to Los Angeles, where my younger brother had promised me floor space until I could find a job and a place to live. (Unbeknownst to me, he didn't think I'd make it in LA. I've been here over ten years, and he probably still doesn't think I will.)

But if we've learned one thing from watching *Buffy*, we've learned that there's no limit to the obstacles Whedon and his writers will throw in Buffy's way. Or, you know. At her head.

I was supposed to leave for the west coast on the auspicious 9/9/1999. I had a lump removed from my breast instead. It was benign, but try telling that to my terrified, lonely self as I stood outside the doctor's office after the procedure, leaned against a tree in the parking lot, and sobbed.

Big adventures are like that. Ups to downs, confusion to confidence, "all is lost" to "happily ever after." Or, in the case of Buffy's universe, "Happily ever... Oh my god, is that a demon?"

I made it to LA. I slept on a hardwood floor for five weeks, got a job at a dot com before the bubble burst, lived on my own for the first time in my life, had my car stolen, earned some promotions, got laid off and started studying martial arts. I wrote a screenplay, more short stories and my first novel. I "took a meeting" in Hollywood. I ghost wrote a few nonfiction books. I made friends. I made a home.

Through it all, *Buffy* was my favorite show. It was one of the only real constants in a life full of new jobs, new relationships and an evolving sense of self. If our lives have soundtracks, then Buffy was mine. When I made life-changing decisions or accepted new challenges, *Buffy the Vampire Slayer* was in the background, singing about courage and heroes, about failure and loss and the power of friends.

I sometimes wonder: how would my life be different if I'd been obsessed with a different show during such a tumultuous time in my life? If I'd fallen in love with *Ally McBeal*, would I have ever found the courage to leave Maryland in the first place? If I'd become obsessed with *Dawson's Creek*, would I be *the same person I am today?*

"This is my lucky stake... I call it Mr. Pointy."
—Kendra, "Becoming (Part I)"

I'd always enjoyed martial arts movies from a distance, and during *Buffy's* TV run, I decided to give kung fu a try. Did this decision have anything to do with *Buffy?* Maybe, maybe not. But I can't help thinking that seeing a petite blonde girl kick ass every week had more than a little influence on this sudden departure from my sedentary lifestyle. I mean there she was – a tiny slip of a girl – able to defend herself, defend her friends, and save the world on a regular basis.

I didn't find a martial arts school in Maryland, and then my life went all Hellmouth on me. It wasn't until 2001, newly laid off from my dot com job in Los Angeles, that I decided it was time.

I spent five years at that first school, until the aura of misogyny became too much. That was four and half years too many. When I finally decided to leave, I spent months searching for a new school. And hey, guess what? I found a whole heap more misogyny. Where was my Watcher with private lessons and an arsenal of weapons to teach me?

At one school, I waited for ten minutes for the head instructor to get off the phone with his girlfriend before he deigned to speak with me. I ran through my questions, including my favorite: "How many women train here?"

"None," he told me. "Women don't really like martial arts."

But the real kicker? He was teaching Wing Chun, a martial art commonly believed to have been created by a woman, for women.

Seriously. That actually happened. That man actually said those words in a non-ironic way, as if we both lived in a universe where they made sense.

I guess he never watched *Buffy* – never saw the Slayer sweat as she trained with Giles, never saw her take on her enemies with wary confidence, never saw the transcendent glow of a woman with power. Women don't just belong in the world of martial arts, they *thrive* in it.

Perhaps you won't be surprised to learn that I didn't sign up for Wing Chun. I kept looking and, a few weeks later, found my dream school: White Lotus Kung Fu. The head instructor? The most bad-ass (and graceful and kind and freakin' awesome) woman you will ever meet.

Last year, I started learning the spear. I named mine Mr. Pointy.

**"She saved the world. A lot."**
                                          —Buffy's headstone, "The Gift"


When *Buffy the Vampire Slayer* ended in 2003, I mourned. I wrote an impassioned journal entry full of words like "kick-ass" and "glorious" and "hope." I talked about how much I've learned from Joss Whedon and *Buffy* in terms of character, plot and metaphor. I thanked everyone involved in the show, and I said "good-bye to one of my closest friends."

How naive.

Characters like Buffy don't disappear just because their TV show ends. They transform into something even greater. They become *icons*.

The episodes or snippets of dialogue you don't like fade away. The show becomes distilled, filtered through your memory, until only the most important, most powerful aspects remain.

In my own life, *Buffy's* influence had barely been tapped by the time the show ended. I had no idea how much I'd need it in the years that followed.

"God, why do my all shirts have to have stupid things on them?"
—Willow, "The Body"

My second husband and I had spent almost 18 grueling hours moving into our new apartment. All we'd managed to do was put the bed frame together before we'd collapsed, two exhausted people surrounded by an landscape of boxes with cryptic labels such as "Bedroom, maybe" and "Open third."

The phone rang at 7am. I think I answered it. Or maybe he did. Was it his cell? I'll never remember. But the call itself, I'll never forget. Just a few Los Angeles towns away, my husband's brother had shot himself. Shot himself in his own backyard, while just a few feet away, his pregnant wife made their morning coffee in the kitchen.

We were supposed to meet the rest of the family at the hospital. No one said aloud that he was going to die... but no one thought he was going to live.

When something horrific happens and you're lucky, your brain goes into emergency mode. While some deep-down part of you is shrieking and wailing and screaming and dissolving into tears of anger and anguish, the surface part is concerned with more practical matters. The surface part tries to find clothes.

I tore into the boxes, ripping cardboard and flinging the pieces to the floor. I cursed my hasty labeling system. Were his shirts in "Bedroom #6" or "Big closet"? And where the hell were *my* clothes? We couldn't wear jeans to the hospital... or could we? He found a shirt first and I dismissed it. We needed to look like somber, responsible adults. Now was not the time for oranges or yellows, for shirts with slogans or geeky references or faded stains.

As we accomplished one step, we moved on to the next. *Find clothes. Dress. Brush teeth. Grab wallet. Find shoes. Tie shoes. Comb hair. Find tissues for the drive.*

In the middle of the chaos, there was also a memory. Willow trying to find her purple sweater, Anya blunt and clueless, Xander angry at the world, at the wall, at death itself.

"The Body" makes me sob. I cried the first time I watched it, from the very beginning when Buffy shakes her mother's body, calls her name, can't wake her. If I happen upon the episode while channel surfing, even for just a second, I become transfixed all over again, thumb poised on the remote but incapable of changing the channel.

On that morning, October 7th, 2003, I was so grateful for "The Body." I was grateful for the assurance that, no matter how I was reacting to the shooting – to the suicide – it was okay. It was normal. It was well within the acceptable parameters of grief and shock and awkwardness. In the midst of everything, I wasted no emotional energy on self recrimination. That was an incredible gift on such a terrible day.

My brother-in-law died before we got to the hospital. In true bizarre Whedon form, the first person I called was the editor who was waiting for short story revisions for an upcoming publication. I left a message on his machine full of tears and "I need more time. He shot himself. I haven't finished the edits."

In the episode, Anya said, "Am I supposed to be changing my clothes a lot? Is that the helpful thing to do?"

The answer is yes. Because there is no rhyme or reason or logic or common sense in those moments. There's only humanity – confused, sad, angry humanity.

(These are difficult things for me to write about. Scary things. Dark things. But I'm writing about *Buffy*. What did you expect?)

> Cordelia: "Does looking at guns make you want to have sex?"
> Xander: "I'm 17. Looking at linoleum makes me want to have sex."
> —"Innocence"

I don't have anything to say about this quote, I just thought you might enjoy a laugh right about now. And besides, making us laugh – even when we're sad, even when we've just plunged a sword into the heart of our beloved and condemned him to an eternity of hell – is kind of what Joss Whedon does best.

> "Nothing here is real, nothing here is right."
> —Buffy, "Once More With Feeling"

Remember that whole regret and sadness thing I mentioned earlier? How it makes us interesting, more well-rounded people capable of learning and growing and becoming better humans?

Well sometimes, it just sucks.

A year after my brother-in-law's suicide, my second marriage began to crumble. I found myself smothered in regret, pinned to my couch by self-loathing and more than one pint of Ben & Jerry's ice cream. It was a dark time for me, my first real bout with depression. I pulled away from my friends, retreated into my own personal Hell, and fell into a deep pit of despair.

I didn't know what depression was. Not really. Sure, I'd had my fair share of bad days, but I could usually point to a reason, a situation, an excuse. This time, I had nothing. All I knew was that the sofa had its own sort of gravitational pull, and that I was helpless against it. For weeks, I did nothing but cry, and lie there, and wonder what the hell had happened to me. I longed for that person I used be, that person I used to love.

The best way to end this tale of misery and woe is to say that the "Once More With Feeling," the musical at the heart of *Buffy* Season Six, rescued me from hell. That Buffy's depression in that episode taught me about my own. That I learned to talk to my friends again, to get help, to forgive myself.

But that sort of pat ending isn't good enough for Joss Whedon, and it's certainly not good enough for real life. Buffy continued to punish herself the rest of the season, and I stayed on the couch.

Except... somewhere out there, someone understood. No one could write those songs, those lyrics, without truly knowing what it was like. "Once More With Feeling" is full of apathy, of despair, of Buffy's desperate longing to once again be the person she was. "I can't even see if this is really me ..."

Did she say that, or did I?

At the end of Season Two's "When She Was Bad," Buffy feels terrible about acting like a "B-I-T-C-H" and putting her friends in danger. She jokes about spending the rest of her life inside a cave rather than facing them. In an effort to comfort her, Giles says, "Believe me, that was hardly the worst mistake you'll ever make."

I made it out of the pit eventually, and if I ever fall back in, *Buffy* will still be there for me.

> "Make your choice. Are you ready to be strong?"
> —Buffy, "Chosen"

When I first started watching *Buffy*, I identified with Willow. I, too, was fashion-challenged, insecure, and more at home with my computer than other people. Willow was my hero.

Years passed, chaos ensued. I went on big adventures, faced new challenges, failed frequently, and occasionally did a little demon-slaying of my own. I emerged... Buffy. (Without the super strength, fashion sense, or destructive taste in boys, natch.)

I have five *Buffy the Vampire Slayer* statues created by Tooned Up Television, but only "Buffy Summers: End of Days" gets to sit on my desk. I particularly love the style in which she was sculpted. She's not modeled after the actor; she reflects an idealized cartoon version of the role itself. I look at the statue and see Buffy Summers, not Sarah Michelle Gellar. I see a hero. I see an archetype.

I can't imagine any better inspiration for facing my fears, spanking my inner moppet, and squaring off against the Big Bad. (Or in this case, against my dread of writing a personal essay.)

I love *Buffy the Vampire Slayer,* and in my own way, I love Joss Whedon for creating it.

Nowadays, I spend my time writing novels about brave, spirited women and girls who want to save the world. They're stories I believe in. Stories that, in my opinion, we will never have enough of.

Maybe this is one of those stories, too.

# Malcom Reynolds, the Myth of the West, and Me

**Emma Bull** is best known as the author of *War for the Oaks*, one of the earliest Urban Fantasy novels. Her works have been nominated for Hugo, Nebula, and World Fantasy Awards. A former member of the folk-goth group the Flash Girls and the rock-funk group Cats Laughing, and a long-time member of the Scribblies writing group, she has taught at Clarion West and the Pima Writer's Workshop. She is also one of the producers of *Shadow Unit*, a collaborative online fiction project of a television series that never existed. She lives in Arizona with her husband, Will Shetterly.

I grew up in the golden age of the TV Western. My family watched *Maverick* and *Paladin, Gunsmoke, Rawhide, Death Valley Days* and *Bonanza*. I remember, in a fuzzy way, *Batt Masterson* and *The Life and Legend of Wyatt Earp*. The shows I thought of as *my* Westerns began to show up in the mid-60s: *The Virginian, The Big Valley, The Wild Wild West* and half a decade later, *Alias Smith and Jones*.

I'd always loved science fiction, too. *Supercar* and *Fireball XL5* on television, *Mystery in Space* comic books, Andre Norton's *Daybreak 2250 AD* bought from the Scholastic Book Service flyer in school. A few years later, I appropriated my brother's copy of Keith Laumer's *Galactic Odyssey*. (He retaliated by disappearing my copy of Peter Beagle's *I See By My Outfit*.)

But I didn't watch the original *Star Trek* on TV. By that time, I knew I wasn't a Federation kind of girl. I was a child of the 60s: anti-establishment, anti-hierarchy, and anti-military, and Romanticism was my philosophy and my aesthetic. I preferred tortured but indomitable loner protagonists facing impossible odds – brave heroes who, all alone, changed the world. I wasn't interested in people who wore uniforms, followed orders, and answered to a giant intergalactic government.

When I was doing research for my novel *Territory*, a fantasy Western about the Matter of Tombstone, I discovered Old West reenactment. Adults could dress up and play cowboy? It took me less time to realize I'd missed my Western heroes than it did to say, "Count me in."

I learned the Romantic ideal of the lone hero was a staple of a lot of cowboy reenactors and Old West history buffs. That, they said, was how the West was won – with rugged individualism and self-reliance. Those who settled the American frontier were beholden to no one.

Malcom Reynolds, captain-owner of the Firefly-class ship *Serenity*, would have agreed. Because, really, he was as dumb as I was – at least at the beginning.

Listen to him talking his old army buddy Zoe into joining his then-nonexistent crew in "Out of Gas":

> **Mal:** Try to see past what she is, and on to what she can be.
> **Zoe:** What's that, sir?
> **Mal:** Freedom, is what.
> **Zoe:** I meant, what's that?
> **Mal:** Oh. Yeah, just step around that. I think something must have been living in here. Tell you, Zoe, we get a mechanic, get her up and running again, hire a good pilot, maybe a cook – live like real people. Small crew, them as feel the need to be free. Take jobs as they come. Ain't never have to be under the heel of nobody ever again. No matter how long the arm of the Alliance might get, we'll just get ourselves a little further.

Oh, Mal, honey. You just keep telling yourself that.

When *Firefly* begins, Malcom Reynolds is hanging onto independence so hard his knuckles are white. In the opening scenes of "Serenity," the original pilot, he counts on God and the Independents' air support; if he and the rest of the ground troops in Serenity Valley can just hold on long enough, one or the other or both will turn the tide and scatter the Alliance forces.

Neither God nor the air strike comes through. And Malcom Reynolds loses his faith, in God and in humanity.

> **Kaylee:** He's nice.
> **Mal:** Don't go workin' too hard on that crush, mei-mei. Doc won't be with us for long.
> **Kaylee:** You're nice, too.
> **Mal:** No, I'm not. I'm a mean old man.

But the independence Mal is determined to rely on instead is a myth. Because the frontier – whether it's the Old American West or the Outer Planets – is the most communal of societies.

Few people set off alone into the wilderness. In wagon trains, in voyageurs' big canoes, in flocks of Mormon handcarts, they travel together to share work and protection. Once they reach the frontier, the new settlers need help with jobs too big for an individual: erecting buildings, clearing land, catching and corralling stock, digging for ore and processing it. They rely on others for tools and supplies they can't fashion themselves. And once they have whatever they came for, they need someone to trade or sell it to.

If nature or their fellow humans turn threatening, those pioneers have a better chance if they band together to resist the danger. But how do they know whom to trust?

Trust, it turns out, is a survival trait on the frontier. Those who reach out to the people around them to offer and request help, who trust their neighbors to watch their backs or their kids or their buckboard, are seen as trustworthy. Those who trust no one, on the other hand, are mistrusted in turn. Trust builds the bonds of community and extends family relationships into the ranks of one's acquaintances.

That trust is why reputation is such a precious commodity in frontier societies. The cowboy phrase is, "He's a good man to ride the river with." That means the person in question can be counted on to do what needs to be done in a crisis. Not that he's personally charming or likeable, mind you, or someone you'll go carousing with when you get the herd to town. But he'll save your life in a jam, and if you value that, you'll be just as prepared to save his.

That's the real Code of the West, right there: you step in and give aid when it's needed, because someday it could be you who needs it. In harsh country (which most of the American West could be when it felt like it) there was an assumed law of hospitality. If a household turned away a traveler requesting food, water and shelter, they could be condemning that traveler to death. So ranchers would harbor even known rustlers overnight; those who requested shelter knew better than to abuse the privilege when they had it.

Of course, some folks did abuse others' trust. The Bender family of Labette County, Kansas, bumped off at least 11 travelers and possibly as many as two dozen between 1872 and 1873 in their rough-and-ready inn. With a hammer. But you can't really expect serial killers to adhere to the social contract.

Humans are a sociable species; with a few noteworthy exceptions, we can't go without each other's company indefinitely. We'll pay for that company with a few restrictions on our independence, and the (mostly unspoken) obligation to step up when a neighbor or a stranger falls on hard times.

**Kaylee:** You *are* a nice man, Captain. Always lookin' after us. You just gotta have faith in people.

Mal has visions of living without obligations, of not needing other people. In his speech to Zoe, he admits to requiring a little assistance – a mechanic, a pilot, someone who doesn't suck at cooking – but he plans to make his relationship with them a purely financial one. The hired help. He's able to handwave his friendship and mutual assistance pact with Zoe, I suspect, because it's built on the template of army rank and soldiers' dependence on one another in wartime. She still calls him "sir," after all.

Compare the realities of life on the frontier with life on *Serenity*. Everyone on board relies on their fellow crew members' work and knowledge. Without Kaylee, *Serenity* doesn't fly. Without Wash, she *does* fly... but where, and how well, and does she arrive in one piece? Without Jayne, crew members might be picked off by hostile locals. (They might also be picked off by Jayne, but let's ignore that.) Without Mal, there's no work for the ship and crew. Without Zoe, there's no one to keep Mal from doing something even further beyond his abilities (not to mention the laws of probability) than usual.

*Serenity* is a trading ship. She needs customers, people to ship cargo, dealers in goods that are readily resalable on the Outer Planets, and even, sometimes, paying passengers. On the surface of it, those relationships are as manageable as Mal's platonic ideal of a crew: it's just money changing hands. But *Serenity* gets cargo and customers on the basis of her captain's reputation for success and honest dealing. Even smugglers prefer to get what they pay for, after all. As Badger says in the *Firefly* pilot: "Now you got yourself a ship and you're a captain. Only I think you're still a sergeant, see? Still a soldier. Man of honor in a den of thieves."

Badger's offended because Mal seems to think that makes him better than Badger. But that's exactly the quality that makes Mal the kind of captain Badger wants to hire. Adelai Niska is another customer who's less concerned about rates than about respect; in "The Train Job," he says, "Yes, good! You have reputation! Malcom Reynolds gets it done, is the talk."

Because Mal's self-image is of someone who stands apart from his community, he doesn't hesitate to take commissions from questionable types like Badger or outright psychos like Niska. It's not personal; it's just a job. He can take money from people who ignore the social contract without violating it himself. Right?

In "The Train Job," Mal runs smack up against that question. He can take the money or the high road, but not both. When he has to choose, he comes down on the side of the real code of the frontier: the expectation that those who can will help those in need.

That code is so much a part of the *Firefly* universe's frontier that *Serenity*'s crew counts on it in the pilot episode. They lure off an Alliance cruiser with a fake distress beacon, knowing the Alliance ship will place the rescue of stranded travelers above the capture of illegal salvagers.

As well they should. I frown on this bit of cunning from *Serenity*'s crew; too much of this, and ships might think twice before they follow a distress call. Mal gets the karmic backlash in "Out of Gas," however, when pirates follow *Serenity*'s distress beacon, intending to prey on a weakened ship and crew.

Because, again, not everyone obeys the frontier code of conduct. Just as the Old West had its killers and thieves, the Outer Planets have people who prey on the weak.

**Inara:** You're lost in the woods. We all are. Even the captain. The only difference is, he likes it that way.

Those people aren't always breaking the written law when they scorn the social code of the frontier. Rance Burgess, in "Heart of Gold," *is* the law in those parts, like the cattle barons who hired men to hang Ella Watson (better known as "Cattle Kate"). His relationships are purchased: his hired hands, the prostitute who's pregnant with his child, even the wife whose function is hostess and society accessory, not friend and helpmeet. He may surround himself with people, but he has no real ties to any of them, beyond the bonds of money. He is as self-reliant as Mal claims he wants to be.

Bounty hunter Jubal Early, in "Objects in Space," is another lawful man in violation of the unwritten laws. He's focused on his job – collecting River Tam – and everything, every *human*, who stands between him and her is just a problem to be dealt with. He brutalizes and terrorizes *Serenity*'s crew while maintaining a chilling emotional distance from them, and from his own actions. His preferred social environment is absolute zero and hard vacuum, metaphorically speaking, and his capacity for bonding with others was broken long before we meet him.

Those two characters fit the concept of "rugged individualist," though they're not quite what those who embrace the Old West myth have in mind. How does Mal's conduct compare to that kind of hard-headed self-reliance?

In the *Firefly* pilot, an Alliance agent sneaks on board *Serenity* to arrest Simon and River. An Alliance ship is on its way to intercept *Serenity* and take the Tams into custody, when the agent panics in a confrontation and accidentally shoots Kaylee.

Mal could surrender the Tams to the Alliance. He didn't know they were wanted when he took them aboard. If he hands them over, the Alliance will let *Serenity* and her crew go about their business. But Kaylee's gut-shot, and needs medical aid immediately – sooner than the Alliance ship will arrive. And Simon Tam is a trauma surgeon.

Kaylee's the second mechanic Mal has hired for *Serenity*; he can hire a third if this one dies. Once *Serenity* has been identified as carrying fugitives, the Alliance will never cease to stick its nose into Mal's business. A coldly rational man, one who values self-reliance and the freedom to do as he pleases, would hand Simon and River over to the authorities to protect that freedom.

Instead, Mal sacrifices it. He chooses to run from the Alliance and save Kaylee's life. It's not an automatic decision. He knows he's dooming himself and his ship to endless Alliance pursuit. But when he's forced to choose between the myth of the frontier and the reality of it, he chooses the reality. Those who can, help those who can't. That code of conduct turns strangers into families-of-choice whose members' well-being is everyone's first priority.

> **Simon:** Captain – Why'd you come back for us?
> **Mal:** You're on my crew.
> **Simon:** Yeah, but you don't even like me. Why'd you come back?
> **Mal:** You're on my crew. Why are we still talking about this?

In "Safe," Mal doesn't abandon Simon and River when Simon's kidnapped by an isolated village in need of a doctor. Again, it's not a snap decision. Even Zoe points out that life in the Black and on-planet will be easier without a pair of Alliance fugitives aboard. So this time, when he makes his choice, he's aware of what's changed. When the village's Patron objects to letting River go, and says, "The girl is a witch," Mal replies, "Yeah, but she's *our* witch." And means it.

To paraphrase the Duke of Wellington, no life plan survives contact with actual living. To Mal, his hypothetical crew was a means to an end: freedom. When they become real people, rather than the population of Mal's dream, something's got to give. What gives is his sense of his own boundaries. *Serenity*'s crew are no longer hired help but family, and he'll compromise even his own freedom for them.

"Out of Gas" is my favorite *Firefly* episode. As a writer, I love it for its use of point of view and non-linear narrative. But what I love most is the way the episode illustrates both Mal's assumptions about self-reliance and the actuality of survival on the frontier.

An early scene in the episode shows the crew at dinner. It echoes the final scene of "Safe," which I like to think was a conscious choice. Both scenes evoke a family dinner table (complete with siblings behaving badly). In "Safe," it's the family reunited. In "Out of Gas," the family is about to be broken. But the scene reminds us of the relationships between these people, the bonds of work and need and affection that have grown up among them.

But the first scene in "Out of Gas" is of the ship empty and Mal alone. This is the reality behind the lone adventurer's life that Mal once envisioned for himself. He's alone on his ship. And he's bleeding to death.

The narrative structure rocks back and forth between the family-crew in crisis and the captain struggling to get the engines and life support running in the hollow, echoing shell that is *Serenity* without her crew.

> **Inara:** Mal, you don't have to die alone!
> **Mal:** Everybody dies alone.

But Mal isn't alone, not the way he once imagined he wanted to be. He's knotted into a net of human relationships and mutual assistance, and it's that net that catches and draws him back from death in the end, when his crew disobeys his order and returns for him.

Those who weave the net of family and community survive on the frontier. It's those who are actually alone, beholden to no one, who die alone. Jubal Early, the bounty hunter, drifts in the Black. Rance Burgess, stripped of henchmen and power, dies at the hand of the woman he impregnated. Tracey, Mal and Zoe's old army friend in "The Message," untrusting and untrustworthy, treats that friendship as nothing more than a lever and a bargaining chip, and betrays himself right into a box. Twice.

> **Mal:** You know the old saying.
> **Tracey:** When you can't run, you crawl. And when you can't crawl... When you can't do that...
> **Zoe:** You find someone to carry you.

In the end *Serenity's* crew incorporates even Tracey into their communal net. They carry him, both back to his home and out of life, and he doesn't quite die alone.

By the end of the series, Malcom Reynolds has learned the hard way that the myth of the frontier and its lone-wolf hero is a recipe for disaster. He's accepted the responsibility of friendship and its support. He can even trust River Tam and follow her lead when she masterminds the plot against Early in "Objects in Space."

And in the movie *Serenity*, Mal and the crew draw their boundaries and allegiances even wider. They're prepared to die to get the truth about what happened on Miranda to the rest of the 'verse. They have a responsibility to their community, and that community is *everyone*.

By the time *Firefly* aired, I'd already realized that my youthful idol, the tormented, solo Romantic protagonist, was actually pretty lousy at his job. If the world gets fixed, it gets fixed by people working together, giving a little of their power into each others' hands, giving trust, strength and wisdom to whoever needs it without worrying about the payback.

But it's one thing to know; it's something else to have stories that turn that knowledge into narrative, into the ground your own actions and tales grow out of. That's what *Firefly* became for me: a set of folktales that were as personal as my own experience, yet were shared with a larger community, touchstones that could make strangers into friends on the frontier of daily life. Those inner stories are what keep us all in the air when it looks as if we ought to fall down. We're beholden to those who make them, who pass them on, and who experience them with us.

We're on each others' crew. Why are we still talking about this?

# Acknowledgements

Books like these don't happen without lots of support, both material and moral. In addition to our loving families and friends, the editors would like to thank, in alphabetical order: Carole Barrowman, Elizabeth Bolton-Gabrielsen, K. Tempest Bradford, Jenny Christodal, Sara Charney Cohen, Paul Cornell, Keith R.A. DeCandido, Joanne Ferlas, Christopher Golden, Emmy Gustafson, Maryelizabeth Hart, Mary Robinette Kowal, Ellen Kushner, Nnedi Okorafor, Tara O'Shea, Patrick Rothfuss, Jen Swantson, Evonne Tsang, Steven H Silver and Terri Windling.

# Editors' Bios

**Lynne M. Thomas** is the Head of Rare Books and Special Collections at Northern Illinois University, where she is responsible for archiving popular culture materials, including science fiction and fantasy literature, comic books, dime novels, and historical children's literature. She has published scholarly articles about cross-dressing in dime novels, as well as articles on science fiction archiving for the Hugo-nominated fanzine *Argentus* and the Nebula Awards blog. She is the co-author of *Special Collections 2.0*, a book about web 2.0 technologies and special collections in libraries with Beth Whittaker of Ohio State University, published by Libraries Unlimited in 2009. She co-edited *Chicks Dig Time Lords: A Celebration of Doctor Who by the Women Who Love It* (Mad Norwegian Press, 2010).

**Deborah Stanish** is a Philadelphia-area writer whose works have been published in collections such as *Chicks Dig Time Lords: A Celebration of Doctor Who by the Women Who Love It,* and two volumes of *Time Unincorporated: The Doctor Who Fanzine Archives* series from Mad Norwegian Press. She is a regular columnist for *Enlightenment,* the award-winning fanzine of the Doctor Who Information Network.

# Chicks Dig Time Lords

### A Celebration of Doctor Who by the Women Who Love It

## This book has three settings!

**OUT NOW...** In *Chicks Digs Time Lords*, a host of award-winning female novelists, academics and actresses come together to celebrate the phenomenon that is *Doctor Who*, discuss their inventive involvement with the show's fandom and examine why they adore the series.

These essays will delight male and female readers alike by delving into the extraordinary aspects of being a female *Doctor Who* enthusiast. Contributors include Carole Barrowman (*Anything Goes*), Elizabeth Bear (the Jenny Casey trilogy), Lisa Bowerman (Bernice Summerfield), Jackie Jenkins (*Doctor Who Magazine*), Mary Robinette Kowal (*Shades of Milk and Honey*), Jody Lynn Nye (Mythology series), Kate Orman (*Seeing I*), Lloyd Rose (*Camera Obscura*) and Catherynne M. Valente (*The Orphan's Tales*).

Also featured: a comic from the "Torchwood Babiez" creators, and interviews with *Doctor Who* companions India Fisher (Charley) and Sophie Aldred (Ace).

**ISBN:** 978-1935234043    **MSRP:** 14.95

**mad norwegian press**

**www.madnorwegian.com**
1150 46th St, Des Moines, IA 50311 . madnorwegian@gmail.com

# Credits

**Publisher / Editor-in-Chief**
Lars "Sexy Boy" Pearson

**Design Manager / Senior Editor**
Christa "Says Smart, Dirty Things" Dickson

**Associate Editor (Whedonistas)**
Michael D. "Works for Action Figures" Thomas

**Associate Editor (Mad Norwegian Press)**
Joshua "Ultra Boy" Wilson

**The publisher wishes to thank...**
A very special thank you to Lynne and Deb, for so expertly pulling this book together, and for once again proving that the best strategy to success is to hire the right people to do a task, then do everything you can to stand back and let them get on with it. Also, extra thanks to whichever of them saw fit to include the nicknames seen above. (I'm not so vain that I would dub myself "sexy boy," but I'm hardly going to turn it down when someone else offers it.) Also, thanks are due to all of the writers who contributed to this book, as well as to Christa Dickson, Jane Espenson, Shawne Kleckner, Juliet Landau, Shaun Lyon, Katy Shuttleworth, Michael D. Thomas, Josh Wilson and that nice lady who sends me newspaper articles.

**mad norwegian press**

1150 46th Street
Des Moines, Iowa 50311
madnorwegian@gmail.com
**www.madnorwegian.com**

And please join the Whedonistas and Mad Norwegian Press groups on Facebook!